The Gathering Dark

Book I of *The Grisha Trilogy*

LEIGH BARDUGO

Indigo

First published in Great Britain in 2012
by Indigo
a division of the Orion Publishing Group Ltd
Orion House
5 Upper St Martin's Lane
London WC2H 9EA
An Hachette UK Company

Originally published as *Shadow and Bone* by
Henry Holt and Company, LLC.
Published by arrangement with Rights People, London

1 3 5 7 9 10 8 6 4 2

ISBN 978 1 78062 110 4

Printed and bound by CPI Group (UK) Ltd, Coydon, CRO 4YY

www. orionbooks.co.uk

YA

For my grandfather:
Tell me some lies.

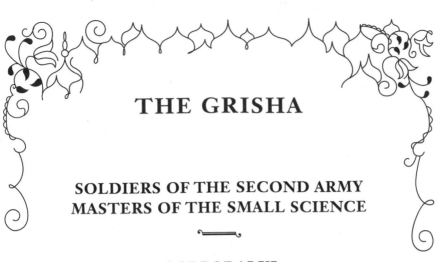

THE GRISHA

SOLDIERS OF THE SECOND ARMY
MASTERS OF THE SMALL SCIENCE

CORPORALKI
(The Order of the Living and the Dead)

Heartrenders
Healers

ETHEREALKI
(The Order of Summoners)

Squallers
Inferni
Tidemakers

MATERIALKI
(The Order of Fabrikators)

Durasts
Alkemi

 *Before*

The servants called them *malenchki*, little ghosts, because they were the smallest and the youngest, and because they haunted the Duke's house like giggling phantoms, darting in and out of rooms, hiding in cupboards to eavesdrop, sneaking into the kitchen to steal the last of the summer peaches.

The boy and the girl had arrived within weeks of each other, two more orphans of the border wars, dirty-faced refugees plucked from the rubble of distant towns and brought to the Duke's estate to learn to read and write, and to learn a trade. The boy was short and stocky, shy but always smiling. The girl was different, and she knew it.

Huddled in the kitchen cupboard, listening to the grown-ups gossip, she heard the Duke's housekeeper, Ana Kuya, say, "She's an ugly little thing. No child should look like that. Pale and sour, like a glass of milk that's turned."

"And so skinny!" the cook replied. "Never finishes her supper."

Crouched beside the girl, the boy turned to her and whispered, "Why *don't* you eat?"

"Because everything she cooks tastes like mud."

"Tastes fine to me."

"You'll eat anything."

They bent their ears back to the crack in the cupboard doors.

A moment later the boy whispered, "I don't think you're ugly."

"Shhhh!" the girl hissed. But hidden by the deep shadows of the cupboard, she smiled.

In the summer, they endured long hours of chores followed by even longer hours of lessons in stifling classrooms. When the heat was at its worst, they escaped into the woods to hunt for birds' nests or swim in the muddy little creek, or they would lie for hours in their meadow, watching the sun pass slowly overhead, speculating on where they would build their dairy farm and whether they would have two white cows or three. In the winter, the Duke left for his city house in Os Alta, and as the days grew shorter and colder, the teachers grew lax in their duties, preferring to sit by the fire and play cards or drink *kvas*. Bored and trapped indoors, the older children doled out more frequent beatings. So the boy and the girl hid in the disused rooms of the estate, putting on plays for the mice and trying to keep warm.

On the day the Grisha Examiners came, the boy and the girl were perched on the window seat of a dusty upstairs bedroom, hoping to catch a glimpse of the mail coach. Instead, they saw a sleigh, a troika pulled by three black horses, pass through the white stone gates onto the estate. They watched its silent progress through the snow to the Duke's front door.

Three figures emerged in elegant fur hats and heavy wool *kefta*: one in crimson, one in darkest blue and one in vibrant purple.

"Grisha!" the girl whispered.

"Quick!" said the boy.

In an instant, they had shaken off their shoes and were running silently down the hall, slipping through the empty music room and darting behind a column in the gallery that overlooked the sitting room where Ana Kuya liked to receive guests.

Ana Kuya was already there, bird-like in her black dress, pouring tea from the samovar, her large key ring jangling at her waist.

"There are just the two this year then?" said a woman's low voice.

They peered through the railing of the balcony to the room below. Two of the Grisha sat by the fire: a handsome man in blue and a woman in red robes with a haughty, refined air. The third, a young blond man, ambled about the room, stretching his legs.

"Yes," said Ana Kuya. "A boy and a girl, the youngest here by quite a bit. Both around eight, we think."

"You think?" asked the man in blue.

"When the parents are deceased . . ."

"We understand," said the woman. "We are, of course, great admirers of your institution. We only wish more of the nobility took an interest in the common people."

"Our Duke is a very great man," said Ana Kuya.

Up in the balcony, the boy and the girl nodded sagely to each other. Their benefactor, Duke Keramsov, was a celebrated war hero and a friend to the people. When he had returned from the front lines, he had converted his estate into an orphanage and a home for war widows. They were told to keep him nightly in their prayers.

"And what are they like, these children?" asked the woman.

"The girl has some talent for drawing. The boy is most at home in the meadow and the wood."

"But what are they *like*?" repeated the woman.

Ana Kuya pursed her withered lips. "What are they like? They are undisciplined, contrary, far too attached to each other. They—"

"They are listening to every word we say," said the young man in purple.

The boy and the girl jumped in surprise. He was staring directly at their hiding spot. They shrank behind the column, but it was too late.

Ana Kuya's voice lashed out like a whip. "Alina Starkov! Malyen Oretsev! Come here at once!"

Reluctantly, Alina and Mal made their way down the narrow spiral staircase at the end of the gallery. When they reached the bottom, the woman in red rose from her chair and gestured them forward.

"Do you know who we are?" the woman asked. Her hair was steel grey. Her face lined, but beautiful.

"You're witches!" blurted Mal.

"Witches?" she snarled. She whirled on Ana Kuya. "Is that what you teach at this school? Superstition and lies?"

Ana Kuya flushed with embarrassment. The woman in red turned back to Mal and Alina, her dark eyes blazing. "We are not witches. We are practitioners of the Small Science. We keep this country and this kingdom safe."

"As does the First Army," Ana Kuya said quietly, an

unmistakeable edge to her voice.

The woman in red stiffened, but after a moment she conceded, "As does the King's Army."

The young man in purple smiled and knelt before the children. He said gently, "When the leaves change colour, do you call it magic? What about when you cut your hand and it heals? And when you put a pot of water on the stove and it boils, is it magic then?"

Mal shook his head, his eyes wide.

But Alina frowned and said, "Anyone can boil water."

Ana Kuya sighed in exasperation, but the woman in red laughed.

"You're very right. Anyone can boil water. But not just anyone can master the Small Science. That's why we've come to test you." She turned to Ana Kuya. "Leave us now."

"Wait!" exclaimed Mal. "What happens if we're Grisha? What happens to us?"

The woman in red looked down at them. "If, by some small chance, *one* of you is Grisha, then that lucky child will go to a special school where Grisha learn to use their talents."

"You will have the finest clothes, the finest food, whatever your heart desires," said the man in purple. "Would you like that?"

"It is the greatest way that you may serve your King," said Ana Kuya, still hovering by the door.

"That is very true," said the woman in red, pleased and willing to make peace.

The boy and the girl glanced at each other and, because the adults were not paying close attention, they did not see the girl reach out to clasp the boy's hand or the look that passed between them. The Duke would have recognised that look. He had spent long years on the ravaged northern borders, where the villages were constantly under siege and the peasants fought their battles with little aid from the King or anyone else. He had seen a woman, barefoot and unflinching in her doorway, face down a row of bayonets. He knew the look of a man defending his home with nothing but a rock in his hand.

Chapter 1

Standing on the edge of a crowded road, I looked down onto the rolling fields and abandoned farms of the Tula Valley and got my first glimpse of the Shadow Fold. My regiment was two weeks' march from the military encampment at Poliznaya and the autumn sun was warm overhead, but I shivered in my coat as I eyed the haze that lay like a dirty smudge on the horizon.

A heavy shoulder slammed into me from behind. I stumbled and nearly pitched face-first into the muddy road.

"Hey!" shouted the soldier. "Watch yourself!"

"Why don't you watch your fat feet?" I snapped, and took some satisfaction from the surprise that came over his broad face. People, particularly big men carrying big rifles, don't expect lip from a scrawny thing like me. They always look a bit dazed when they get it.

The soldier got over the novelty quickly and gave me a dirty look as he adjusted the pack on his back, then disappeared into the caravan of horses, men, carts and wagons streaming over the crest of the hill and into the valley below.

I quickened my steps, trying to peer through the crowd. I'd lost sight of the yellow flag of the surveyors' cart hours ago, and I knew I was far behind.

As I walked, I took in the green and gold smells of the autumn wood, the soft breeze at my back. We were on the Vy, the wide road that had once led all the way from Os Alta to the wealthy port cities on Ravka's western coast. But that was before the Shadow Fold.

Somewhere in the crowd, someone was singing. *Singing? What idiot is singing on his way into the Fold?* I glanced again at that smudge on the horizon and had to suppress a shudder. I'd seen the Shadow Fold on many maps, a black slash that had severed Ravka from its only coastline and left it landlocked. Sometimes it was shown as a stain, sometimes as a bleak and shapeless cloud. And then there were the maps that just showed the Shadow Fold as a long, narrow lake and labelled it by its other name, "the Unsea", a name intended to put soldiers and merchants at their ease and encourage crossings.

I snorted. That might fool some fat merchant, but it was little comfort to me. Ravka's only link to the outside world – to weapons, to commerce, to the hope of survival – lay through the Fold. We would cross because we had to, because we'd been ordered to, but that didn't mean I had to like it.

I tore my attention from the sinister haze hovering in the distance and looked down onto the ruined farms of the Tula. The valley had once been home to some of Ravka's richest estates. One day it was a place where farmers tended crops and sheep grazed in green fields. The next, a dark slash had appeared on the landscape, a swathe of nearly impenetrable darkness that grew with every passing year and crawled with horrors. Where the farmers had gone, their herds, their crops, their homes and families, no one knew.

Stop it, I told myself firmly. *You're only making things worse. People have been crossing the Fold for years . . . usually with massive casualties, but all the same.* I took a deep breath to steady myself.

"No fainting in the middle of the road," said a voice close to my ear as a heavy arm landed across my shoulders and gave me a squeeze. I looked up to see Mal's familiar face, a smile in his bright blue eyes as he fell into step beside me. "C'mon," he said. "One foot in front of the other. You know how it's done."

"You're interfering with my plan."

"Oh really?"

"Yes. Faint, get trampled, grievous injuries all around."

"That sounds like a brilliant plan."

"Ah, but if I'm horribly maimed, I won't be able to cross the Fold."

Mal nodded slowly. "I see. I can shove you under a cart if that would help."

"I'll think about it," I grumbled, but I felt my mood lifting all the same. Despite my best efforts, Mal still had that effect on me. And I wasn't the only one. A pretty blonde girl strolled by and waved, throwing Mal a flirtatious glance over her shoulder.

"Hey, Ruby," he called. "See you later?"

Ruby giggled and scampered off into the crowd. Mal grinned broadly until he caught my eye roll.

"What? I thought you liked Ruby."

"As it happens, we don't have much to talk about," I said drily. I actually had liked Ruby – at first. When Mal and I had left the orphanage at Keramzin to train for our military service in Poliznaya, I'd been nervous about meeting new people. But lots of girls had been excited to befriend me, and Ruby had been among the most eager. Those friendships lasted as long as it took me to figure out that their only interest lay in my proximity to Mal.

Now I watched him stretch his arms expansively and turn his face up to the autumn sky, looking perfectly content. There was even, I noted with some disgust, a little bounce in his step.

"What is wrong with you?" I whispered furiously.

"Nothing," he said, surprised. "I feel great."

"But how can you be so . . . so jaunty?"

"Jaunty? I've never been jaunty. I hope never to be jaunty."

"Well, then what's all this?" I asked, waving a hand at him. "You look as if you're on your way to a really good dinner instead of possible death and dismemberment."

Mal laughed. "You worry too much. The King's sent a whole group of Grisha fire-summoners to cover the skiffs, and even a few of those creepy Heartrenders. We have our rifles," he said, patting the one on his back. "We'll be fine."

"A rifle won't make much difference if there's a bad attack."

Mal shot me a bemused glance. "What's the matter with you lately? You're even grumpier than usual. And you look terrible."

"Thanks," I groused. "I haven't been sleeping well."

"What else is new?"

He was right, of course. I'd never slept well. But it had been even worse over the last few days. Saints knew I had plenty of good reasons to dread going into the Fold, reasons shared by every member of our regiment who had been unlucky enough to be chosen for the crossing.

But there was something else, a deeper sense of unease that I couldn't quite name.

I glanced at Mal. There had been a time when I could have told him anything. "I just . . . have this feeling."

"Stop worrying so much. Maybe they'll put Mikhael on the skiff. The volcra will take one look at that big juicy belly of his and leave us alone."

Unbidden, a memory came to me: Mal and I, sitting side by side in a chair in the Duke's library, flipping through the pages of a large leather-bound book. We'd happened on an illustration of a volcra: long, filthy claws; leathery wings; and rows of razor-sharp teeth for feasting on human flesh. They were blind from generations spent living and hunting in the Fold, but legend had it they could smell human blood from miles away. I'd pointed to the page and asked, "What is it holding?"

I could still hear Mal's whisper in my ear. "I think – I think it's a foot." We'd slammed the book shut and run squealing out into the safety of the sunlight . . .

Without realising it, I'd stopped walking, frozen in place, unable to shake the memory from my mind. The ports of West Ravka lay on the other side of the Fold – wealth, opportunity, the promised blue infinity of the True Sea. Some merchants crossed the Unsea several times each year to trade their goods and stock their shelves. Soldiers and sailors had made it through the Fold countless times before. I knew that. But I still couldn't seem to breathe.

When Mal saw I wasn't with him, he gave a great beleaguered sigh and marched back to me. He rested his hands on my shoulders and gave me a little shake.

"I was kidding. No one's going to eat Mikhael."

"I know," I said, staring down at my boots. "You're hilarious."

"Alina, come on. We'll be fine."

"You can't know that."

"Look at me." I willed myself to raise my eyes to his. "I know you're scared. I am too. But we're going to do this, and we're going to be fine. We always are. Okay?" He smiled, and my heart gave a very loud thud in my chest.

I rubbed my thumb over the scar that ran across the palm of my right hand and took a shaky breath. "Okay," I said grudgingly, and I actually felt myself smiling back.

"Madam's spirits have been restored!" Mal shouted. "The sun can once more shine!"

"Oh will you shut up?"

I turned to give him a punch, but before I could, he'd grabbed hold of me and lifted me off my feet. A clatter of hooves and shouts split the air. Mal yanked me to the side of the road just as a huge black coach roared past, scattering people before it as they ran to avoid the pounding hooves of four black horses. Beside the whip-wielding driver perched two soldiers in charcoal coats.

The Darkling. There was no mistaking his black coach or the uniform of his personal guard.

Another coach, this one lacquered red, rumbled past us at a more leisurely pace.

I looked up at Mal, my heart racing from the close call. "Thanks," I whispered. Mal suddenly seemed to realise that he had his arms around me. He let go and hastily stepped back. I brushed the dust from my coat, hoping he wouldn't notice the flush on my cheeks.

A third coach rolled by, lacquered in blue, and a girl

leaned out of the window. She had curling black hair and wore a hat of silver fox. She scanned the watching crowd and, predictably, her eyes lingered on Mal.

You were just mooning over him, I chided myself. *Why shouldn't some gorgeous Grisha do the same?*

Her lips curled into a small smile as she held Mal's gaze, watching him over her shoulder until the coach was out of sight. Mal goggled dumbly after her, his mouth slightly open.

"Close your mouth before something flies in," I snapped.

Mal blinked, still looking dazed.

"Did you see that?" a voice bellowed. I turned to see Mikhael loping towards us, wearing an almost comical expression of awe. Mikhael was a huge redhead with a wide face and an even wider neck. Behind him, Dubrov, reedy and dark, hurried to catch up. They were both trackers in Mal's unit and never far from his side.

"Of course I saw it," Mal said, his dopey expression evaporating into a cocky grin. I rolled my eyes.

"She looked right at you!" shouted Mikhael, clapping Mal on the back.

Mal gave a casual shrug, but his smile widened. "So she did," he said smugly.

Dubrov shifted nervously. "They say Grisha girls can put spells on you."

I snorted.

Mikhael looked at me as if he hadn't even known I was there. "Hey, Sticks," he said, and gave me a little jab on the arm. I scowled at the nickname, but he had already turned back to Mal. "You know she'll be staying at camp," he said with a leer.

"I hear the Grisha tent's as big as a cathedral," added Dubrov.

"Lots of nice shadowy nooks," said Mikhael, and actually waggled his brows.

Mal whooped. Without sparing me another glance, the three of them strode off, shouting and shoving one another.

"Great seeing you, guys," I muttered under my breath. I readjusted the strap of the satchel slung across my shoulders and started back along the road, joining the last few stragglers down the hill and into Kribirsk. I didn't bother to hurry. I'd probably get yelled at when I finally made it to the Documents Tent, but there was nothing I could do about it now.

I rubbed my arm where Mikhael had punched me. *Sticks.* I hated that name. *You didn't call me Sticks when you were drunk on* kvas *and trying to paw me at the spring bonfire, you miserable oaf,* I thought spitefully.

Kribirsk wasn't much to look at. According to the Senior Cartographer, it had been a sleepy market town in the days before the Shadow Fold, little more than a dusty main square and an inn for weary travellers on the Vy. But now it had become a kind of ramshackle port city, growing up around a permanent military encampment and the drydocks where the sandskiffs waited to take passengers through the darkness to West Ravka. I passed taverns and pubs and what I was pretty sure were brothels meant to cater to the troops of the King's Army. There were shops selling rifles and crossbows, lamps and torches, all necessary equipment for a trek across the Fold. The little church with its whitewashed walls and gleaming onion domes was in surprisingly good repair. *Or maybe not so surprising*, I considered. Anyone contemplating a trip across the Shadow Fold would be smart to stop and pray.

I found my way to where the surveyors were billeted, deposited my pack on a cot, and hurried over to the Documents Tent. To my relief, the Senior Cartographer was nowhere in sight, and I was able to slip inside unseen.

Entering the white canvas tent, I felt myself relax for the first time since I'd caught sight of the Fold. The Documents Tent was essentially the same in every camp I'd seen, full of bright light and rows of drafting tables where artists and surveyors bent to their work. After the noise and jostle of the journey, there was something soothing about the crackle of paper, the smell of ink and the soft scratching of nibs and brushes.

I pulled my sketchbook from my coat pocket and slid onto a workbench beside Alexei, who turned to me and whispered irritably, "Where have you been?"

"Nearly getting trampled by the Darkling's coach," I replied, grabbing a clean piece of paper and flipping through my sketches to try to find a suitable one to copy. Alexei and I were both junior cartographers' assistants and, as part of our training, we had to submit two finished sketches or renderings at the end of every day.

Alexei drew in a sharp breath. "Really? Did you actually see him?"

"*Actually*, I was too busy trying not to die."

"There are worse ways to go." He caught sight of the sketch of a rocky valley I was about to start copying. "Ugh. Not that one." He flipped through my sketchbook to an elevation of a mountain ridge and tapped it with his finger. "There."

I barely had time to put pen to paper before the Senior Cartographer entered the tent and came swooping down the aisle, observing our work as he passed.

"I hope that's the second sketch you're starting, Alina Starkov."

"Yes," I lied. "Yes, it is."

As soon as the Cartographer had passed on, Alexei whispered, "Tell me about the coach."

"I have to finish my sketches."

"Here," he said in exasperation, sliding one of his sketches over to me.

"He'll know it's your work."

"It's not that good. You should be able to pass it off as yours."

"Now there's the Alexei I know and tolerate," I grumbled, but I didn't give back the sketch. Alexei was one of the most talented assistants and he knew it.

Alexei extracted every last detail from me about the three Grisha coaches. I was grateful for the sketch, so I did my best to satisfy his curiosity as I finished up my elevation of the mountain ridge and worked in my thumb measurements of some of the highest peaks.

By the time we were finished, dusk was falling. We handed in our work and walked to the mess tent, where we stood in line for muddy stew ladled out by a sweaty cook and found seats with some of the other surveyors.

I passed the meal in silence, listening to Alexei and the others exchange camp gossip and jittery talk about tomorrow's crossing. Alexei insisted that I retell the story of the Grisha coaches, and it was met by the usual mix of fascination and fear that greeted any mention of the Darkling.

"He's not natural," said Eva, another assistant; she had pretty green eyes that did little to distract from her pig-like nose. "None of them are."

Alexei sniffed. "Please spare us your superstition, Eva."

"It was a Darkling who made the Shadow Fold to begin with."

"That was hundreds of years ago!" protested Alexei. "And that Darkling was completely mad."

"This one is just as bad."

"Peasant," Alexei said, and dismissed her with a wave. Eva gave him an affronted look and deliberately turned away from him to talk to her friends.

I stayed quiet. I was more a peasant than Eva, despite her superstitions. It was only by the Duke's charity that I could read and write, but by unspoken agreement, Mal and I avoided mentioning Keramzin.

As if on cue, a raucous burst of laughter pulled me from my thoughts. I looked over my shoulder. Mal was holding court at a rowdy table of trackers.

Alexei followed my glance. "How did you two become friends anyway?"

"We grew up together."

"You don't seem to have much in common."

I shrugged. "I guess it's easy to have a lot in common when you're kids." Like loneliness, and memories of parents we were meant to forget, and the pleasure of escaping chores to play tag in our meadow.

Alexei looked so skeptical that I had to laugh. "He wasn't always the Amazing Mal, expert tracker and seducer of Grisha girls."

Alexei's jaw dropped. "He seduced a Grisha girl?"

"No, but I'm sure he will," I muttered.

"So what *was* he like?"

"He was short and pudgy and afraid of baths," I said with some satisfaction.

Alexei glanced at Mal. "I guess things change."

I rubbed my thumb over the scar in my palm. "I guess they do."

We cleared our plates and drifted out of the mess tent into the cool night. On the way back to the barracks, we took a detour so that we could walk by the Grisha camp. The Grisha pavilion really was the size of a cathedral, covered in black silk, its blue, red, and purple pennants flying high above. Hidden somewhere behind it were the Darkling's tents, guarded by Corporalki Heartrenders and the Darkling's personal guard. He travelled constantly between the capital and the military outposts on Ravka's borders. He must have come to Kribirsk to oversee our crossing.

When Alexei had looked his fill, we wended our way back to our quarters. Alexei grew quiet and started cracking his knuckles, and I knew we were both thinking about tomorrow's crossing. Judging by the gloomy mood in the barracks, we weren't alone. Some people were already on their cots, sleeping – or trying to – while others huddled by lamplight, talking in low tones. A few sat clutching their icons, praying to their Saints.

I unfurled my bedroll on a narrow cot, removed my boots and hung up my coat. Then I wriggled down into the fur-lined blankets and stared up at the roof, waiting for sleep. I stayed that way for a long time, until the lamplights had all been extinguished and the sounds of conversation gave way to soft snores and the rustle of bodies.

Tomorrow, if everything went as planned, we would pass safely through to West Ravka, and I would get my first glimpse of the True Sea. There, Mal and the other trackers would hunt for red wolves and sea foxes and other coveted creatures that could only be found in the west. I would stay with the cartographers in Os Kervo to finish my training and help draft whatever information we managed to glean in the Fold. And then, of course, I'd have to cross the Fold again in order to return home. But it was hard to think that far ahead.

I was still wide awake when I heard it. *Tap tap.* Pause. *Tap.* Then again. *Tap tap.* Pause. *Tap.*

"What's going on?" mumbled Alexei drowsily from the cot nearest mine.

"Nothing," I whispered, already slipping out of my bedroll and shoving my feet into my boots.

I grabbed my coat and crept out of the barracks as quietly as I could. As I opened the door I heard a giggle, and a female voice called from somewhere in the dark room, "If it's that tracker, tell him to come inside and keep me warm."

"If he wants to catch *tsifil*, I'm sure you'll be his first stop," I said sweetly, and slipped out into the night.

The cold air stung my cheeks and I buried my chin in my collar, wishing I'd taken the time to grab my scarf and gloves. Mal was sitting on the rickety steps, his back to me. Beyond him, I could see Mikhael and Dubrov passing a bottle back and forth beneath the glowing lights of the footpath.

I scowled. "Please tell me you didn't just wake me up to inform me that you're going to the Grisha tent. What do you want, advice?"

"You weren't sleeping. You were lying awake worrying."

"Wrong. I was planning how to sneak into the Grisha pavilion and snag myself a cute Corporalnik."

Mal laughed. I hesitated by the door. This was the hardest part of being around him – other than the way he made my heart do clumsy acrobatics. I hated hiding how much the stupid things he did hurt me, but I hated the idea of him finding out even more. I thought about turning around and going back inside. Instead, I swallowed my jealousy and sat down beside him.

"I hope you brought me something nice," I said. "Alina's Secrets of Seduction do not come cheap."

He grinned. "Can you put it on my tab?"

"I suppose. But only because I know you're good for it."

I peered into the dark and watched Dubrov take a swig from the bottle and then lurch forward. Mikhael put his arm out to steady him, and the sounds of their laughter floated back to us on the night air.

Mal shook his head and sighed. "He always tries to keep up with Mikhael. He'll probably end up throwing up on my boots."

"Serves you right," I said. "So what *are* you doing here?" When we'd first started our military service a year ago, Mal had visited me almost every night. But he hadn't come by in months.

He shrugged. "I don't know. You looked so miserable at dinner."

I was surprised he'd noticed. "Just thinking about the crossing," I said carefully. It wasn't exactly a lie. I *was* terrified of entering the Fold, and Mal definitely didn't need to know that Alexei and I had been talking about him. "But I'm touched by your concern."

"Hey," he said with a grin, "I worry."

"If you're lucky, a volcra will have me for breakfast tomorrow and then you won't have to fret any more."

"You know I'd be lost without you."

"You've never been lost in your life," I scoffed. I was the mapmaker, but Mal could find true north blindfolded and standing on his head.

He bumped his shoulder against mine. "You know what I mean."

"Sure," I said. But I didn't. Not really.

We sat in silence, watching our breath make plumes in the cold air.

Mal studied the toes of his boots and said, "I guess I'm nervous too."

I nudged him with my elbow and said with confidence I didn't feel, "If we can take on Ana Kuya, we can handle a few volcra."

"If I remember right, the last time we crossed Ana Kuya, you got your ears boxed and we both ended up mucking out the stables."

I winced. "I'm trying to be reassuring. You could at least pretend I'm succeeding."

"You know the funny thing?" he asked. "I actually miss her sometimes."

I did my best to hide my astonishment. We'd spent more than ten years of our lives in Keramzin, but usually I got the impression that Mal wanted to forget everything about the place, maybe even me. There he'd been another lost refugee, another orphan made to feel grateful for every mouthful of food, every used pair of boots. In the army, he'd carved out a real place for himself where no one needed to know that he'd once been an unwanted little boy.

"Me too," I admitted. "We could write to her."

"Maybe," Mal said.

Suddenly, he reached out and took my hand. I tried to ignore the little jolt that went through me. "This time tomorrow, we'll be sitting in the harbour at Os Kervo, looking out at the ocean and drinking *kvas.*"

I glanced at Dubrov weaving back and forth and smiled. "Is Dubrov buying?"

"Just you and me," Mal said.

"Really?"

"It's always just you and me, Alina."

For a moment, it seemed as if it were true. The world was this step, this circle of lamplight, the two of us suspended in the dark.

"Come on!" bellowed Mikhael from the path.

Mal started like a man waking from a dream. He gave my hand a last squeeze before he dropped it. "Gotta go," he said, his brash grin sliding back into place. "Try to get some sleep."

He hopped lightly from the stairs and jogged off to join his friends. "Wish me luck!" he called over his shoulder.

"Good luck," I said automatically and then wanted to kick myself. *Good luck? Have a lovely time, Mal. Hope you find a pretty Grisha, fall deeply in love, and make lots of gorgeous, disgustingly talented babies together.*

I sat frozen on the steps, watching them disappear down the path, still feeling the warm pressure of Mal's hand in mine. *Oh well*, I thought as I got to my feet. *Maybe he'll fall into a ditch on his way there.*

I edged back into the barracks, closed the door tightly behind me, and gratefully snuggled into my bedroll.

Would that black-haired Grisha girl sneak out of the pavilion to meet Mal? I pushed the thought away. It was none of my business, and really, I didn't want to know. Mal had never looked at me the way he'd looked at that girl or even the way he looked at Ruby, and he never would. But the fact that we were still friends was more important than any of that.

For how long? said a nagging voice in my head. Alexei was right: things change. Mal had changed for the better. He'd got more handsome, braver, cockier. And I'd got . . . taller. I sighed and rolled onto my side. I wanted to believe that Mal and I would always be friends, but I had to face the fact that we were on different paths. Lying in the dark, waiting for sleep, I wondered if those paths would just keep taking us further and further apart, and if a day might come when we would be strangers to each other once again.

Chapter 2

The morning passed in a blur: breakfast, a brief trip to the Documents Tent to pack additional inks and paper, then the chaos of the dry dock. I stood with the rest of the surveyors, waiting our turn to board one of a small fleet of sand skiffs. Behind us, Kribirsk was waking up and going about its business. Ahead lay the strange, shifting darkness of the Fold.

Animals were too noisy and scared too easily for travel on the Unsea, so crossings were made on sand skiffs, shallow sleds rigged with enormous sails that let them skate almost soundlessly over the dead grey sands. The skiffs were loaded with grain, timber, and raw cotton, but on the trip back they would be stocked with sugar, rifles, and all manner of finished goods that passed through the seaports of West Ravka. Looking out at the skiff's deck, equipped with little more than a sail and a rickety railing, all I could think was that it offered no place to hide.

At the mast of each sled, flanked by heavily armed soldiers, stood two Grisha Etherealki, the Order of Summoners, in dark blue *kefta*. The silver embroidery at their cuffs and the hems of their robes indicated that they were Squallers, Grisha who could raise or lower the pressure of the air and fill the skiffs' sails with wind that would carry us across the long miles of the Fold.

Soldiers armed with rifles and overseen by a grim officer lined the railings. Between them stood more Etherealki, but their blue robes bore the red cuffs that indicated they could raise fire.

At a signal from the skiff's captain, the Senior Cartographer herded me, Alexei, and the rest of the assistants onto the skiff to join the other passengers. Then he took his place beside the Squallers at the mast, where he would help them navigate through the dark. He had a compass in his hand, but it would be of little use once we were on the Fold. As we crowded on deck, I caught a glimpse of Mal standing with the trackers on the other side of the skiff. They were also armed with rifles. A row of archers stood behind them, the quivers on their backs bristling with arrows tipped in Grisha steel. I fingered the hilt of the army-issue knife tucked into my belt. It didn't give me much confidence.

A shout rang out from the foreman on the docks, and crews of burly men on the ground began pushing the skiffs into the colourless sand that marked the furthest reaches of the Fold. They stepped back hurriedly, as if that pale, dead sand would burn their feet.

Then it was our turn, and with a sudden jolt our skiff lurched forward, creaking against the earth as the dockworkers heaved. I grabbed the railing to steady myself, my heart beating wildly. The Squallers lifted their arms. The sails billowed open with a loud snap, and our skiff surged forward into the Fold.

At first, it was like drifting into a thick cloud of smoke, but there was no heat, no smell of fire. Sounds seemed to dampen and the world became still. I watched the sand skiffs ahead of us slide into the darkness, fading from view, one after another. I realised that I could no longer see the prow of our skiff and then that I could not see my own hand on the railing. I looked back over my shoulder. The living world had disappeared. Darkness fell around us, black, weightless, and absolute. We were in the Fold.

It was as if we were standing at the end of everything. I held tight to the railing, feeling the wood dig into my hand, grateful for its solidity. I focused on that and the feel of my toes in my boots, gripping the deck. To my left, I could hear Alexei breathing.

I tried to think about the soldiers with their rifles and the blue-robed Grisha pyros. The hope in crossing the Fold was that we would pass through silently and unnoticed; no shot would sound, no fire would be summoned. But their presence comforted me all the same.

I don't know how long we went on that way, the skiffs floating forward, the only sound the gentle rasp of sand on their hulls. It seemed like minutes, but it might have been hours. *We're going to be okay*, I thought to myself. *We're going to be okay.* Then I felt Alexei's hand fumbling for mine. He seized hold of my wrist.

"Listen!" he whispered, and his voice was hoarse with terror. For a moment, all I heard was his ragged breathing and the steady hiss of the skiff. Then, somewhere out in the darkness, another sound, faint but relentless: the rhythmic flapping of wings.

I grabbed Alexei's arm with one hand and clutched the hilt of my knife with the other, my heart pounding, my eyes straining to see something, anything in the blackness. I heard the sound of triggers being cocked, the tap of arrows being notched. Someone whispered, "Be ready."

We waited, listening to the sound of wings beating the air, growing louder as they drew nearer, like the drums of an oncoming army. I thought I could feel the wind stir against my cheek as they circled closer, closer.

"Burn!" The command rang out, followed by the crackle of flint striking stone and an explosive *whoosh* as rippling blooms of Grisha flame erupted from each of the skiffs.

I squinted into the sudden brightness, waiting for my vision to adjust. In the firelight, I saw them. Volcra were supposed to move in small flocks, but there they were . . . not tens but hundreds, hovering and swooping in the air around the skiff. They were more frightening than anything I had ever seen in any book, than any monster I could have imagined. Shots rang out. The archers let fly, and the shrieks of volcra split the air, high and horrible.

They dived. I heard a shrill wail and watched in horror as a soldier was lifted from his feet and carried into the air, kicking and struggling. Alexei and I huddled together, crouched low against the railing, clinging to our flimsy knives and muttering our prayers as the world dissolved into nightmare. All around us, men shouted, people screamed, soldiers were locked in combat with the massive, writhing forms of winged beasts, and the unnatural darkness of the Fold was broken in fits and starts by bursts of golden Grisha flame.

Then a cry rent the air next to me. I gasped as Alexei's arm was yanked away. In a spurt of flame, I saw him clutching at the railing with one hand. I saw his howling mouth, his wide, terrified eyes, and the monstrous thing that held him in its glistening grey arms, its wings beating the air as it lifted him from his feet, its thick claws sunk deep into his back, its talons already wet with his blood. Alexei's hand slipped on the railing. I lunged forward and grabbed his arm.

"Hold on!" I cried.

The flame vanished, and in the darkness I felt Alexei's fingers pulled from mine.

"Alexei!" I shouted.

His screams faded into the sounds of battle as the volcra carried him into the dark. Another burst of flame lit the sky, but he was gone.

"Alexei!" I yelled, leaning over the side of the railing. "Alexei!"

The answer came in a gust of wings as another volcra swooped down on me. I careened backwards, barely avoiding its grasp, my knife held out before me with trembling hands. The volcra lunged forward, the firelight glinting off its milky, sightless eyes, its gaping mouth crowded with rows of sharp, crooked black teeth. I saw a flash of powder from the corner of my eye, heard a rifle shot, and the volcra stumbled, yowling in rage and pain.

"Move!" It was Mal, rifle in hand, face streaked with blood. He grabbed my arm and pulled me behind him.

The volcra was still coming, clawing its way across the deck, one of its wings hanging at a crooked angle. Mal was trying to reload in the firelight, but the volcra was too fast. It rushed at us, claws slashing, its talons tearing across Mal's chest. He screamed.

I caught hold of the volcra's broken wing and stabbed my knife deep between its shoulders. Its muscled flesh felt slimy beneath my hands. It screeched and thrashed free of my grip, and I fell back, hitting the deck hard. It lunged at me in a frenzy, its huge jaws snapping.

Another shot rang out. The volcra stumbled and fell in a grotesque heap, black blood pouring from its mouth. In the dim light, I saw Mal lowering his rifle. His torn shirt was dark with blood. The rifle slid from his fingers as he swayed and fell to his knees, then collapsed onto the deck.

"Mal!" I was at his side in an instant, my hands pressing down on his chest in a desperate attempt to stop the bleeding. "Mal!" I sobbed, the tears streaming down my cheeks.

The air was thick with the smell of blood and gunpowder. All around us, I heard rifle fire, people weeping . . . and the obscene sound of something feeding. The flames of the Grisha were growing weaker, more sporadic, and worst of all, I realised the skiff had stopped moving. *This is it*, I thought hopelessly. I bent low over Mal, keeping pressure on the wound.

His breathing was laboured. "They're coming," he gasped.

I looked up and saw, in the feeble, fading glow of Grisha fire, two volcra swooping down upon us.

I huddled over Mal, shielding his body with mine. I knew it was futile, but it was all I could offer. I smelled the fetid stench of the volcra, felt the air gusting from their wings. I pressed my forehead to Mal's and heard him whisper, "I'll meet you in the meadow."

Something inside me gave way, in fury, in hopelessness, in the certainty of my own death. I felt Mal's blood beneath my palms, saw the suffering on his beloved face. A volcra screeched in triumph as its talons sank into my shoulder. Pain shot through my body.

And the world went white.

I closed my eyes as a sudden, piercing flood of light exploded across my vision. It seemed to fill my head, blinding me, drowning me. From somewhere above, I heard a horrible shriek. I felt the volcra's claws loosen their grip, felt the thud as I fell forward and my head connected with the deck, and then I felt nothing at all.

Chapter 3

I woke with a start. I could feel the rush of air on my skin, and I opened my eyes to see what looked like dark clouds of smoke. I was on my back, on the deck of the skiff. It took me only a moment to realise that the clouds were getting thinner, giving way to dark wisps and, between them, a bright autumn sun. I closed my eyes again, feeling relief wash over me. *We're on our way out of the Fold*, I thought. *Somehow, we made it through.* Or had we? Memories of the volcra attack flooded back in a frightening rush. Where was Mal?

I tried to sit up and a bolt of pain sliced through my shoulder. I ignored it and pushed myself up. I found myself looking down a rifle barrel.

"Get that thing away from me," I snapped, batting it aside.

The soldier swung the rifle back around, jabbing it threateningly at me. "Stay where you are," he commanded.

I stared at him, stunned. "What's wrong with you?"

"She's awake!" he shouted over his shoulder. He was joined by two more armed soldiers, the captain of the skiff and a Corporalnik. With a thrum of panic, I saw that the cuffs of her red *kefta* were embroidered in black. What did a Heartrender want with me?

I looked around. A Squaller still stood by the mast, arms raised, driving us forward on a strong wind, a single soldier by his side. The deck was slick with blood in places. My stomach turned as I remembered the horror of the battle. A Corporalki Healer was tending to the wounded. *Where was Mal?*

There were soldiers and Grisha standing by the railings, bloodied, singed and considerably fewer in number than when we had set out. They were all watching me warily. With growing fear, I realised that the soldiers and the Corporalnik were actually guarding me. Like a prisoner.

I said, "Mal Oretsev. He's a tracker. He was injured during the attack. Where is he?" No one said anything. "Please," I begged. "Where is he?"

There was a jolt as the skiff came aground. The captain gestured at me with his rifle. "Up."

I thought about simply refusing to get up until they told me what had happened to Mal, but a glance at the Heartrender made me reconsider. I got to my feet, wincing at the pain in my shoulder, then I stumbled as the skiff started to move again, pulled forward by the dry dock workers on land. Instinctively, I reached out to steady myself, but the soldier I touched shrank back from me as if burned. I managed to find my footing, but my thoughts were reeling.

The skiff halted again.

"Move," the captain commanded.

The soldiers led me at riflepoint from the skiff. I passed the other survivors, acutely aware of their curious and frightened stares, and caught sight of the Senior Cartographer babbling excitedly to a soldier. I wanted to stop to tell him what had happened to Alexei, but I didn't dare.

As I stepped onto the dry dock, I was surprised to see that we were back in Kribirsk. We hadn't even made it across the Fold. I shuddered. Better to be marching through camp with a rifle at my back than to be on the Unsea.

But not much better, I thought anxiously.

As the soldiers marched me up the main road, people turned from their work to gawk. My mind was whirring, searching for answers and finding nothing. Had I done something wrong in the Fold? Broken some kind of military protocol? And how had we got out of the Fold, anyway? The wounds near my shoulder throbbed. The last thing I remembered was the agony of the volcra's claws piercing my back, that searing burst of light. How had we survived?

These thoughts were driven from my mind as we approached the Officers' Tent. The captain called the guards to a halt and stepped towards the entrance.

The Corporalnik reached out a hand to stop him. "This is a waste of time. We should proceed immediately to—"

"Take your hand off me, bloodletter," the captain snapped and shook his arm free.

For a moment, the Corporalnik stared at him, her eyes dangerous, then she smiled coldly and bowed. "*Da, kapitan.*"

I felt the hair on my arms rise.

The captain disappeared inside the tent. We waited. I glanced nervously at the Corporalnik, who had apparently forgotten her feud with the captain and was scrutinising me once again. She was young, maybe even younger than I was, but that hadn't stopped her from confronting a superior officer. Why would it? She could kill the captain where he stood without ever raising a weapon. I rubbed my arms, trying to shake the chill that had settled over me.

The tent flap opened, and I was horrified to see the captain emerge followed by a stern Colonel Raevsky. What could I possibly have done that would require the involvement of a senior officer?

The colonel peered at me, his weathered face grim. "What are you?"

"Assistant Cartographer Alina Starkov. Royal Corps of Surveyors—"

He cut me off. "*What* are you?"

I blinked. "I . . . I'm a mapmaker, sir."

Raevsky scowled. He pulled one of the soldiers aside and muttered something to him that sent the soldier sprinting back towards the dry docks. "Let's go," he said tersely.

I felt the jab of a rifle barrel in my back and marched forward. I had a very bad feeling about where I was being taken. *It can't be*, I thought desperately. *It makes no sense.* But as the huge black tent loomed larger and larger before us, there could be no doubt about where we were going.

The entrance to the Grisha tent was guarded by more Corporalki Heartrenders and charcoal-clad *oprichniki*, the elite soldiers who made up the Darkling's personal guard. The *oprichniki* weren't Grisha, but they were just as frightening.

The Corporalnik from the skiff conferred with the

guards at the front of the tent, then she and Colonel Raevsky disappeared inside. I waited, my heart racing, aware of the whispers and stares behind me, my anxiety rising.

High above, four flags fluttered in the breeze: blue, red, purple, and above them all, black. Just last night, Mal and his friends had been laughing about trying to get into this tent, wondering what they might find there. And now it seemed I would be the one to find out. *Where is Mal?* The thought kept returning to me, the only clear thought I seemed to be able to form.

After what felt an eternity, the Corporalnik returned and nodded at the captain, who led me into the Grisha tent.

For a moment, all my fear disappeared, eclipsed by the beauty that surrounded me. The tent's inner walls were draped with cascades of bronze silk that caught the glimmering candlelight from chandeliers sparkling high above. The floors were covered in rich rugs and furs. Along the walls, shimmering silken partitions separated compartments where Grisha clustered in their vibrant *kefta*. Some stood talking, others lounged on cushions drinking tea. Two were bent over a game of chess. From somewhere, I heard the strings of a balalaika being plucked. The Duke's estate had been beautiful, but it was a melancholy beauty of dusty rooms and peeling paint, the echo of something that had once been grand. The Grisha tent was like nothing I had ever seen before, a place alive with power and wealth.

The soldiers marched me down a long carpeted aisle at the end of which I could see a black pavilion on a raised dais. A ripple of curiosity spread through the tent as we passed. Grisha men and women stopped their conversations to gape at me; a few even rose to get a better look.

By the time we reached the dais, the room was all but silent, and I felt sure that everyone must hear my heart hammering in my chest. In front of the black pavilion, a few richly attired ministers wearing the King's double eagle and a group of Corporalki clustered around a long table spread with maps. At the head of the table was an ornately carved, high-backed chair of blackest ebony, and upon it lounged a figure in a black *kefta*, his chin resting on one pale hand. Only one Grisha wore black, was *permitted* to wear black. Colonel Raevsky stood beside him, speaking in tones far too low for me to hear.

I stared, torn between fear and fascination. *He's too young*, I thought. This Darkling had been commanding the Grisha since before I was born, but the man seated above me on the dais didn't look much older than I did. He had a sharp, beautiful face, a shock of thick black hair, and clear grey eyes that glimmered like quartz. I knew that the more powerful Grisha were said to live long lives, and Darklings were the most powerful of them all. But I felt the wrongness of it and I remembered Eva's words: *He's not natural. None of them are.*

A high, tinkling laugh sounded from the crowd that had formed near me at the base of the dais. I recognised the beautiful girl in blue, the one from the Etherealki coach who had been so taken with Mal. She whispered something to her chestnut-haired friend, and they both laughed again. My cheeks burned as I imagined what I must look like in a torn, shabby coat, after a journey into the Shadow Fold and a battle with a flock of hungry volcra. But I lifted my chin and looked the beautiful girl right in the eye. *Laugh all you want*, I thought grimly. *Whatever you're whispering, I've heard worse.* She held my gaze for a moment and then looked away. I enjoyed a brief flash of satisfaction before Colonel Raevsky's voice brought me back to the reality of my situation.

"Bring them," he said. I turned to see more soldiers leading a battered and bewildered group of people into the tent and up the aisle. Among them, I saw the soldier who had been beside me when the volcra attacked and the Senior Cartographer, his usually tidy coat torn and dirty, his face frightened. My distress grew as I realised that they were the survivors from my sand skiff and that they had been brought before the Darkling as witnesses. What had happened out there on the Fold? What did they think I had done?

My breath caught as I spotted the trackers in the group. I saw Mikhael first, his shaggy red hair bobbing above the crowd on his thick neck, and leaning on him, bandages peeking out from his bloodied shirt, was a very pale, very tired-looking Mal. My legs went weak and I pressed a hand to my mouth to stifle a sob.

Mal was alive. I wanted to push through the crowd and throw my arms around him, but it was all I could do to stay standing as relief flooded through me. Whatever happened here, we would be all right. We had survived the Fold, and we would survive this madness too.

I looked back at the dais and my elation withered. The Darkling was looking directly at me. He was still listening to Colonel Raevsky, his posture just as relaxed as it had been before, but his gaze was focused, intent. He turned his attention back to the colonel and I realised that I had been holding my breath.

When the bedraggled group of survivors reached the base of the dais, Colonel Raevsky ordered, "*Kapitan*, report."

The captain stood to attention and answered in an expressionless voice: "Approximately thirty minutes into the crossing, we were set upon by a large flock of volcra. We were pinned down and sustaining heavy casualties. I was fighting on the starboard side of the skiff. At that point, I saw . . ." The soldier hesitated, and when he spoke again, his voice sounded less sure. "I don't know exactly what I saw. A blaze of light. Bright as noon, brighter. Like staring into the sun."

The crowd erupted into murmurs. The survivors from the skiff were nodding, and I found myself nodding along with them. I had seen the blaze of light too.

The soldier snapped back to attention and continued, "The volcra scattered and the light disappeared. I ordered us back to dry dock immediately."

"And the girl?" asked the Darkling.

With a cold stab of fear, I realised he was talking about me.

"I didn't see the girl, *moi soverenyi*."

The Darkling raised an eyebrow, turning to the other survivors. "Who actually saw what happened?" His voice was cool, distant, almost disinterested.

The survivors broke into muttered discussion with one another. Then slowly, timidly, the Senior Cartographer stepped forward. I felt a keen twinge of pity for him. I'd never seen him so dishevelled. His sparse brown hair was standing at all angles on his head; his fingers plucked nervously at his ruined coat.

"Tell us what you saw," said Raevsky.

The Cartographer licked his lips. "We . . . we were under attack," he said tremulously. "There was fighting all around. Such noise. So much blood . . . One of the boys, Alexei, was taken. It was terrible, terrible." His hands fluttered like two startled birds.

I frowned. If the Cartographer had seen Alexei attacked, then why hadn't he tried to help?

The old man cleared his throat. "They were everywhere. I saw one go after her—"

"Who?" asked Raevsky.

"Alina . . . Alina Starkov, one of my assistants."

The beautiful girl in blue smirked and leaned over to whisper to her friend. I clenched my jaw. How nice to know that the Grisha could still maintain their snobbery in the midst of hearing about a volcra attack.

"Go on," Raevsky pressed.

"I saw one go after her and the tracker," the Cartographer said, gesturing to Mal.

"And where were you?" I asked angrily. The question was out of my mouth before I could think better of it. Every face turned to look at me, but I didn't care. "You saw the volcra attack us. You saw that thing take Alexei. Why didn't you help?"

"There was nothing I could do," he pleaded, his hands spread wide. "They were everywhere. It was chaos!"

"Alexei might still be alive if you'd tried to help us!"

There was a gasp and a burble of laughter from the crowd. The Cartographer flushed angrily and I felt instantly sorry. If I got out of this mess, I was going to be in very big trouble.

"Enough!" boomed Raevsky. "Tell us what you saw,

Cartographer."

The crowd hushed and the Cartographer licked his lips again. "The tracker went down. She was beside him. That thing, the volcra, was coming at them. I saw it on top of her and then . . . she lit up."

The Grisha erupted into exclamations of disbelief and derision. A few of them laughed. If I hadn't been so scared and baffled, I might have been tempted to join them. *Maybe I shouldn't have been so hard on him*, I thought, looking at the rumpled Cartographer. *The poor man clearly took a bump to the head during the attack.*

"I saw it!" he shouted over the din. "Light came *out* of her!"

Some of the Grisha were jeering openly now, but others were yelling, "Let him speak!" The Cartographer looked desperately to his fellow survivors for support, and to my amazement, I saw some of them nod. Had everyone gone mad? Did they actually think *I* had chased off the volcra?

"This is absurd!" said a voice from the crowd. It was the beautiful girl in blue. "What are you suggesting, old man? That you've found us a Sun Summoner?"

"I'm not suggesting anything," he protested. "I'm only telling you what I saw!"

"It's not impossible," said a heavyset Grisha. He wore the purple *kefta* of a Materialnik, a member of the Order of Fabrikators. "There are stories—"

"Don't be ridiculous," the girl laughed, her voice thick with scorn. "The man's had his wits rattled by the volcra!"

The crowd erupted into loud argument.

I suddenly felt very tired. My shoulder throbbed

where the volcra had dug its talons into me. I didn't know what the Cartographer or any of the others on the skiff thought they had seen. I just knew this was all some kind of terrible mistake, and at the end of this farce, I would be the one looking foolish. I cringed when I thought of the teasing I would take when this was over. And hopefully, it would be over soon.

"Quiet." The Darkling barely seemed to raise his voice, but the command sliced through the crowd and silence fell.

I suppressed a shiver. He might not find this joke so funny. I just hoped he wouldn't blame me for it. The Darkling wasn't known for mercy. Maybe I should be worrying less about being teased and more about being exiled to Tsibeya. Or worse. Eva said that the Darkling had once ordered a Corporalki Healer to seal a traitor's mouth shut permanently. The man's lips had been grafted together and he had starved to death. At the time, Alexei and I had laughed and dismissed it as another of Eva's crazy stories. Now I wasn't so sure.

"Tracker," the Darkling said softly, "what did you see?"

As one, the crowd turned towards Mal, who looked uneasily at me and then back at the Darkling. "Nothing. I didn't see anything."

"The girl was right beside you."

Mal nodded.

"You must have seen something."

Mal glanced at me again, his look weighted with worry and fatigue. I'd never seen him so pale, and I wondered how much blood he had lost. I felt a surge of helpless anger. He was badly hurt. He should be resting instead of standing here answering ridiculous questions.

"Just tell us what you remember, tracker," commanded Raevsky.

Mal shrugged slightly and winced at the pain from his wounds. "I was on my back on the deck. Alina was next to me. I saw the volcra diving, and I knew it was coming for us. I said something and—"

"What did you say?" The Darkling's cool voice cut through the room.

"I don't remember," Mal said. I recognised the stubborn set of his jaw and knew he was lying. He did remember. "I smelled the volcra, saw it swooping down on us. Alina screamed and then I couldn't see anything. The world was just . . . shining."

"So you didn't see where the light was coming from?" Raevsky asked.

"Alina isn't . . . She couldn't . . ." Mal shook his head. "We're from the same . . . village." I noticed that tiny pause, the orphan's pause. "If she could do anything like that, I would know."

The Darkling looked at Mal for a long moment and then glanced back at me.

"We all have our secrets," he said.

Mal opened his mouth as if to say more, but the Darkling put up a hand to silence him. Anger flashed across Mal's features. He shut his mouth, his lips pressed into a grim line.

The Darkling rose from his chair. He gestured and the soldiers stepped back, leaving me alone to face him. The tent seemed eerily quiet. Slowly, he descended the steps.

I had to fight the urge to back away as he came to a halt in front of me.

"Now, what do *you* say, Alina Starkov?" he asked pleasantly.

I swallowed. My throat was dry and my heart was careening from beat to beat, but I knew I had to speak. I had to make him understand that I'd had no part in any of this. "There's been some kind of mistake," I said hoarsely. "I didn't do anything. I don't know how we survived."

The Darkling appeared to consider this. Then he crossed his arms, cocked his head to one side. "Well," he said, his voice bemused. "I like to think that I know everything that happens in Ravka, and that if I had a Sun Summoner living in my own country, I'd be aware of it." Soft murmurs of assent rose from the crowd, but he ignored them, watching me closely. "But *something* powerful stopped the volcra and saved the King's skiffs."

He paused and waited as if he expected me to solve this conundrum for him.

My chin rose stubbornly. "I didn't do anything," I said. "Not one thing."

The side of the Darkling's mouth twitched, as if he were repressing a smile. His eyes slid over me from head to toe and back again. I felt like something strange and shiny, a curiosity that had washed up on a lake shore, that he might kick aside with his boot.

"Is your memory as faulty as your friend's?" he asked and bobbed his head towards Mal.

"I don't . . ." I faltered. What *did* I remember? Terror. Darkness. Pain. Mal's blood. His life flowing out of him beneath my hands. The rage that filled me at the thought of my own helplessness.

"Hold out your arm," said the Darkling.

"What?"

"We've wasted enough time. Hold out your arm."

A cold spike of fear went through me. I looked around in panic, but there was no help to be had. The soldiers stared forward, stony-faced. The survivors from the skiff looked frightened and tired. The Grisha regarded me curiously. The girl in blue was smirking. Mal's pale face seemed to have gone even whiter, but there was no answer in his worried eyes.

Shaking, I held out my left arm.

"Push up your sleeve."

"I didn't do anything." I'd meant to say it loudly, to proclaim it, but my voice sounded frightened and small.

The Darkling looked at me, waiting. I pushed up my sleeve.

He spread his arms and terror washed through me as I saw his palms filling with something black that pooled and curled through the air like ink in water.

"Now," he said in that same soft, conversational voice, as if we were sitting together drinking tea, as if I did not stand before him shaking, "let's see what you can do."

He brought his hands together and there was a sound like a thunderclap. I gasped as undulating darkness spread from his clasped hands, spilling in a black wave over me and the crowd.

I was blind. The room was gone. Everything was gone. I cried out in terror as I felt the Darkling's fingers close around my bare wrist. Suddenly, my fear receded. It was still there, cringing like an animal inside me, but it had been pushed aside by something calm and sure and powerful, something vaguely familiar.

I felt a call ring through me and, to my surprise, I felt

something in me rise up to answer. I pushed it away, pushed it down. Somehow I knew that if that thing got free, it would destroy me.

"Nothing there?" the Darkling murmured. I felt how very close he was to me in the dark. My panicked mind seized on his words. *Nothing there. That's right, nothing. Nothing at all. Now leave me be!*

And to my relief, that struggling thing inside me seemed to lie back down, leaving the Darkling's call unanswered.

"Not so fast," he whispered. I felt something cold press against the inside of my forearm. In the same moment that I realised it was a knife, the blade cut into my skin.

Pain and fear rushed through me. I cried out. The thing inside me roared to the surface, speeding towards the Darkling's call. I couldn't stop myself. I answered. The world exploded into blazing white light.

The darkness shattered around us like glass. For a moment, I saw the faces of the crowd, their mouths wide with shock as the tent filled with shining sunlight, the air shimmering with heat. Then the Darkling released his grip, and with his touch went that peculiar sense of certainty that had possessed me. The radiant light disappeared, leaving ordinary candlelight in its place, but I could still feel the warm and inexplicable glow of sunshine on my skin.

My legs gave way and the Darkling caught me up against his body with one surprisingly strong arm.

"I guess you only look like a mouse," he whispered in my ear, and then beckoned to one of his personal guard. "Take her," he said, handing me over to the *oprichnik* who reached out his arm to support me. I felt myself flush at the indignity of being handed over like a sack of potatoes, but I was too shaky and confused to protest. Blood was running down my arm from the cut the Darkling had given me.

"Ivan!" shouted the Darkling. A tall Heartrender rushed from the dais to the Darkling's side. "Get her to my coach. I want her surrounded by an armed guard at all times. Take her to the Little Palace and stop for nothing." Ivan nodded. "And bring a Healer to see to her wounds."

"Wait!" I protested, but the Darkling was already turning away. I clutched at his arm, ignoring the gasp that rose from the Grisha onlookers. "There's been some kind of mistake. I don't . . . I'm not . . ." My voice trailed off as the Darkling turned slowly to me, his slate eyes drifting to where my hand gripped his sleeve. I let go, but I wasn't giving up that easily. "I'm not what you think I am," I whispered desperately.

The Darkling stepped closer to me and spoke, his voice so low that only I could hear, "I doubt you have any idea what you are." Then he nodded to Ivan. "Go!"

The Darkling turned his back on me and walked swiftly towards the raised dais, where he was swarmed by advisers and ministers, all talking loudly and rapidly.

Ivan grabbed me roughly by the arm. "Come on."

"Ivan," called the Darkling, "mind your tone. She is Grisha now."

Ivan reddened slightly and gave a small bow, but his grip on my arm didn't slacken as he pulled me down the aisle.

"You have to listen to me," I gasped as I struggled to

keep up with his long strides. "I'm not Grisha. I'm a mapmaker. I'm not even a very good mapmaker."

Ivan ignored me.

I looked back over my shoulder, searching the crowd. Mal was arguing with the captain from the sand skiff. As if he felt my eyes on him, he looked up and met my gaze. I could see my own panic and confusion mirrored in his white face. I wanted to cry out to him, to run to him, but the next moment he was gone, swallowed up by the crowd.

Chapter 4

Tears of frustration welled in my eyes as Ivan dragged me out of the tent and into the late-afternoon sun. He pulled me down a low hill to the road where the Darkling's black coach was already waiting, surrounded by a ring of mounted Grisha Etherealki and flanked by lines of armed cavalry. Two of the Darkling's grey-clad guards waited by the door to the coach with a woman and a fair-haired man, both of whom wore Corporalki red.

"Get in," commanded Ivan. Then, seeming to remember the Darkling's order, he added, "If you please."

"No," I said.

"What?" Ivan seemed genuinely surprised. The other Corporalki looked shocked.

"No!" I repeated. "I'm not going anywhere. There's been some kind of mistake. I—"

Ivan cut me off, taking a firmer grip on my arm. "The Darkling doesn't make mistakes," he said through gritted teeth. "Get in the coach."

"I don't want—"

Ivan lowered his head until his nose was just inches from mine and practically spat, "Do you think I care what you want? In a few hours' time, every Fjerdan spy and Shu Han assassin will know what happened on the Fold, and they'll be coming for you. Our only chance is to get you to Os Alta and behind the palace walls before anyone else realises what you are. Now, *get in the coach*."

He shoved me through the door and followed me inside, throwing himself down on the seat opposite me in disgust. The other Corporalki joined him, followed by the *oprichniki* guards, who settled on either side of me.

"So I'm the Darkling's prisoner?"

"You're under his protection."

"What's the difference?"

Ivan's expression was unreadable. "Pray you never find out."

I scowled and slumped back on the cushioned seat, then hissed in pain. I'd forgotten my wounds.

"See to her," Ivan said to the female Corporalnik. Her cuffs were embroidered in Healer's grey.

The woman switched places with one of the *oprichniki* so that she could sit beside me.

A soldier ducked his head inside the door. "We're ready," he said.

"Good," replied Ivan. "Stay alert and keep moving."

"We'll only stop to change horses. If we stop before then, you'll know something is wrong."

The soldier disappeared, closing the door behind him. The driver didn't hesitate. With a cry and the snap of a whip, the coach lurched forward. I felt an icy tumble of panic. What was happening to me? I thought about just throwing open the coach door and making a run for it. But where would I run? We were surrounded by armed men in the middle of a military camp. And even if we weren't, where could I possibly go?

"Please remove your coat," said the woman beside me.

"What?"

"I need to see to your wounds."

I considered refusing, but what was the point? I shrugged awkwardly out of my coat and let the Healer ease my shirt over my shoulders. The Corporalki were the Order of the Living and the Dead. I tried to focus on the *living* part, but I'd never been healed by a Grisha and every muscle in my body tensed with fear.

She took something out of a little satchel and a sharp chemical scent filled the coach. I flinched as she cleaned the wounds, my fingers digging into my knees. When she had finished, I felt a hot, prickling sensation between my shoulders. I bit down hard on my lip. The urge to scratch my back was almost unbearable. Finally, she stopped and pulled my shirt back into place. I flexed my shoulders carefully. The pain was gone.

"Now the arm," she said.

I'd almost forgotten the cut from the Darkling's knife, but my wrist and hand were sticky with blood. She wiped the cut clean and then held my arm up to the light. "Try to stay still," she said, "or there will be a scar."

I did my best, but the jostling of the coach made it difficult. The Healer passed her hand slowly over the wound. I felt my skin throb with heat. My arm began to itch furiously and, as I watched in amazement, my flesh seemed to shimmer and move as the two sides of the cut knitted together and the skin sealed shut.

The itching stopped and the Healer sat back. I reached out and touched my arm. There was a slightly raised scar where the cut had been, but that was all.

"Thank you," I said in awe.

The Healer nodded.

"Give her your *kefta*," Ivan said to her.

The woman frowned but hesitated only a moment before she shrugged out of her red *kefta* and handed it to me.

"Why do I need this?" I asked.

"Just take it," Ivan growled.

I took the *kefta* from the Healer. She kept her face blank, but I could tell it pained her to part with it.

Before I could decide whether or not to offer her my blood-stained coat, Ivan tapped the roof and the coach began to slow. The Healer didn't even wait for it to stop moving before she opened the door and swung outside.

Ivan pulled the door shut. The *oprichnik* slipped back into the seat beside me, and we were on our way once more.

"Where is she going?" I asked.

"Back to Kribirsk," replied Ivan. "We'll travel faster with less weight."

"You look heavier than she does," I muttered.

"Put on the *kefta*," he said.

"Why?"

"Because it's made with Materialki corecloth. It can withstand rifle fire."

I stared at him. Was that even possible? There were stories of Grisha withstanding direct gunshots and surviving what should have been fatal wounds. I'd never taken them seriously, but maybe Fabrikator handiwork was the truth behind those peasant tales.

"Do you all wear this stuff?" I asked as I pulled on the *kefta*.

"When we're in the field," said an *oprichnik*. I nearly

jumped. It was the first time either of the guards had spoken.

"Just don't get shot in the head," Ivan added with a condescending grin.

I ignored him. The *kefta* was far too large. It felt soft and unfamiliar, the fur lining warm against my skin. I chewed my lip. It didn't seem fair that *oprichniki* and Grisha wore corecloth while ordinary soldiers went without. Did our officers wear it too?

The coach picked up speed. In the time it had taken for the Healer to do her work, dusk had begun to fall and we had left Kribirsk behind. I leaned forward, straining to see out of the window, but the world outside was a twilight blur. I felt tears threatening again and blinked them back. A few hours ago, I'd been a frightened girl on my way into the unknown, but at least I'd known who and what I was. With a pang, I thought of the Documents Tent. The other surveyors might be at their work right now. Would they be mourning Alexei? Would they be talking about me and what had happened on the Fold?

I clutched the crumpled army-issue coat I had bundled up on my lap. Surely this all had to be a dream, some crazy hallucination brought on by the terrors of the Shadow Fold. I couldn't really be wearing a Grisha's *kefta*, sitting in the Darkling's coach – the same coach that had almost crushed me only yesterday.

Someone lit a lamp inside the coach, and in the flickering light I could better see the silken interior. The seats were heavily cushioned black velvet. On the windows, the Darkling's symbol had been cut into the glass: two overlapping circles, the sun in eclipse. Sun Summoner. I'd never heard the term before. If the Darkling could summon darkness, then I supposed it was possible for someone to summon light. Was that what I had done? I rubbed my thumb across the scar on my palm. It wasn't possible.

Across from me, the two Grisha were studying me with open curiosity. Their red *kefta* were of the finest wool, embroidered lavishly in black and lined with black fur. The fair-haired Heartrender was lanky and had a long, melancholy face. Ivan was taller, broader, with wavy brown hair and sun-bronzed skin. Now that I bothered to look, I had to admit he was handsome. *And knows it too. A big handsome bully.*

I shifted restlessly in my seat, uncomfortable with their stares. I looked out of the window, but there was nothing to see except the growing darkness and my own pale reflection. I looked back at the Grisha and tried to quash my irritation. They were still gawking at me. I reminded myself that these men could make my heart explode in my chest, but eventually I just couldn't stand it.

"I don't do tricks, you know," I snapped.

The Grisha exchanged a glance.

"That was a pretty good trick back in the tent," Ivan said.

I rolled my eyes. "Well, if I plan on doing anything exciting, I promise to give fair warning so just . . . go to sleep or something."

Ivan looked affronted. I felt a little snap of fear, but the fair-haired Corporalnik let out a bark of laughter.

"I am Fedyor," he said. "And this is Ivan."

"I know," I replied. Then, picturing Ana Kuya's disapproving glare, I added, "Very pleased to meet you."

They exchanged an amused glance. I ignored them

and wriggled back in my seat, trying to get comfortable. It wasn't easy with two heavily armed soldiers taking up most of the room.

The coach jolted as we hit a bump.

"Is it safe?" I asked. "To be travelling at night?"

"No," Fedyor said. "But it would be considerably more dangerous to stop."

"Because people are after me now?" I said sarcastically.

"If not now, then soon."

I snorted. Fedyor raised his eyebrows and said, "For hundreds of years, the Shadow Fold has been doing our enemies' work, closing off our ports, choking us, making us weak. If you're truly a Sun Summoner, then your power could be the key to opening up the Fold – or maybe even destroying it. Fjerda and the Shu Han won't just stand by and let that happen."

I gaped at him. What did these people expect from me? And what would they do to me when they realised I couldn't deliver? "This is ridiculous," I muttered.

Fedyor looked me up and down and then smiled slightly. "Maybe," he said.

I frowned. He was agreeing with me, but I still felt insulted.

"How did you hide it?" Ivan asked abruptly.

"What?"

"Your power," Ivan said impatiently. "How did you hide it?"

"I didn't hide it. I didn't know it was there."

"That's impossible."

"And yet here we are," I said bitterly.

"Weren't you tested?"

A dim memory flashed through my mind: three cloaked figures in the sitting room at Keramzin, a woman's haughty brow.

"Of course I was tested."

"When?"

"When I was eight."

"That's very late," commented Ivan. "Why didn't your parents have you tested earlier?"

Because they were dead, I thought but didn't say. *And no one paid much attention to Duke Keramsov's orphans.* I shrugged.

"It doesn't make any sense," Ivan grumbled.

"That's what I've been trying to tell you!" I leaned forward, looking desperately from Ivan to Fedyor. "I'm not what you think I am. I'm not Grisha. What happened in the Fold . . . I don't know what happened, but I didn't do it."

"And what happened in the Grisha tent?" asked Fedyor calmly.

"I can't explain that. But it wasn't my doing. The Darkling did something when he touched me."

Ivan laughed. "He didn't *do* anything. He's an amplifier."

"A what?"

Fedyor and Ivan exchanged another glance.

"Forget it," I snapped. "I don't care."

Ivan reached inside his collar and removed something on a thin silver chain. He held it out for me to examine.

My curiosity got the best of me, and I edged closer to get a better view. It looked like a cluster of sharp black claws.

"What are they?"

"My amplifier," Ivan said with pride. "The claws from the forepaw of a Sherborn bear. I killed it myself when I left school and joined the Darkling's service." He leaned back in his seat and tucked the chain into his collar.

"An amplifier increases a Grisha's power," said Fedyor. "But the power must be there to begin with."

"Do all Grisha have them?" I asked.

Fedyor stiffened. "No," he said. "Amplifiers are rare and hard to obtain."

"Only the Darkling's most favoured Grisha have them," Ivan said smugly. I was sorry I'd asked.

"The Darkling is a living amplifier," Fedyor said. "That's what you felt."

"Like the claws? That's his power?"

"*One* of his powers," corrected Ivan.

I pulled the *kefta* tighter around me, feeling suddenly cold. I remembered the surety that had flooded through me with the Darkling's touch, and that strangely familiar sensation of a call echoing through me, a call that demanded an answer. It had been frightening, but exhilarating too. In that moment, all my doubt and fear had been replaced by a kind of absolute certainty. I was no one, a refugee from an unnamed village, a scrawny, clumsy girl hurtling alone through the gathering dark. But when the Darkling had closed his fingers around my wrist, I'd felt different, like something more. I shut my eyes and tried to focus, tried to remember that feeling, to bring that sure and perfect power into blazing life. But nothing happened.

I sighed and opened my eyes. Ivan looked highly amused. The urge to kick him was almost overwhelming.

"You're all in for a big disappointment," I muttered.

"For your sake, I hope you're wrong," said Ivan.

"For all our sakes," said Fedyor.

I lost track of time. Night and day passed through the windows of the coach. I stared out at the landscape, searching for landmarks to give me some sense of the familiar. I'd expected that we would take side roads, but instead we stuck to the Vy, and Fedyor explained that the Darkling had opted for speed over stealth. He was hoping to get me safely behind Os Alta's double walls before rumour of my power spread to the enemy spies and assassins who operated within Ravka's borders.

We kept a brutal pace. Occasionally, we stopped to change horses and I was allowed to stretch my legs. When I was able to sleep, my dreams were plagued by monsters.

Once, I awoke with a start, my heart pounding, to find Fedyor watching me. Ivan was asleep beside him, snoring loudly.

"Who's Mal?" he asked.

I realised I must have been talking in my sleep. Embarrassed, I glanced at the *oprichniki* guards flanking me. One stared impassively forward. The other was dozing. Outside, the afternoon sun shone through a grove of birchwood trees as we rumbled past.

"No one," I said. "A friend."

"The tracker?"

I nodded. "He was with me on the Shadow Fold. He saved my life."

"And you saved his."

I opened my mouth to disagree, but stopped. Had I saved Mal's life? The thought brought me up short.

"It's a great honour," said Fedyor. "To save a life. You saved many."

"Not enough," I murmured, thinking of the terrified look on Alexei's face as he was pulled into the darkness. If I had this power, why hadn't I been able to save him? Or any of the others who had perished on the Fold? I looked at Fedyor. "If you really believe that saving a life is an honour, then why not become a Healer instead of a Heartrender?"

Fedyor considered the passing scenery. "Of all Grisha, Corporalki have the hardest road. We hold the highest rank, but we require the most training and study. At the end of it all, I felt I could save more lives as a Heartrender."

"As a killer?" I asked in surprise.

"As a soldier," Fedyor corrected. He shrugged. "To kill or to cure?" he said with a sad smile. "We each have our own gifts." Abruptly, his expression changed. He sat up straight and jabbed Ivan in the side. "Wake up!"

The coach had stopped. I looked around in confusion. "Are we—" I began, but the guard beside me clapped a hand over my mouth and put a finger to his lips.

The coach door flew open and a soldier ducked his head in.

"There's a fallen tree across the road," he said. "But it could be a trap. Be alert and—"

He never finished his sentence. A shot rang out and he fell forward, a bullet in his back. Suddenly, the air was full of panicked cries and the teeth-rattling sound of rifle fire as a volley of bullets struck the coach.

"Get down!" yelled the guard beside me, shielding my body with his own as Ivan kicked the dead soldier out of the way and pulled the door closed.

"Fjerdans," said the guard, peering outside.

Ivan turned to Fedyor and the guard beside me. "Fedyor, go with him. You take this side. We'll take the other. At all costs, defend the coach."

Fedyor pulled a large knife from his belt and handed it to me. "Stay close to the floor and stay quiet."

The Grisha waited with the guards, crouching by the windows, then at a signal from Ivan they leapt from either side of the coach, slamming the doors behind them. I huddled on the floor, clutching the knife's heavy hilt, my knees to my chest, my back pressed against the base of the seat. Outside, I could hear the sounds of fighting, metal on metal, grunts and shouts, horses whinnying. The coach shook as a body slammed against the glass of the window. I saw with horror that it was one of my guards. His body left a red smear against the glass as he slid from view.

The coach door flew open and a man with a wild, yellow-bearded face appeared. I scrambled to the other side of the coach, holding the knife before me. He barked something to his compatriots in his strange Fjerdan tongue and reached for my leg. As I kicked out at him, the door behind me opened and I nearly tumbled into another bearded man. He grabbed me under the arms, pulling me roughly from the coach as I howled and slashed out with the knife.

I must have made contact, because he cursed and loosened his grip. I struggled to my feet and ran. We were in a wooded glen where the Vy narrowed to pass between two sloping hills. All around me, soldiers and Grisha were fighting with bearded men. Trees burst into flames, caught in the line of Grisha fire. I saw Fedyor throw his hand out, and the man before him crumpled to the ground, clutching his chest, blood trickling from his mouth.

I ran without direction, clambering up the nearest hill, my feet slipping on the fallen leaves that covered the forest floor, my breath coming in gasps. I made it halfway up the slope before I was tackled from behind. I fell forward, the knife flying from my hands as I put up my arms to break my fall.

I twisted and kicked as the yellow-bearded man grabbed hold of my legs. I looked desperately down to the glen. The soldiers and Grisha below me were fighting for their lives, clearly outnumbered and unable to come to my aid. I struggled and thrashed, but the Fjerdan was too strong. He climbed on top of me, using his knees to pin my arms to my sides, and reached for his knife.

"I'll gut you right here, witch," he snarled in a heavy Fjerdan accent.

At that moment, I heard the pounding of hooves and my attacker turned his head to look down at the road.

A group of riders roared into the glen, their *kefta* streaming red and blue, their hands blazing fire and thunder. The lead rider was dressed in black.

The Darkling slid from his mount and threw his hands wide, then brought them together with a resounding boom. Skeins of darkness shot from his clasped hands, snaking through the glen, finding the Fjerdan assassins, then slithering up their bodies to swathe their faces in seething shadow. They screamed. Some dropped their swords; others waved them blindly.

From the hillside, I watched in mingled awe and horror as the Ravkan fighters seized the advantage, cutting down the blinded, helpless men with ease.

The bearded man on top of me muttered something I did not understand. I thought it might be a prayer. He was staring down at the slaughter in the glen, frozen, his terror palpable. I took my chance.

"I'm here!" I called.

The Darkling's head turned. He raised his hands.

"*Nej!*" bleated the Fjerdan, his knife held high. "I don't need to see to put my knife through her heart!"

I held my breath. Silence fell in the glen, broken only by the moans of dying men. The Darkling dropped his hands.

"You must know that you're surrounded," he said calmly, his voice carrying through the trees.

The assassin's gaze darted right and left, then up to the crest of the hill where Ravkan soldiers were emerging, rifles at the ready. As the Fjerdan looked around frantically, the Darkling edged a few steps up the slope.

"No closer!" the man shrieked.

The Darkling stopped. "Give her to me," he said, "and I'll let you scurry back to your King."

The assassin gave a crazed little giggle. "Oh no, oh no. I don't think so," he said, shaking his head, his knife held high above my pounding heart, its cruel point gleaming in the sun. "The Darkling doesn't spare lives." He looked down at me. His lashes were light blond, almost invisible. "He will not have you," he crooned softly. "He will not have the witch. He will not have this power too." He raised the knife higher and yowled, "*Skirden Fjerda!*"

The knife plunged down in a shining arc. I turned my head, squeezing my eyes shut in terror, and as I did, I glimpsed the Darkling, his arm slashing through the air in front of him. I heard another crack like thunder and then . . . nothing.

Slowly, I opened my eyes and took in the horror before me. I opened my mouth to scream, but no sound would come. The man on top of me had been cut in two. His head, his right shoulder and his arm lay on the forest floor, his white hand still clasping the knife. The rest of him swayed for a moment above me, a dark wisp of smoke fading in the air beside the wound that ran the length of his severed torso. Then what remained of him fell forward.

I found my voice and screamed. I crawled backwards, scrambling away from the mutilated body, unable to get to my feet, unable to look away from the awful sight, my body shaking uncontrollably.

The Darkling hurried up the hill and knelt beside me, blocking my view of the corpse. "Look at me," he instructed.

I tried to focus on his face, but all I could see was the assassin's severed body, his blood pooling in the damp leaves. "What . . . what did you do to him?" I asked, my voice quavering.

"What I had to do. Can you stand?"

I nodded shakily. He took my hands and helped me to my feet. When my gaze slid back to the corpse, he took hold of my chin and drew my eyes back to his. "At me," he commanded.

I nodded and tried to keep my eyes trained on the Darkling as he led me down the hill and called out orders to his men.

"Clear the road. I need twenty riders."

"The girl?" Ivan asked.

"Rides with me," said the Darkling.

He left me by his horse as he went to confer with Ivan and his captains. I was relieved to see Fedyor with them, clutching his arm but looking otherwise uninjured. I patted the horse's sweaty flank and breathed in the clean leather smell of the saddle, trying to slow the beating of my heart and to ignore what I knew lay behind me on the hillside.

A few minutes later, I saw soldiers and Grisha mounting their horses. Several men had finished clearing the tree from the road, and others were riding out with the much-battered coach.

"A decoy," said the Darkling, coming up beside me. "We'll take the southern trails. It's what we should have done in the first place."

"So you do make mistakes," I said without thinking.

He paused in the act of pulling on his gloves, and I pressed my lips together nervously. "I didn't mean—"

"Of course I make mistakes," he said. His mouth curved into a half smile. "Just not often."

He raised his hood and offered me his hand to help me onto the horse. For a moment, I hesitated. He stood before me, a dark rider, cloaked in black, his features in shadow. The image of the severed man loomed up in my mind, and my stomach turned.

As if he'd read my thoughts, he repeated, "I did what I had to, Alina."

I knew that. He had saved my life. And what other choice did I have? I put my hand in his and let the Darkling help me into the saddle. He slid up behind me and kicked the horse into a trot.

As we left the glen, I felt the reality of what had just happened sink into me.

"You're shaking," he said.

"I'm not used to people trying to kill me."

"Really? I hardly notice any more."

I turned to look at him. That trace of a smile was still there, but I wasn't entirely sure he was joking. I turned back around and said, "And I did just see a man get sliced in half." I kept my voice light, but I couldn't hide the fact that I was still trembling.

The Darkling switched his reins to one hand and pulled off one of his gloves. I stiffened as I felt him slide his bare palm under my hair and rest it on the nape of my neck. My surprise gave way to calm as that same sense of power and surety flooded through me. With one hand cupping my head, he kicked the horse into a canter. I closed my eyes and tried not to think, and soon, despite the movement of the horse, despite the terrors of the day, I fell into a troubled sleep.

Chapter 5

The next few days passed in a blur of discomfort and exhaustion. We stayed off the Vy and kept to side roads and narrow hunting trails, moving as quickly as the hilly and sometimes treacherous terrain would allow. I lost all sense of where we were or how far we had gone.

After the first day, the Darkling and I had ridden separately, but I found that I was always aware of where he was in the column of riders. He didn't say a word to me, and as the hours and days wore on, I started to worry that I'd somehow offended him. (Though, given how little we'd spoken, I wasn't sure how I could have managed it.) Occasionally, I caught him looking at me, his eyes cool and unreadable.

I'd never been a particularly good rider, and the pace the Darkling set was taking its toll. No matter which way I shifted in my saddle, some part of my body ached. I stared listlessly at my horse's twitching ears and tried not to think of my burning legs or the throbbing in my lower back. On the fifth night, when we stopped to make camp at an abandoned farm, I wanted to leap from my horse in joy. But I was so stiff that I settled for sliding awkwardly to the ground. I thanked the soldier who saw to my mount and waddled slowly down a small hill to where I could hear the soft gurgle of a stream.

I knelt by the bank on shaky legs and washed my face and hands in the cold water. The air had changed over the last couple of days, and the bright blue skies of autumn were giving way to sullen grey. The soldiers seemed to think that we would reach Os Alta before any real weather came on. And then what? What would happen to me when we reached the Little Palace? What would happen when I couldn't do what they wanted me to do? It wasn't wise to disappoint kings. Or Darklings. I doubted they'd just send me back to the regiment with a pat on the back. I wondered if Mal was still in Kribirsk. If his wounds had healed, he might already have been sent back across the Fold or on to some other assignment. I thought of his face disappearing into the crowd in the Grisha tent. I hadn't even had a chance to say goodbye.

In the gathering dusk, I stretched my arms and back and tried to shake the feeling of gloom that had settled over me. *It's probably for the best*, I told myself. How would I have said goodbye to Mal anyway? *Thanks for being my best friend and making my life bearable. Oh, and sorry I fell in love with you for a while there. Make sure to write!*

"What are you smiling at?"

I whirled, peering into the gloom. The Darkling's voice seemed to float out of the shadows. He walked down to the stream, crouching on the bank to splash water on his face and through his dark hair.

"Well?" he asked, looking up at me.

"Myself," I admitted.

"Are you that funny?"

"I'm hilarious."

The Darkling regarded me in what remained of the twilight. I had the disquieting sensation that I was being studied. Other than a bit of dust on his *kefta*, our trek seemed to have had little effect on him. My skin prickled with embarrassment as I became keenly aware of my torn, too-large *kefta*, my dirty hair, and the bruise the Fjerdan assassin had left on my cheek. Was he looking at me and regretting his decision to drag me all this way? Was he thinking that he'd made another of his infrequent mistakes?

"I'm not Grisha," I blurted.

"The evidence suggests otherwise," he said. "What makes you so certain?"

"Look at me!"

"I'm looking."

"Do I look like a Grisha to you?" Grisha were beautiful. They didn't have spotty skin and dull brown hair and scrawny arms.

He shook his head and rose. "You don't understand at all," he said, and began walking back up the hill.

"Are you going to explain it to me?"

"Not right now, no."

I was so furious I wanted to smack him on the back of his head. And if I hadn't seen him cut a man in half, I might have done just that. I settled for glaring at the space between his shoulder blades as I followed him up the hill.

Inside the farm's broken-down barn, the Darkling's men had cleared a space on the earthen floor and built a fire. One of them had caught and killed a grouse and was roasting it over the flames. It made a poor meal shared among all of us, but the Darkling did not want to send his men ranging into the woods for game.

I took a place by the fire and ate my small portion in

silence. When I'd finished, I hesitated for only a moment before wiping my fingers on my already filthy *kefta*. It was probably the nicest thing I'd ever worn or would wear, and something about seeing the fabric stained and torn made me feel particularly low.

In the light from the fire, I watched the *oprichniki* sitting side by side with the Grisha. Some of them had already drifted away from the fire to bed down for the night. Others had been posted to the first watch. The rest sat talking as the flames ebbed, passing a flask back and forth. The Darkling sat with them. I'd noticed that he had taken no more than his share of the grouse. And now he sat beside his soldiers on the cold ground, a man second in power only to the King.

He must have felt my gaze, because he turned to look at me, his granite eyes glimmering in the firelight. I flushed. To my dismay, he rose and came to sit beside me, offering me the flask. I hesitated and then took a sip, grimacing at the taste. I'd never liked *kvas*, but the teachers at Keramzin had drunk it like water. Mal and I had stolen a bottle once. The beating we'd taken when we were caught had been nothing compared to how miserably sick we'd been.

Still, it burned going down, and the warmth was welcome. I took another sip and handed the flask back to him. "Thank you," I said with a little cough.

He drank, staring into the fire, and then said, "All right. Ask me."

I blinked at him, taken aback. I wasn't sure where to begin. My tired mind had been brimming with questions, whirring in a state between panic and exhaustion and disbelief since we'd left Kribirsk. I wasn't sure that I had the energy to form a thought, and when I opened my mouth, the question that came out surprised me.

"How old are you?"

He looked at me, bemused. "I don't know exactly."

"How can you not know?"

The Darkling shrugged. "How old are *you* exactly?"

I flashed him a sour look. I didn't know the date of my birth. All the orphans at Keramzin were given the Duke's birthday in honour of our benefactor. "Well, then, roughly how old are you?"

"Why do you want to know?"

"Because I've heard stories about you since I was a child, but you don't look much older than I am," I said honestly.

"What kind of stories?"

"The usual kind," I said with some annoyance. "If you don't want to answer me, just say so."

"I don't want to answer you."

"Oh."

Then he sighed and said, "One hundred and twenty. Give or take."

"What?" I squeaked. The soldiers sitting across from me glanced over. "That's impossible," I said more quietly.

He looked into the flames. "When a fire burns, it uses up the wood. It devours it, leaving only ash. Grisha power doesn't work that way."

"How does it work?"

"Using our power makes us stronger. It feeds us instead of consuming us. Most Grisha live long lives."

"But not one hundred and twenty years."

"No," he admitted. "The length of a Grisha's life is

proportional to his or her power. The greater the power, the longer the life. And when that power is amplified . . ." He trailed off with a shrug.

"And you're a living amplifier. Like Ivan's bear."

The hint of a smile tugged at the corner of his mouth. "Like Ivan's bear."

An unpleasant thought occurred to me. "But that means—"

"That my bones or a few of my teeth would make another Grisha very powerful."

"Well, that's completely creepy. Doesn't it worry you a little bit?"

"No," he said simply. "Now you answer my question. What kind of stories were you told about me?"

I shifted uncomfortably. "Well . . . our teachers told us that you strengthened the Second Army by gathering Grisha from outside of Ravka."

"I didn't have to gather them. They came to me. Other countries don't treat their Grisha so well as Ravka," he said grimly. "The Fjerdans burn us as witches, and the Kerch sell us as slaves. The Shu Han carve us up seeking the source of our power. What else?"

"They said you were the strongest Darkling in generations."

"I didn't ask you for flattery."

I fingered a loose thread on the cuff of my *kefta*. He watched me, waiting.

"Well," I said, "there was an old serf who worked on the estate . . ."

"Go on," he said. "Tell me."

"He . . . he said that Darklings are born without souls. That only something truly evil could have created the

Shadow Fold." I glanced at his cold face and added hastily, "But Ana Kuya sent him packing and told us it was all peasant superstition."

The Darkling sighed. "I doubt that serf is the only one who believes it."

I said nothing. Not everyone thought like Eva or the old serf, but I'd been in the First Army long enough to know that most ordinary soldiers didn't trust Grisha and felt no allegiance to the Darkling.

After a moment, the Darkling said, "My great-great-great-grandfather was the Black Heretic, the Darkling who created the Shadow Fold. It was a mistake, an experiment born of his greed, maybe his evil. I don't know. But every Darkling since then has tried to undo the damage he did to our country, and I'm no different." He turned to me then, his expression serious, the firelight playing over the perfect planes of his features. "I've spent my life searching for a way to make things right. You're the first glimmer of hope I've had for a long time."

"Me?"

"The world is changing, Alina. Muskets and rifles are just the beginning. I've seen the weapons they're developing in Kerch and Fjerda. The age of Grisha power is coming to an end."

It was a terrifying thought. "But . . . but what about the First Army? They have rifles. They have weapons."

"Where do you think their rifles come from? Their ammunition? Every time we cross the Fold, we lose lives. A divided Ravka won't survive the new age. We need our ports. We need our harbours. And only you can give them back to us."

"How?" I pleaded. "How am I supposed to do that?"

"By helping me destroy the Shadow Fold."

I shook my head. "You're crazy. This is all crazy."

I looked up through the broken beams of the barn's roof to the night sky. It was full of stars, but I could only see the endless reaches of darkness between them. I imagined myself standing in the dead silence of the Shadow Fold, blind, frightened, with nothing to protect me but my supposed power. I thought of the Black Heretic. He had created the Fold, a Darkling, just like the one who sat watching me so closely in the firelight.

"What about that thing you did?" I asked before I could lose my nerve. "To the Fjerdan?"

He looked back into the fire. "It's called the Cut. It requires great power and great focus; it's something few Grisha can do."

I rubbed my arms, trying to stave off the chill that had taken hold of me.

He glanced at me and then back to the fire. "If I had cut him down with a sword, would that make it any better?"

Would it? I had seen countless horrors in the last few days. But even after the nightmares of the Fold, the image that stayed with me, that reared up in my dreams and chased me into waking, was of the bearded man's severed body, swaying in the dappled sunlight before it toppled onto me.

"I don't know," I said quietly.

Something flashed across his features, something that looked like anger or maybe even pain. Without another word, he rose and walked away from me.

I watched him disappear into the darkness and felt suddenly guilty. *Don't be a fool,* I chastised myself. *He's the Darkling. He's the second most powerful man in Ravka. He's*

one hundred and twenty years old! You didn't hurt his feelings.
But I thought of the look that had flickered over his face,
the shame in his voice when he'd talked about the Black
Heretic, and I couldn't shake the feeling that I had failed
some kind of test.

Two days later, just after dawn, we passed through a
massive gate and the famous double walls of Os Alta.

Mal and I had taken our training not far from here,
in the military stronghold at Poliznaya, but we had never
been inside the city itself. Os Alta was reserved for the
very wealthy, for the homes of military and government
officials, their families, their mistresses, and all the
businesses that catered to them.

I felt a twinge of disappointment as we passed
shuttered shops, a wide marketplace where a few vendors
were already setting up their stalls, and crowded rows
of narrow houses. Os Alta was called the dream city.
It was the capital of Ravka, home to the Grisha and
the King's Grand Palace. But if anything, it just looked
like a bigger, dirtier version of the market town at
Keramzin.

All that changed when we reached the bridge. It
spanned a wide canal where little boats bobbed in the
water beneath it. And on the other side, rising from the
mist, white and gleaming, lay the other Os Alta. As we
crossed the bridge, I saw that it could be raised to turn
the canal into a giant moat that would separate the dream
city before us from the common mess of the market town
that lay behind.

When we reached the other side of the canal, it was as if we had passed into another world. Everywhere I looked, I saw fountains and plazas, verdant parks, and broad boulevards lined with perfect rows of trees. Here and there, I saw lights on in the lower storeys of the grand houses, where kitchen fires were being lit and the day's work was starting.

The streets began to slope upward, and as we climbed higher, the houses became larger and more imposing, until finally we arrived at another wall and another set of gates, these wrought in gleaming gold and emblazoned with the King's double eagle. Along the wall, I could see heavily armed men at their posts, a grim reminder that for all its beauty, Os Alta was still the capital of a country that had long been at war.

The gate swung open.

We rode along a wide path paved in glittering gravel and bordered by rows of elegant trees. To the left and right, stretching into the distance, I saw manicured gardens, rich with green and hazy in the mist of early morning. Above it all, atop a series of marble terraces and golden fountains, loomed the Grand Palace, the Ravkan King's winter home.

When we finally reached the huge double-eagle fountain at its base, the Darkling brought his horse up beside mine.

"So what do you think of it?" he asked.

I glanced at him, then back at the elaborate façade. It was larger than any building I had ever seen, its terraces crowded with statues, its three storeys gleaming with row after row of shining windows, each ornamented extensively in what I suspected was real gold.

"It's very . . . grand?" I said carefully.

He looked at me, a little smile playing on his lips. "I think it's the ugliest building I've ever seen," he said, and nudged his horse forward.

We followed a path that curved behind the palace and deeper into the grounds, passing a hedge maze, a rolling lawn with a columned temple at its centre, and a vast greenhouse, its windows clouded with condensation. Then we entered a thick stand of trees, large enough that it felt like a small wood, and passed through a long, dark corridor where the branches made a dense, braided roof above us.

The hair rose on my arms. I had the same feeling I'd had as we were crossing the canal, that sense of crossing the boundary between two worlds.

When we emerged from the tunnel into weak sunshine, I looked down a gentle slope and saw a building like nothing I'd ever seen.

"Welcome to the Little Palace," said the Darkling.

It was a strange name, because though it was smaller than the Grand Palace, the "Little" Palace was still huge. It rose from the trees surrounding it like something carved from an enchanted forest, a cluster of dark wood walls and golden domes. As we drew closer, I saw that every inch of it was covered in intricate carvings of birds and flowers, twisting vines and magical beasts.

A charcoal-clad group of servants waited on the steps. I dismounted, and one of them rushed forward to take my horse, while others pushed open a large set of double doors. As we passed through them, I couldn't resist the urge to reach out and touch the exquisite carvings. They had been inlaid with mother-of-pearl so that they sparkled in the early-morning light. How many hands, how many years had it taken to create such a place?

We passed through an entry chamber and then into a vast hexagonal room with four long tables arranged in a square at its centre. Our footsteps echoed off the stone floor, and a massive gold dome seemed to float above us at an impossible height.

The Darkling took aside one of the servants, an older woman in a charcoal dress, and spoke to her in hushed tones. Then he gave me a small bow and strode away across the hall, followed by his men.

I felt a surge of annoyance. The Darkling had said little to me since that night in the barn, and he'd given me no idea what I might expect once we arrived. But I didn't have the nerve or the energy to run after him, so I meekly followed the woman in grey through another pair of double doors and into one of the smaller towers.

When I saw all the stairs, I almost broke down and wept. *Maybe I'll just ask if I can stay here in the middle of the hall*, I thought miserably. Instead, I put my hand on the carved banister and dragged myself upward, my stiff body protesting every step. When we reached the top, I felt like celebrating by lying down and going to sleep, but the servant was already moving along the hallway. We passed door after door, until finally we reached a chamber where another uniformed maid stood waiting by an open doorway.

Dimly, I registered a large room, heavy golden curtains, a fire burning in a beautifully tiled grate, but all I really cared about was the huge canopied bed.

"Can I get you anything? Something to eat?" asked the woman. I shook my head. I just wanted sleep.

"Very good," she said, and nodded to the maid, who curtseyed and disappeared down the hall. "Then I'll let you rest. Make sure to lock your door."

I blinked.

"As a precaution," said the woman and left, closing the door gently behind her.

A precaution against what? I wondered. But I was too tired to think about it. I locked the door, peeled off the *kefta* and my boots, and fell into bed.

Chapter 6

I dreamed that I was back in Keramzin, slipping through the darkened hallways on stockinged feet, trying to find Mal. I could hear him calling to me, but his voice never seemed to get any closer. Finally, I reached the top floor and the door to the old blue bedroom where we liked to sit in the window seat and look out at our meadow. I heard Mal laughing. I threw open the door . . . and screamed. There was blood everywhere. The volcra was perched on the window seat and, as it turned on me and opened its horrible jaws, I saw that it had grey quartz eyes.

I bolted awake, my heart thudding in my chest, and looked around in terror. For a moment I couldn't remember where I was. Then I groaned and flopped back onto the pillows.

I had just started to doze again when someone pounded on the door.

"Go away," I mumbled from beneath the covers. But the pounding only grew louder. I sat up, feeling my whole body shriek in rebellion. My head ached, and when I tried to stand, my legs did not want to cooperate.

"All right!" I shouted. "I'm coming!" The knocking stopped. I stumbled over to the door and reached for the lock, but then I hesitated. "Who is it?"

"I don't have time for this," a female voice snapped from behind the door. "Open. Now!"

I shrugged. Let them kill me or kidnap me or whatever they wanted. As long as I didn't have to ride a horse or climb stairs, I wouldn't complain.

I had barely unlocked the door when it flew open and a tall girl pushed past me, surveying the room and then me with a critical eye. She was easily the most beautiful person I'd ever seen. Her wavy hair was deepest auburn, her irises large and golden; her skin was so smooth and flawless that she looked as if her perfect cheekbones had been carved from marble. She wore a cream-coloured *kefta* embroidered in gold and lined in reddish fox fur.

"All Saints," she said, looking me over. "Have you even bathed? And what happened to your face?"

I flushed bright red, my hand flying to the bruise on my cheek. It had been nearly a week since I'd left camp, and longer since I'd bathed or brushed my hair. I was covered in dirt and blood and the smell of horses. "I—"

But the girl was already shouting to the servants who had followed her into the room. "Draw a bath. A hot one. I'll need my kit, and get her out of those clothes."

The servants descended upon me, pulling at my buttons.

"Hey!" I shouted, batting their hands away.

The Grisha rolled her eyes. "Hold her down if you have to."

The servants redoubled their efforts.

"Stop!" I shouted again, backing away from them. They hesitated, looking from me to the girl.

Honestly, nothing sounded better than a hot bath and a change of clothes, but I wasn't about to let some tyrannical redhead push me around. "*What* is going on? Who are you?"

"I don't have ti—"

"Make time!" I snapped. "I've covered almost two hundred miles on horseback. I haven't had a good night's sleep in a week, and I've nearly been killed twice. So before I do anything else, you're going to have to tell me who you are and why it's so very important that you get my clothes off."

The redhead took a deep breath and said slowly, as if she were speaking to a child, "My name is Genya. In less than an hour, you will be presented to the King and it is my job to make you look presentable."

My anger evaporated. I was going to meet the *King*? "Oh," I said meekly.

"Yes, 'oh'. So, shall we?"

I nodded mutely, and Genya clapped her hands. The servants flew into action, yanking at my clothes and dragging me into the bathroom. Last night I'd been too tired to notice the room, but now, even shivering and scared witless at the prospect of having to meet a king, I marvelled at the tiny bronze tiles that rippled over every surface and the sunken oval bath of beaten copper that the servants were filling with steaming water. Beside the bath, the wall was covered in a mosaic of shells and shimmering abalone.

"In! In!" said one of the servants, giving me a nudge.

I climbed in. The water was painfully hot, but I endured it rather than try to ease in slowly. Military life had long ago cured me of most of my modesty, but there was something very different about being the only naked person in the room, especially when everyone kept shooting curious glances at me.

I squeaked as one of the servants grabbed my head and began furiously washing my hair. Another leaned over the bath and started scrubbing at my nails.

Once I'd adjusted to it, the heat of the water felt good on my aching body. I hadn't had a hot bath in well over a year, and I had never even dreamed that there might be one such as this. Clearly, being Grisha had its benefits. I could have spent an hour just paddling around. But once I had been thoroughly dunked and scoured, a servant pulled my arm and ordered, "Out! Out!"

Reluctantly, I climbed from the bath, letting the women dry me roughly with thick towels. One of the younger servants stepped forward with a heavy velvet robe and led me into the bedroom. Then she and the others backed out of the door, leaving me alone with Genya.

I watched the redhead warily. She had thrown open the curtains and pulled an elaborately carved wooden table and chair over by the windows.

"Sit," she commanded. I bridled at her tone, but I obeyed.

A small trunk lay open by her hand, its contents spread out on the tabletop: squat glass jars full of what looked like berries, leaves, and coloured powders. I didn't have a chance to investigate further, because Genya took my chin in hand, peering closely at my face and turning my bruised cheek towards the light from the window. She took a breath and let her fingers travel over my skin. I felt the same prickling sensation I'd experienced when the Healer took care of my wounds from the Fold.

Long minutes passed as I clenched my hands into fists to keep from scratching. Then Genya stepped back and the itching receded. She handed me a small golden hand mirror. The bruise was completely gone. I pressed the skin tentatively, but there was no soreness.

"Thank you," I said, setting the mirror down and starting to stand. But Genya pushed me right back down into the chair.

"Where do you think you're going? We're not finished."

"But—"

"If the Darkling just wanted you healed, he would have sent a Healer."

"You're not a Healer?"

"I'm not wearing red, am I?" Genya retorted, an edge of bitterness to her voice. She gestured to herself. "I'm a Tailor."

I was baffled. I realised I'd never seen a Grisha in a white *kefta*. "You're going to make me a dress?"

Genya blew out an exasperated breath. "Not the robes! *This*," she said, waving her long, graceful fingers before her face. "You don't think I was born looking like this, do you?"

I stared at the smooth marble perfection of Genya's features as understanding set in and, with it, a wave of indignation. "You want to change my face?"

"Not change it. Just . . . freshen you up a bit."

I scowled. I knew what I looked like. In fact, I was acutely aware of my shortcomings. But I really didn't need a gorgeous Grisha pointing them out to me. And worse was the fact that the Darkling had sent her to do it.

"Forget it," I said, jumping to my feet. "If the Darkling doesn't like the way I look, that's his problem."

"Do you like the way you look?" Genya asked with

what seemed to be genuine curiosity.

"Not particularly," I snapped. "But my life has become confusing enough without seeing a stranger's face in the mirror."

"It doesn't work that way," Genya said. "I can't make big changes, just small ones. Even out your skin. Do something with that mousy hair of yours. I've perfected myself, but I've had my whole life to do it."

I wanted to argue, but she actually was perfect. "Get out."

Genya cocked her head to one side, studying me. "Why are you taking this so personally?"

"Wouldn't you?"

"I have no idea. I've always been beautiful."

"And humble too?"

She shrugged. "So I'm beautiful. That doesn't mean much among Grisha. The Darkling doesn't care what you look like, just what you can do."

"Then why did he send you?"

"Because the King loves beauty and the Darkling knows that. In the King's court, appearances are everything. If you're to be the salvation of all of Ravka . . . well, it would be better if you looked the part."

I crossed my arms and looked out of the window. Outside, the sun was shining off a small lake, a tiny island at its centre. I had no idea what time it was or how long I'd slept.

Genya walked over to me. "You're not ugly, you know."

"Thanks," I said drily, still staring out at the wooded grounds.

"You just look a little . . ."

"Tired? Sickly? Skinny?"

"Well," Genya said reasonably, "you said yourself, you've been travelling hard for days and—"

I sighed. "This is how I always look." I rested my head on the cool glass, feeling the anger and embarrassment drain out of me. What was I fighting for? If I was honest with myself, the prospect of what Genya was offering was tempting. "Fine," I said. "Do it."

"Thank you!" exclaimed Genya, clapping her hands together. I looked at her sharply, but there was no sarcasm in her voice or expression. *She's relieved*, I realised. The Darkling had set Genya a task, and I wondered what might have happened to her if I'd refused. I let her lead me back to the chair.

"Just don't get carried away," I said.

"Don't worry," said the redhead. "You'll still look like yourself, just as if you've had more than a few hours of sleep. I'm very good."

"I can see that," I said. I closed my eyes.

"It's okay," she said. "You can watch." She handed me the gold mirror. "But no more talk. And stay still."

I held up the mirror and watched as Genya's cool fingertips descended slowly over my forehead. My skin prickled, and I watched with growing amazement as Genya's hands travelled across my face. Every blemish, every scrape, every flaw seemed to disappear beneath her fingers. She placed her thumbs under my eyes.

"Oh!" I exclaimed in surprise as the dark circles that had plagued me since childhood disappeared.

"Don't get too excited," Genya said. "It's temporary." She reached for one of the roses on the table and plucked a pale pink petal. She held it up to my cheek, and the colour bled from the petal onto my skin, leaving what looked like a pretty flush. Then she held a fresh petal to my lips and repeated the process. "It only lasts for a few days," she informed me. "Now the hair."

She plucked a long comb made of bone from her trunk along with a glass jar full of something shiny.

Stunned, I asked, "Is that real gold?"

"Of course," Genya said, lifting a chunk of my dull brown hair. She shook some of the gold leaf onto the crown of my head and, as she pulled the comb through my hair, the gold seemed to dissolve into shimmering strands. As Genya finished with each section, she wound it around her fingers, letting the hair fall in waves.

Finally she stepped back, wearing a smug smile. "Better, no?"

I examined myself in the mirror. My hair shone. My cheeks held a rosy flush. I still wasn't pretty, but I couldn't deny the improvement. I wondered what Mal would think if he saw me, then shoved the thought away. "Better," I agreed grudgingly.

Genya gave a plaintive sigh. "It's really the best I can do for now."

"Thanks," I said tartly, but then Genya winked at me and smiled.

"Besides," she said, "you don't want to attract too much attention from the King." Her voice was light, but I saw a shadow pass over her features as she strode across the room and opened the door to let the servants rush back in.

They pushed me behind an ebony screen inlaid with mother-of-pearl stars so that it resembled a night sky. In a few moments, I was dressed in a clean tunic and trousers, soft leather boots, and a grey coat. With disappointment, I saw that it was just a clean version of my army uniform. There was even a little cartographer's patch showing a compass rose on the right sleeve. My feelings must have shown on my face.

"Not what you expected?" Genya asked with some amusement.

"I just thought . . ." But what had I thought? Did I really think I belonged in Grisha robes?

"The King expects to see a humble girl plucked from the ranks of his army, an undiscovered treasure. If you appear in a *kefta*, he'll think the Darkling's been hiding you."

"Why would the Darkling hide me?"

Genya shrugged. "For leverage. For profit. Who knows? But the King is . . . well, you'll see what the King is."

My stomach turned. I was about to be presented to the King. I tried to steady myself, but as Genya hurried me out of the door and down the hall, my legs felt leaden and shaky.

Near the bottom of the stairs, she whispered, "If anyone asks, I just helped you get dressed. I'm not supposed to work on Grisha."

"Why not?"

"Because the ridiculous Queen and her more ridiculous court think it's not fair."

I gaped at her. Insulting the Queen could be considered treason, but Genya seemed unconcerned.

When we entered the huge domed hall, it was crowded with Grisha in robes of crimson, purple and darkest blue. Most of them looked to be around my age, but a few older Grisha were gathered in a corner. Despite the silver in their hair and their lined faces, they were strikingly attractive. In fact, everyone in the room was unnervingly good-looking.

"The Queen may have a point," I murmured.

"Oh, this isn't my handiwork," said Genya.

I frowned. If Genya was telling the truth, then this was just further evidence that I didn't belong here.

Someone had seen us enter the hall, and a hush fell as every eye in the room fastened onto me.

A tall, broad-chested Grisha in red robes came forward. He had deeply tanned skin and seemed to exude good health. He made a low bow and said, "I am Sergei Beznikov."

"I'm—"

"I know who you are, of course," Sergei interrupted, his white teeth flashing. "Come, let me introduce you. You'll be walking with us." He took me by the elbow and began to steer me towards a group of Corporalki.

"She's a Summoner, Sergei," said a girl in a blue *kefta* with flowing brown curls. "She walks with us." There were murmurs of assent from the other Etherealki behind her.

"Marie," said Sergei with an insincere smile, "you can't possibly be suggesting that she enter the hall as a lower-order Grisha."

Marie's alabaster skin went suddenly blotchy, and several of the Summoners got to their feet. "Need I remind you that the Darkling is himself a Summoner?"

"So you're ranking yourself with the Darkling now?"

Marie sputtered, and in an attempt to make peace, I interjected, "Why don't I just go with Genya?"

There were a few low snickers.

"With the Tailor?" Sergei asked, looking aghast.

I glanced at Genya, who simply smiled and shook her head.

"She belongs with us," protested Marie, and argument broke out all around us.

"She'll walk with me," said a low voice, and the room went silent.

Chapter 7

I turned and saw the Darkling standing in an archway, flanked by Ivan and several other Grisha whom I recognised from the journey. Marie and Sergei backed away hastily. The Darkling surveyed the crowd and said, "We are expected."

Instantly, the room bustled with activity as the Grisha rose and began to file through the large double doors that led outside. They arranged themselves two abreast in a long line. First the Materialki, then the Etherealki, and finally the Corporalki, so that the highest-ranked Grisha would enter the throne room last.

Unsure what to do, I stayed where I was, watching the crowd. I looked around for Genya, but she seemed to have disappeared. A moment later, the Darkling was beside me. I glanced up at his pale profile, the sharp jaw, the granite eyes.

"You look well rested," he said.

I bristled. I wasn't comfortable with what Genya had done, but standing in a room full of beautiful Grisha, I had to admit that I was grateful for it. I still didn't look as if I belonged, but I would have stuck out much worse without Genya's help.

"Are there other Tailors?" I asked.

"Genya is unique," he answered, glancing at me. "Like us."

I ignored the little thrill that went through me at the word *us* and said, "Why isn't she walking with the rest of the Grisha?"

"Genya must attend to the Queen."

"Why?"

"When Genya's abilities began to show themselves, I could have had her choose between becoming a Fabrikator or a Corporalnik. Instead, I cultivated her particular affinity and made a gift of her to the Queen."

"A gift? So a Grisha is no better than a serf?"

"We all serve someone," he said, and I was surprised by the harsh edge in his voice. Then he added, "The King will expect a demonstration."

I felt as if I'd been dunked in ice water. "But I don't know how to—"

"I don't expect you to," he said calmly, moving forward as the last of the red-robed Corporalki disappeared through the door.

We emerged onto the gravel path and into the last of the afternoon sunshine. I was finding it hard to breathe. I felt as if I were walking to my execution. *Maybe I am*, I thought with a surge of dread.

"This isn't fair," I whispered angrily. "I don't know what the King thinks I can do, but it isn't fair to throw me out there and expect me to just . . . make things happen."

"I hope you don't expect fairness from me, Alina. It isn't one of my specialties."

I stared at him. What was I supposed to make of that?

The Darkling glanced down at me. "Do you really believe I brought you all this way to make a fool out of you? Out of both of us?"

"No," I admitted.

"And it's completely out of your hands now, isn't it?" he said as we made our way through the dark wooded tunnel of branches. That was true too, if not particularly comforting. I had no choice but to trust that he knew what he was doing. I had a sudden unpleasant thought.

"Are you going to cut me again?" I asked.

"I doubt I'll have to, but it all depends on you."

I was not reassured.

I tried to calm myself and to slow the beating of my heart but, before I knew it, we had made our way through the grounds and were climbing the white marble steps to the Grand Palace. As we moved through a spacious entry hall into a long corridor lined with mirrors and ornamented in gold, I thought how different this place was from the Little Palace. Everywhere I looked, I saw marble and gold, soaring walls of white and palest blue, gleaming chandeliers, liveried footmen, polished parquet floors laid out in elaborate geometric designs. It wasn't without beauty, but there was something exhausting about the extravagance of it all. I'd always assumed that Ravka's hungry peasants and poorly supplied soldiers were the result of the Shadow Fold. But as we walked by a tree of jade embellished with diamond leaves, I wasn't so sure.

The throne room was three storeys high, every window sparkling with gold double eagles. A long, pale blue carpet ran the length of the room to where the members of the court milled about a raised throne. Many of the men wore military dress, black trousers and white coats laden with medals and ribbons. The women sparkled in gowns of liquid silk with little puffed sleeves and low necklines. Flanking the carpeted aisle, the Grisha stood arranged in their separate orders.

A hush fell as every face turned to me and the Darkling. We walked slowly towards the golden throne. As we drew closer, the King sat up straighter, tense with excitement. He looked to be in his forties, slender and round-shouldered with big watery eyes and a pale moustache. He wore full military dress, a thin sword at his side, his narrow chest covered with medals. Beside him on the raised dais stood a man with a long, dark beard. He wore priest's robes, but a gold double eagle was emblazoned on his chest.

The Darkling gave my arm a gentle squeeze to warn me that we were stopping.

"Your Highness, *moi tsar*," he said in clear tones. "Alina Starkov, the Sun Summoner." A rush of murmurs came from the crowd. I wasn't sure if I should bow or curtsey. Ana Kuya had insisted that all the orphans know how to greet the Duke's few noble guests, but somehow, it didn't feel right to curtsey in army-issue trousers. The King saved me from making a blunder when he waved us forward impatiently. "Come, come! Bring her to me."

The Darkling and I walked to the base of the dais.

The King scrutinised me. He frowned, and his lower lip jutted out slightly. "She's very plain."

I flushed and bit my tongue. The King wasn't much to look at either. He was practically chinless, and close up, I could see the broken blood vessels in his nose.

"Show me," the King commanded.

My stomach clenched. I looked at the Darkling. This was it. He nodded at me and spread his arms wide. A tense silence descended as his hands filled with dark, swirling ribbons of blackness that bled into the air. He brought his hands together with a resounding *crack*. Nervous cries burst from the crowd as darkness blanketed the room.

This time, I was better prepared for the dark that engulfed me, but it was still frightening. Instinctively, I reached forward, searching for something to hold on to. The Darkling caught my arm and his bare hand slid into mine. I felt that same powerful certainty wash through me and then the Darkling's call, pure and compelling, demanding an answer. With a mixture of panic and relief, I felt something rising up inside me. This time, I didn't try to fight it. I let it have its way.

Light flooded the throne room, drenching us in warmth and shattering the darkness like black glass. The court erupted into applause. People were weeping and hugging one another. A woman fainted. The King was clapping the loudest, rising from his throne and applauding furiously, his expression exultant.

The Darkling let go of my hand and the light faded.

"Brilliant!" the King shouted. "A miracle!" He descended the steps of the dais, the bearded priest gliding silently behind him, and took my hand in his own, raising it to his wet lips. "My dear girl," he said. "My dear, dear girl." I thought of what Genya had said about the King's attention and felt my skin crawl, but I didn't dare pull my hand away. Soon, though, he had relinquished me and was clapping the Darkling on the back.

"Miraculous, simply miraculous," he effused. "Come, we must make plans immediately."

As the King and the Darkling stepped away to talk,

the priest drifted forward. "A miracle indeed," he said, staring at me with a disturbing intensity. His eyes were so brown they were almost black, and he smelled faintly of mildew and incense. *Like a tomb*, I thought with a shiver. I was grateful when he slithered away to join the King.

I was quickly surrounded by beautifully dressed men and women, all wishing to make my acquaintance and to touch my hand or my sleeve. They crowded on every side of me, jostling and pushing to get closer. Just as I felt fresh panic setting in, Genya appeared at my side. But my relief was short-lived.

"The Queen wants to meet you," she murmured into my ear. She steered me through the crowd and out of a narrow side door into the hall, then into a jewel-like sitting room where the Queen reclined on a divan, a snuffling dog with a pushed-in face cradled on her lap.

The Queen was beautiful, with shining blonde hair in a perfect coiffure, her delicate features cold and lovely. But there was also something a little odd about her face. Her irises seemed a little too blue, her hair too yellow, her skin too smooth. I wondered just how much work Genya had done on her.

She was surrounded by ladies in exquisite gowns of petal pink and soft blue, their low necklines embroidered with gilded thread and tiny riverpearls. And yet, they all paled beside Genya in her simple cream wool *kefta*, her bright red hair burning like a flame.

"*Moya tsaritsa*," Genya said, sinking into a low, graceful curtsey. "The Sun Summoner."

This time, I had to make a choice. I executed a small bow and heard a few low titters from the ladies.

"Charming," said the Queen. "I loathe pretence." It

took all my willpower not to snort at this. "You are from a Grisha family?" she asked.

I glanced nervously at Genya, who nodded encouragement.

"No," I said, and then quickly added, "*moya tsaritsa.*"

"A peasant then?"

I nodded.

"We are so lucky in our people," the Queen said, and the ladies murmured soft assent. "Your family must be notified of your new status. Genya will send a messenger."

Genya nodded and gave another little curtsey. I thought about just nodding right along with her, but I wasn't sure I wanted to start lying to royalty.

"Actually, your Highness, I was raised in Duke Keramsov's household."

The ladies buzzed in surprise, and even Genya looked curious.

"An orphan!" exclaimed the Queen, sounding delighted. "How marvellous!"

I wasn't sure that I would describe my parents being dead as "marvellous", but at a loss for anything else to say, I mumbled, "Thank you, *moya tsaritsa.*"

"This all must seem so very strange to you. Take care that life at court does not corrupt you the way it has others," she said, her blue marble eyes sliding to Genya. The insult was unmistakeable, but Genya's expression betrayed nothing, a fact which did not seem to please the Queen. She dismissed us with a flick of her ring-laden fingers. "Go now."

As Genya led me back into the hallway, I thought I heard her mutter, "Old cow". But before I could decide whether or not to ask her about what the Queen had said, the Darkling was there, steering us down an empty corridor.

"How did you fare with the Queen?" he asked.

"I have no idea," I said honestly. "Everything she said was perfectly nice, but the whole time she was looking at me as if I were something her dog coughed up."

Genya laughed, and the Darkling's lips quirked in what was nearly a smile.

"Welcome to court," he said.

"I'm not sure I like it."

"No one does," he admitted. "But we all make a good show of it."

"The King seemed pleased," I offered.

"The King is a child."

My mouth fell open in shock and I looked around nervously, afraid someone had overheard. These people seemed to speak treason as easily as breathing. Genya didn't look remotely disturbed by the Darkling's words.

The Darkling must have noticed my discomfort, because he said, "But today, you've made him a very happy child."

"Who was that bearded man with the King?" I asked, eager to change the subject.

"The Apparat?"

"Is he a priest?"

"Of a sort. Some say he's a fanatic. Others say he's a fraud."

"And you?"

"I say he has his uses." The Darkling turned to Genya. "I think we've asked enough of Alina for today," he said. "Take her back to her chambers and have her fitted for her *kefta*. She will start instruction tomorrow."

Genya gave a little bow and laid her hand on my arm to lead me away. I was overcome by excitement and relief. My power (*my* power, it still didn't seem real) had shown up again and kept me from making a fool of myself. I'd made it through my introduction to the King and my audience with the Queen. And I was going to be given a Grisha's *kefta*.

"Genya," the Darkling called after us, "the *kefta* will be black."

Genya drew a startled breath. I looked at her stunned face and then at the Darkling, who was already turning to go.

"Wait!" I called before I could stop myself. The Darkling halted and turned those slate-coloured eyes on me. "I . . . If it would be all right, I'd prefer to have blue robes, Summoners' blue."

"Alina!" exclaimed Genya, clearly horrified.

But the Darkling held up a hand to silence her. "Why?" he asked, his expression unreadable.

"I already feel like I don't belong here. I think it might be easier if I weren't . . . singled out."

"Are you so anxious to be like everyone else?"

My chin lifted. He clearly didn't approve, but I wasn't going to back down. "I just don't want to be more conspicuous than I already am."

The Darkling looked at me for a long moment. I wasn't sure if he was thinking over what I'd said or trying to intimidate me, but I gritted my teeth and returned his gaze.

Abruptly, he nodded. "As you wish," he said. "Your *kefta* will be blue." And without another word, he turned his back on us and disappeared down the hall.

Genya stared at me, aghast.

"What?" I asked.

"Alina," Genya said slowly, "no other Grisha has ever been permitted to wear a Darkling's colours."

"Do you think he's angry?"

"That's hardly the point! It would have been a mark of your standing, of the Darkling's esteem. It would have placed you high above all others."

"Well, I don't want to be high above all others."

Genya threw up her hands in exasperation and took me by the elbow, leading me back through the palace to the main entrance. Two liveried servants opened the large golden doors for us. With a jolt, I realised that they were wearing white and gold, the same colours as Genya's *kefta*, a servant's colours. No wonder she thought I was crazy for refusing the Darkling's offer. And maybe she was right.

The thought stayed with me through the long walk back across the grounds to the Little Palace. Dusk was falling, and servants were lighting the lamps that lined the gravel path. By the time we climbed the stairs to my room, my stomach was in knots.

I sat down by the window, staring out at the grounds. While I brooded, Genya rang for a servant, whom she sent to find a seamstress and order up a dinner tray. But before she sent the girl away, she turned to me. "Maybe you'd prefer to wait and dine with the Grisha later tonight?" she asked.

I shook my head. I was far too tired and overwhelmed to even think about being around another crowd of people. "But would you stay?" I asked her.

She hesitated.

"You don't have to, of course," I said quickly. "I'm sure you'll want to eat with everyone else."

"Not at all. Dinner for two then," she said imperiously, and the servant raced off. Genya closed the door and walked to the little dressing table, where she started straightening the items on its surface: a comb, a brush, a pen and pot of ink. I didn't recognise any of them, but someone must have had them brought to my room.

With her back still to me, Genya said, "Alina, you should understand that, when you start your training tomorrow . . . well, Corporalki don't eat with Summoners. Summoners don't dine with Fabrikators, and—"

I felt instantly defensive. "Look, if you don't want to stay for dinner, I promise not to cry into my soup."

"No!" she exclaimed. "It's not that at all! I'm just trying to explain the way things work."

"Forget it."

Genya blew out a frustrated breath. "You don't understand. It's a great honour to be asked to dine with you, but the other Grisha might not approve."

"Why?"

Genya sighed and sat down on one of the carved chairs. "Because I'm the Queen's pet. Because they don't consider what I do valuable. A lot of reasons."

I considered what the other reasons might be and if they had something to do with the King. I thought of the liveried servants standing at every doorway in the Grand Palace, all of them dressed in white and gold. What must it be like for Genya, isolated from her own kind but not a true member of the court?

"It's funny," I said after a while. "I always thought that

being beautiful would make life so much easier."

"Oh it does," Genya said, and laughed. I couldn't help but laugh too.

We were interrupted by a knock on the door, and the seamstress soon had us occupied with fittings and measurements. When she had finished and was gathering up her muslin and pins, Genya whispered, "It isn't too late, you know. You could still—"

But I cut her off. "Blue," I said firmly, though my stomach clenched again.

The seamstress left, and we turned our attention to dinner. The food was less alien than I'd expected, the kind of food we'd eaten on feast days at Keramzin: sweet pea porridge, quail roasted in honey, and fresh figs. I found I was hungrier than I'd ever been and had to resist picking up my plate to lick it.

Genya maintained a steady stream of chatter during dinner, mostly about Grisha gossip. I didn't know any of the people she was talking about, but I was grateful not to have to make conversation, so I nodded and smiled when necessary. When the last servants left, taking our dinner dishes with them, I couldn't suppress a yawn, and Genya rose.

"I'll come get you for breakfast in the morning. It will take a while for you to learn your way around. The Little Palace can be a bit of a maze." Then her perfect lips turned up in a mischievous smile. "You should try to rest. Tomorrow you meet Baghra."

"Baghra?"

Genya grinned wickedly. "Oh yes. She's an absolute treat."

Before I could ask what she meant, she gave me a

little wave and slipped out of the door. I bit my lip. Exactly what was in store for me tomorrow?

As the door closed behind Genya, I felt fatigue creep over me. The thrill of knowing that my power might actually be real, the excitement of meeting the King and Queen, the strange marvels of the Grand Palace and the Little Palace had kept my exhaustion at bay, but now it returned – and, with it, a huge, echoing feeling of loneliness.

I undressed, hung my uniform neatly on a peg behind the star-speckled screen and placed my shiny new boots beneath it. I rubbed the brushed wool of the coat between my fingers, hoping to find some sense of familiarity, but the fabric felt wrong, too stiff, too new. I suddenly missed my dirty old coat.

I changed into a nightdress of soft white cotton and rinsed my face. As I patted it dry, I caught a glimpse of myself in the glass above the basin. Maybe it was the lamplight, but I thought I looked even better than when Genya had first finished her work on me. After a moment, I realised I was just gawking at myself in the mirror and had to smile. For a girl who hated looking at herself, I was at risk of becoming vain.

I climbed onto the high bed, slid beneath the heavy silks and furs, and blew out the lamp. Distantly, I heard a door closing, voices calling their goodnights, the sounds of the Little Palace going to sleep. I stared into the darkness. I'd never had a room to myself before. In Keramzin, I'd slept in an old portrait hall that had been converted into a dormitory, surrounded by countless other girls. In the army, I'd slept in the barracks or tents with the other surveyors. My new room felt huge and empty. In the silence, all the events of the day rushed in on me, and tears pricked my eyes.

Maybe I would wake tomorrow and find that it had all been a dream, that Alexei was still alive and Mal was unhurt, that no one had tried to kill me, that I'd never met the King and Queen or seen the Apparat, or felt the Darkling's hand on the nape of my neck. Maybe I would wake to smell the campfires burning, safe in my own clothes, on my little cot, and I could tell Mal all about this strange and terrifying, but very beautiful, dream.

I rubbed my thumb over the scar in my palm and heard Mal's voice saying, "We'll be okay, Alina. We always are."

"I hope so, Mal," I whispered into my pillow and let my tears carry me to sleep.

Chapter 8

After a restless night, I woke early. I'd forgotten to close the curtains when I went to bed, and sunlight was streaming through the windows. I thought about getting up to close them and trying to go back to sleep, but I just didn't have the energy. I wasn't sure if it was worry and fear that had kept me tossing and turning, or the unfamiliar luxury of sleeping in a real bed after so many months spent on wobbly canvas cots or with nothing but a bedroll between me and the hard ground.

I stretched and reached out to run a finger over the intricately carved birds and flowers on the bedpost. High above me, the canopy of the bed opened to reveal a ceiling painted in bold colours, an elaborate pattern of leaves and flowers and birds in flight. As I was staring up at it, counting the leaves of a juniper wreath and beginning to doze off again, a soft knock came at the door. I threw off the heavy covers and slipped my feet into the little fur-lined slippers set out by the bed.

When I opened the door, a servant was waiting with a stack of clothing, a pair of boots, and a dark blue *kefta* draped over her arm. I barely had time to thank her before she bobbed a curtsey and disappeared.

I closed the door and set the boots and clothing down

on the bed. The new *kefta* I hung carefully over the dressing screen.

For a while, I just looked at it. I'd spent my life in clothes passed down from older orphans, and then in the standard-issue uniform of the First Army. I'd certainly never had anything made for me. And I'd never dreamed that I would wear a Grisha's *kefta*.

I washed my face and combed my hair. I wasn't sure when Genya would be arriving, so I didn't know if I had time for a bath. I was desperate for a glass of tea, but I didn't have the courage to ring for a servant. Finally, there was nothing left for me to do.

I started with the pile of clothes on the bed: close-fitting breeches of a fabric I'd never encountered that seemed to fit and move like a second skin, a long blouse of thin cotton that tied with a dark blue sash, and boots. But to call them boots didn't seem right. I'd owned boots. These were something else entirely, made of the softest black leather and fitted perfectly to my calves. They were strange clothes, similar to what peasant men and farmers wore. But the fabrics were finer and more expensive than any peasant could ever hope to afford.

When I was dressed, I eyed the *kefta*. Was I really going to put that on? Was I really going to be a Grisha? It didn't seem possible.

It's just a coat, I chided myself.

I took a deep breath, pulled the *kefta* off the screen, and slipped it on. It was lighter than it looked, and like the other clothes, it fitted perfectly. I fastened the little hidden buttons in the front and stepped back to try and look at myself in the mirror above the basin. The *kefta* was deepest midnight blue and fell nearly to my feet. The sleeves were wide, and though it was a lot like a coat, it was so elegant I felt as if I were wearing a gown. Then I noticed the embroidery at the cuffs. Like all Grisha, the Etherealki indicated their designation within their order by colour of embroidery: pale blue for Tidemakers, red for Inferni, and silver for Squallers. My cuffs were embroidered in gold. I ran my finger over the gleaming threads, feeling a sharp twinge of anxiety, and nearly jumped when a knock sounded at the door.

"Very nice," said Genya when I opened the door. "But you would have looked better in black."

I did the graceful thing and stuck my tongue out at her, then hurried to follow as she swept down the hallway and descended the stairs. Genya led me to the same domed room where we had gathered the previous afternoon for the processional. It wasn't nearly as crowded today, but there was still a lively buzz of conversation. In the corners, Grisha clustered around samovars and lounged on divans, warming themselves by elaborately tiled ovens. Others breakfasted at the four long tables arranged in a square at the room's centre. Again, a hush seemed to fall as we entered, but this time people at least pretended to carry on their conversations as we passed.

Two girls in Summoners' robes swooped on us. I recognised Marie from her argument with Sergei before the processional.

"Alina!" she said. "We weren't properly introduced yesterday. I'm Marie, and this is Nadia." She gestured to the apple-cheeked girl beside her, who smiled toothily at me. Marie looped her arm through mine, deliberately turning her back on Genya. "Come and sit with us!"

I frowned and opened my mouth to protest, but Genya simply shook her head and said, "Go on. You belong with the Etherealki. I'll fetch you after breakfast to give you a tour."

"We can show her around—" began Marie.

But Genya cut her off. "To give you a tour *as the Darkling requested.*"

Marie flushed. "What are you, her maid?"

"Something like that," Genya said, and walked off to pour herself a glass of tea.

"Far above herself," said Nadia with a little sniff.

"Worse every day," Marie agreed. Then she turned to me and beamed. "You must be starving!"

She led me to one of the long tables, and as we approached, two servants stepped forward to pull out chairs for us.

"We sit here, at the right hand of the Darkling," said Marie, pride in her voice, indicating the length of the table where more Grisha in blue *kefta* sat. "The Corporalki sit there," she said with a disdainful glance at the table opposite ours, where a glowering Sergei and a few other red-robed figures were eating breakfast.

It occurred to me that if we were at the right hand of the Darkling, the Corporalki were just as close to him on the left, but I didn't mention that.

The Darkling's table was empty, the only sign of his presence a large ebony chair. When I asked if he would be eating breakfast with us, Nadia shook her head vigorously.

"Oh no! He hardly ever dines with us," she said.

I raised my eyebrows. All this fuss about who sat nearest the Darkling, and he couldn't be bothered to show up?

Plates of rye bread and pickled herring were placed in front of us, and I had to stifle a gag. I hate herring. Luckily, there was plenty of bread and, I saw with astonishment, sliced plums that must have come from a hothouse. A servant brought us hot tea from one of the large samovars.

"Sugar!" I exclaimed as he set a little bowl before me.

Marie and Nadia exchanged a glance and I blushed. Sugar had been rationed in Ravka for the last hundred years, but apparently it wasn't a novelty in the Little Palace.

Another group of Summoners joined us and, after brief introductions, began peppering me with questions.

Where was I from? The North. (Mal and I never lied about where we were from. We just didn't tell the whole truth.)

Was I really a mapmaker? Yes.

Had I really been attacked by Fjerdans? Yes.

How many volcra had I killed? None.

They all seemed disappointed by this last answer, particularly the boys.

"But I heard you killed hundreds of them when the skiff was attacked!" protested a boy named Ivo with the sleek features of a mink.

"Well, I didn't," I said, and then considered. "At least, I don't think I did. I . . . um . . . kind of fainted."

"You *fainted*?" Ivo looked appalled.

I was exceedingly grateful when I felt a tap on my shoulder and saw that Genya had come to my rescue.

"Shall we?" she asked, ignoring the others.

I mumbled my goodbyes and quickly escaped, conscious of their stares following us across the room.

"How was breakfast?" Genya asked.

"Awful."

Genya made a disgusted sound. "Herring and rye?"

I'd been thinking more about the interrogation, but I just nodded.

She wrinkled her nose. "Vile."

I eyed her suspiciously. "What did *you* eat?"

Genya looked over her shoulder to make sure no one was within earshot and whispered, "One of the cooks has a daughter with terrible spots. I took care of them for her, and now she sends me the same pastries they prepare for the Grand Palace every morning. They're divine."

I smiled and shook my head. The other Grisha might look down on Genya, but she had her own kind of power and influence.

"But don't say anything about it," Genya added. "The Darkling is very keen on the idea that we all eat hearty peasant fare. Saints forbid we forget we're *real* Ravkans."

I restrained a snort. The Little Palace was a storybook version of serf life, no more like the real Ravka than the glitter and gilt of the royal court. The Grisha seemed obsessed with emulating serf ways, right down to the clothes we wore beneath our *kefta*. But there was something a little silly about eating "hearty peasant fare" off porcelain plates, beneath a dome inlaid with real gold. And what peasant wouldn't pick pastry over pickled fish?

"I won't say a word," I promised.

"Good! If you're very nice to me, I might even share," Genya said with a wink. "Now, these doors lead to the library and the workrooms." She gestured to a massive set of double doors in front of us. "That way to get back to your room," she said, pointing to the right. "And that way to the Grand Palace," she said, pointing to the double doors on the left. Genya started to lead me towards the library.

"But what about that way?" I asked, nodding to the closed double doors behind the Darkling's table.

"If those doors open, pay attention. They lead to the Darkling's council room and his quarters."

When I looked more closely at the heavily carved doors, I could make out the Darkling's symbol hidden in the tangle of vines and running animals. I tore myself away and hurried after Genya, who was already on her way out of the domed hall.

I followed her across a corridor to another set of enormous double doors. This pair had been carved to look like the cover of an old book, and when Genya pulled them open, I gasped.

The library was two storeys high, its walls lined from floor to ceiling with books. A balcony ran around the second storey, and its dome was made entirely of glass so that the whole room glowed with morning light. A few reading chairs and small tables were set by the walls. At the room's centre, directly beneath the sparkling glass dome, was a round table ringed by a circular bench.

"You'll have to come here for history and theory," Genya said, leading me around the table and across the room. "I finished with all that years ago. So boring." Then she laughed. "Close your mouth. You look like a trout."

I snapped my mouth shut, but that didn't stop me from gazing around in awe. The Duke's library had seemed so grand to me, but compared to this place it was a hovel. All of Keramzin seemed shabby and faded viewed beside the beauty of the Little Palace, but somehow it made me sad to think of it that way. I wondered what Mal's eyes would see.

My steps slowed. Were the Grisha allowed guests? Could Mal come and visit me in Os Alta? He had his duties with his regiment, but if he could get leave . . . The thought filled me with excitement. The Little Palace didn't seem quite so intimidating when I thought of walking its corridors with my best friend.

We left the library through another set of double doors and passed into a dark hallway. Genya turned left, but I glanced down the hall to the right and saw two Corporalki emerge from a large set of red-lacquered doors. They gave us unfriendly looks before they disappeared into the shadows.

"Come on," Genya whispered, taking my arm and pulling me in the opposite direction.

"Where do those doors lead?" I asked.

"To the anatomy rooms."

A chill rippled through me. The Corporalki. Healers . . . and Heartrenders. They had to practise somewhere, but I hated to think what that practice might entail. I quickened my steps to catch up with Genya. I didn't want to get caught by myself anywhere near those red doors.

At the end of the hallway, we stopped at a set of doors made of light wood, exquisitely carved with birds and blooming flowers. The flowers had yellow diamonds at their centres, and the birds had what looked to be amethyst eyes. The door handles were wrought to look like two perfect hands. Genya took hold of one and pushed the door open.

The Fabrikators' workshops had been positioned to make the most of the clear eastern light, and the walls were made up almost entirely of windows. The brightly lit rooms reminded me a bit of a Documents Tent, but instead of atlases, stacks of paper, and bottles of ink, the large worktables were laden with bolts of fabric, chunks of glass, thin skeins of gold and steel, and strangely twisted hunks of rock. In one corner, terrariums held exotic flowers, insects, and – I saw with a shudder – snakes.

The Materialki in their dark purple *kefta* sat hunched over their work, but looked up to stare at me as we passed. At one table, two female Fabrikators were working a molten lump of what I thought might become Grisha steel, their table scattered with bits of diamond and jars full of silkworms. At another table, a Fabrikator with a cloth tied over his nose and mouth was measuring out a thick black liquid that stank of tar. Genya led me past all of them to where a Fabrikator was hunched over a set of tiny glass discs. He was pale, reed-thin and in dire need of a haircut.

"Hello, David," said Genya.

David looked up, blinked, gave a curt nod and bent back to his work.

Genya sighed. "David, this is Alina."

David gave a grunt.

"The Sun Summoner," Genya added.

"These are for you," he said without looking up.

I looked at the discs. "Oh, um . . . thank you?"

I wasn't sure what else to say, but when I looked at Genya, she just shrugged and rolled her eyes.

"*Goodbye, David,*" she said deliberately. David grunted. Genya led me outside onto an arched wooden arcade that overlooked a rolling green lawn. "Don't take it personally," she said. "David is a great metalworker. He can fold a blade so sharp it will cut through flesh like water. But if you're not made of metal or glass, he isn't interested."

Genya's voice was light, but it had a funny little edge to it, and when I glanced at her, I saw that there were bright spots of colour on her perfect cheekbones. I looked back through the windows to where I could still see David's bony shoulders and messy brown hair. I smiled. If a creature as gorgeous as Genya could fall for a skinny, studious Fabrikator, there might be hope for me yet.

"What?" she said, noticing my smile.

"Nothing, nothing."

Genya squinted suspiciously at me, but I kept my mouth shut. We followed the arcade along the eastern wall of the Little Palace, past more windows that looked into the Fabrikators' workshops. Then we turned a corner and the windows stopped. Genya quickened her pace.

"Why aren't there any windows?" I asked.

Genya glanced nervously at the solid walls. They were the only parts of the Little Palace I'd seen that weren't covered in carvings. "We're on the other side of the Corporalki anatomy rooms."

"Don't they need light to . . . do their work?"

"Skylights," she said. "In the roof, like the library dome. They prefer it that way. It keeps them and their secrets safe."

"But what do they do in there?" I asked, not entirely sure I wanted to hear the answer.

"Only the Corporalki know. But there are rumours

that they've been working with the Fabrikators on new . . . experiments."

I shivered and was relieved when we turned another corner and the windows began again. Through them I saw bedrooms like my own, and I realised I was seeing the downstairs dormitories. I was grateful that I'd been given a room on the third floor. I could have done without all those stairs to climb, but now that I had my own room for the first time, I was glad that people couldn't just walk by my window.

Genya pointed to the lake I'd seen from my room. "That's where we're going," she said, pointing to the little white structures dotting the shore. "To the Summoners' pavilions."

"All the way out there?"

"It's the safest place for you sort to practise. All we need is some overexcited Inferni to burn the whole palace down around us."

"Ah," I said. "I hadn't thought about that."

"That's nothing. The Fabrikators have another place all the way outside the city where they work on blast powders. I can arrange for you to have a tour there too," she said with a wicked grin.

"I'll pass."

We descended a set of steps to a gravel path and made our way to the lake. As we approached it, another building became visible on the far shore. To my surprise, I saw groups of children running and shouting around it. Children in red, blue and purple. A bell rang, and they left their playing and streamed inside.

"A school?" I asked.

Genya nodded. "When a Grisha's talent is discovered,

the child is brought here for training. It's where nearly all of us learned the Small Science."

Again I thought of those three figures looming over me in the sitting room at Keramzin. Why hadn't the Grisha Examiners discovered my abilities all those years ago? It was hard to imagine what my life might have been like if they had. I would have been catered to by servants instead of working side by side with them at chores. I never would have become a cartographer or even learned to draw a map. And what might it have meant for Ravka? If I'd learned to use my power, would the Shadow Fold already be a thing of the past? Mal and I might never have had to fight the volcra. In fact, Mal and I would probably have long forgotten each other.

I looked back across the water to the school. "What happens when they finish?"

"They become members of the Second Army. Many are sent to the great houses to serve with noble families, or they're sent to serve with the First Army on the northern or southern front, or near the Fold. The best are chosen to remain at the Little Palace, to finish their education and join the Darkling's service."

"What about their families?" I asked.

"They're compensated handsomely. A Grisha's family never wants."

"That's not what I meant. Don't you ever go home to visit?"

Genya shrugged. "I haven't seen my parents since I was five. This is my home."

Looking at Genya in her white and gold *kefta*, I wasn't quite convinced. I'd lived at Keramzin for most of my life, but I'd never felt I belonged there. And even after a year, the same had been true for the King's Army. The only place I'd ever felt I belonged was with Mal, and even that hadn't lasted. For all her beauty, maybe Genya and I weren't so different after all.

When we reached the lake shore, we strolled past the stone pavilions, but Genya didn't stop until we reached a path that wound from the shore into the woods.

"Here we are," she said.

I peered up the path. Hidden in the shadows, I could just make out a small stone hut, obscured by trees. "There?"

"I can't go with you. Not that I'd want to."

I looked back up the path and a little shiver ran up my spine.

Genya gave me a pitying look. "Baghra's not so bad once you get used to her. But you don't want to be late."

"Right," I said hastily, and scurried up the path.

"Good luck!" Genya called after me.

The stone hut was round and, I noted apprehensively, didn't seem to have any windows. I climbed the few steps to the door and knocked. When no one answered, I knocked again and waited. I wasn't sure what to do. I looked back up the path, but Genya was long gone. I knocked once more, then screwed up my courage and opened the door.

The heat hit me in a blast, and I instantly began to sweat in my new clothes. As my eyes adjusted to the dimness, I could just make out a narrow bed, a basin and a stove with a kettle on it. In the middle of the room were two chairs and a fire roaring in a large tile oven.

"You're late," said a harsh voice.

I looked around but didn't see anyone in the tiny

room. Then one of the shadows moved. I nearly jumped out of my skin.

"Shut the door, girl. You're letting the heat out."

I closed the door.

"Good, let's have a look at you."

I wanted to turn and run in the other direction, but I told myself to stop being stupid. I forced myself to walk over to the fire. The shadow emerged from behind the oven to peer at me in the firelight.

My first impression was of an impossibly ancient woman, but when I looked closer, I wasn't sure why I'd thought that at all. Baghra's skin was smooth and taut over the sharp angles of her face. Her back was straight, her body wiry like a Suli acrobat, her coal-black hair untouched by grey. And yet the firelight made her features eerily skull-like, all jutting bones and deep hollows. She wore an old *kefta* of indeterminate colour, and with one skeletal hand she gripped a flat-headed cane that looked as if it had been hewn from silvery, petrified wood.

"So," she said in a low, guttural voice, "you're the Sun Summoner. Come to save us all. Where's the rest of you?"

I shifted uneasily.

"Well, girl, are you mute?"

"No," I managed.

"That's something, I suppose. Why weren't you tested as a child?"

"I was."

"Hmph," she said. Then her expression changed. She looked on me with eyes so unfathomably bleak that a chill rippled through me, despite the heat of the room. "I hope you're stronger than you look, girl," she said grimly.

A bony hand snaked out from the sleeve of her robes and fastened hard around my wrist. "Now," she said, "let's see what you can do."

Chapter 9

It was a complete disaster. When Baghra fastened her bony hand around my wrist, I knew instantly that she was an amplifier like the Darkling. I felt the same jolting surety flood through me, and sunlight erupted in the room, shimmering over the stone walls of Baghra's hut. But when she released me and told me to call the power on my own, I was hopeless. She chided me, cajoled me, even hit me once with her stick.

"What am I supposed to do with a girl who can't call her own power?" she growled. "Even children can do this."

She slid her hand around my wrist again, and I felt that thing inside me rising up, struggling to break the surface. I reached for it, grasping, sure I could feel it. Then she let go, and the power slipped from me, sinking like a stone. Finally, she shooed me away with a disgusted wave of her hand.

The day did not improve. I spent the rest of the morning at the library, where I was given a towering stack of books on Grisha theory and Grisha history and informed that this was just a fraction of my reading list. At lunch, I looked for Genya, but she was nowhere to be found. I sat down at the Summoners' table and was quickly swarmed by Etherealki.

I picked at my plate as Marie and Nadia prodded me with questions about my first lesson, where my room was, if I wanted to go with them to the *banya* that night. When they realised they weren't going to get much out of me, they turned to the other Summoners to chat about their classes. While I suffered with Baghra, the other Grisha were studying advanced theory, languages, military strategy. Apparently, this was all to prepare for when they left the Little Palace next summer. Most of them would travel to the Fold or to the northern or southern front to assume command positions in the Second Army. But the greatest honour was to be asked to travel with the Darkling as Ivan did.

I did my best to pay attention, but my mind kept wandering back to my disastrous lesson with Baghra. At some point I realised that Marie must have asked me a question, because she and Nadia were both staring at me.

"Sorry, what?" I said.

They exchanged a glance.

"Do you want to walk with us to the stables?" Marie asked. "For combat training?"

Combat training? I looked down at the little schedule Genya had left with me. Listed after lunch were the words "Combat Training, Botkin, West Stables". So this day was actually going to get worse.

"Sure," I said numbly, and stood up with them. The servants sprang forward to pull our chairs out and clear the dishes. I doubted I'd ever get used to being waited on this way.

"*Ne brinite*," Marie said with a giggle.

"What?" I asked, baffled.

"*To c´e biti zabavno.*"

Nadia giggled. "She said, 'Don't worry. It will be fun.' It's Suli dialect. Marie and I are studying it in case we get sent west."

"Ah," I said.

"*Shi si yuyan Suli*," said Sergei as he strode past us out of the domed hall. "That's Shu for 'Suli is a dead language'."

Marie scowled and Nadia bit her lip.

"Sergei is studying Shu," whispered Nadia.

"I got that," I replied.

Marie spent the entire walk to the stables complaining about Sergei and the other Corporalki and debating the merits of Suli over Shu. Suli was best for missions in the north-west. Shu meant you'd be stuck translating diplomatic papers. Sergei was an idiot who was better off learning to trade in Kerch. She took a brief break to point out the *banya*, an elaborate system of steam baths and cold pools nestled in a birch grove beside the Little Palace, then launched immediately into a rant about selfish Corporalki overrunning the baths every night.

Maybe combat training wouldn't be so bad. Marie and Nadia were definitely making me want to punch something.

As we were crossing the western lawn, I suddenly got the feeling that someone was watching me. I looked up and saw a figure standing off the path, nearly hidden by the shadows from a low stand of trees. There was no mistaking the long brown robes or the dirty black beard, and even from a distance, I could feel the eerie intensity of the Apparat's stare. I hurried to catch up with Marie and Nadia, but I sensed his gaze following me, and when I looked back over my shoulder, he was still there.

The training rooms were next to the stables – large, empty, high-beamed rooms with packed dirt floors and weapons of every variety lining the walls. Our instructor, Botkin Yul-Erdene, wasn't Grisha; he was a former Shu Han mercenary who had fought in wars on every continent for any army that could afford his particular gift for violence. He had straggly grey hair and a gruesome scar across his neck where someone had tried to cut his throat. I spent the next two hours cursing that person for not doing a more thorough job.

Botkin started with endurance drills, racing us across the palace grounds. I did my best to keep up, but I was as weak and clumsy as ever, and I quickly fell behind.

"Is this what they teach in First Army?" he sneered in his heavy Shu accent as I stumbled up a hill.

I was too out of breath to answer.

When we returned to the training rooms, the other Summoners paired off for sparring drills, and Botkin insisted on partnering me. The next hour was a blur of painful jabs and punches.

"Block!" he shouted, knocking me backwards. "Faster! Maybe little girl likes to be hit?"

The sole consolation was that we weren't allowed to use our Grisha abilities in the training rooms. So at least I was spared the embarrassment of revealing that I couldn't call my power.

When I was so tired and sore that I thought I might just lie down and let him kick me, Botkin dismissed the class. Before we were out of the door he called, "Tomorrow, little girl comes early, trains with Botkin."

It was all I could do not to whimper.

By the time I stumbled back to my room and bathed,

I just wanted to slink beneath the covers and hide. But I forced myself to return to the domed hall for dinner.

"Where's Genya?" I asked Marie as I sat down at the Summoners' table.

"She eats at the Grand Palace."

"And sleeps there," added Nadia. "The Queen likes to make sure she's always available."

"So does the King."

"Marie!" Nadia protested, but she was snickering.

I gaped at them. "You mean—"

"It's just a rumour," said Marie. But she and Nadia exchanged a knowing look.

I thought of the King's wet lips, the broken blood vessels in his nose, and beautiful Genya in her servant's colours. I pushed my plate away. The bit of appetite I'd had seemed to have disappeared.

Dinner seemed to last forever. I nursed a glass of tea and endured another round of endless Summoner chatter. I was getting ready to excuse myself and escape back to my room when the doors behind the Darkling's table opened and the hall fell silent.

Ivan emerged and sauntered over to the Summoners' table, seemingly oblivious to the stares of the other Grisha.

With a sinking sensation, I saw he was walking straight towards me.

"Come with me, Starkov," he said when he reached us, then added a mocking, "please."

I pushed my chair back and rose on legs that felt suddenly weak. Had Baghra told the Darkling that I was hopeless? Had Botkin told him just how badly I'd failed at my lessons? The Grisha were goggling at me.

Nadia's jaw was actually hanging open.

I followed Ivan across the silent hall and through the huge ebony doors. He led me down a hallway and through another door emblazoned with the Darkling's symbol. It was easy to tell that I was in the war room. There were no windows, and the walls were covered with large maps of Ravka. The maps were made in the old style, with heated ink on animal hide. Under any other circumstances, I could have spent hours studying them, running my fingers over the raised mountains and twisting rivers. Instead, I stood with my hands bunched into clammy fists, my heart thumping in my chest.

The Darkling was seated at the end of a long table, reading through a pile of papers. He looked up when we entered, his quartz eyes glittering in the lamplight.

"Alina," he said. "Please, sit." He gestured to the chair beside him.

I hesitated. He didn't *sound* angry.

Ivan disappeared back through the door, closing it behind him. I swallowed hard and made myself cross the room and take the seat the Darkling offered.

"How was your first day?"

I swallowed again. "Fine," I croaked.

"Really?" he asked, but he was smiling slightly. "Even Baghra? She can be a bit of a trial."

"Just a bit," I managed.

"You're tired?"

I nodded.

"Homesick?"

I shrugged. It felt strange to say I was homesick for the barracks of the First Army. "A little, I guess."

"It will get better."

I bit my lip. I hoped so. I wasn't sure how many days like this one I could handle.

"It will be harder for you," he said. "An Etherealnik rarely works alone. Inferni pair up. Squallers often partner with Tidemakers. But you're the only one of your kind."

"Right," I said wearily. I wasn't really in the mood to hear about how special I was.

He rose. "Come with me," he said.

My heart started racing again. He led me out of the war room and along another hallway.

He pointed to a narrow door set unobtrusively into the wall. "Keep right and this will lead you back to the dormitories. I thought you might want to avoid the main hall."

I stared at him. "That's it?" I blurted. "You just wanted to ask me about my day?"

He cocked his head to one side. "What were you expecting?"

I was so relieved that a little laugh escaped me. "I have no idea. Torture? Interrogation? A stern talking to?"

He frowned slightly. "I'm not a monster, Alina. Despite what you may have heard."

"I didn't mean that," I said hurriedly. "I just . . . I didn't know what to expect."

"Other than the worst?"

"It's an old habit." I knew I should stop there, but I couldn't help myself. Maybe I wasn't being fair. But neither was he. "Why shouldn't I be afraid of you?" I asked. "You're the Darkling. I'm not saying you *would* throw me in a ditch or ship me off to Tsibeya, but you certainly could. You can cut people in half. I think it's fair to be a little intimidated."

He studied me for a long moment, and I wished fervently that I'd kept my mouth shut. But then that half smile flickered across his face. "You may have a point."

Some of the fear ebbed out of me.

"Why do you do that?" he asked suddenly.

"Do what?"

He reached out and took hold of my hand. I felt that wonderful sense of surety rush through me. "Rub your thumb across your palm."

"Oh," I laughed nervously. I hadn't even been aware I was doing it. "Just another old habit."

He turned my hand over and examined it in the dim light of the hallway. He dragged his thumb along the pale scar that ran across my palm. A shivery hum shot through me.

"Where did you get this?" he asked.

"I . . . Keramzin."

"Where you grew up?"

"Yes."

"The tracker is an orphan too?"

I drew in a sharp breath. Was mind reading another one of his powers? But then I remembered that Mal had given testimony in the Grisha tent.

"Yes," I said.

"Is he any good?"

"What?" I was finding it hard to concentrate. The Darkling's thumb was still moving back and forth, tracing the length of the scar on my palm.

"At tracking. Is he any good at it?"

"The best," I said honestly. "The serfs at Keramzin said he could make rabbits out of rocks."

"I wonder sometimes how much we really understand our own gifts," he mused.

Then he dropped my hand and opened the door. He stepped aside and gave me a little bow.

"Goodnight, Alina."

"Goodnight," I managed.

I ducked through the doorway and into a narrow hall. A moment later, I heard the sound of a door closing behind me.

Chapter 10

Next morning, my body ached so badly that I could barely drag myself out of bed. But I got up and did it all over again. And again. And again. Each day was worse and more frustrating than the one before, but I didn't stop. I couldn't. I wasn't a mapmaker any more, and if I couldn't manage to become a Grisha, where would that leave me?

I thought of the Darkling's words that night beneath the broken beams of the barn. *You're the first glimmer of hope I've had for a long time.* He believed I was the Sun Summoner. He believed I could help him destroy the Fold. And if I could, no soldier, no merchant, no tracker would ever have to cross the Unsea again.

But as the days dragged on, that idea began to seem more and more absurd.

I spent long hours in Baghra's hut learning breathing exercises and holding painful poses that were supposed to help with my focus. She gave me books to read, teas to drink, and repeated whacks with her stick, but nothing helped. "Should I cut you, girl?" she would cry in frustration. "Should I have an Inferni burn you? Should I have them throw you back into the Fold to make food for those abominations?"

My daily failures with Baghra were matched only by

the torture that Botkin put me through. He ran me all over the palace grounds, through the woods, up and down hills until I thought I would collapse. He put me through sparring drills and falling drills until my body was covered in bruises and my ears ached from his constant grumbling: too slow, too weak, too skinny.

"Botkin cannot build house from such little twigs!" he shouted at me, giving my upper arm a squeeze. "Eat something!"

But I wasn't hungry. The appetite that had appeared after my brush with death on the Fold was gone and food had lost all its savour. I slept poorly, despite my luxurious bed, and felt as if I was stumbling through my days. The work Genya had done on me had worn off, and my cheeks were once again sallow, my eyes shadowed, my hair dull and limp.

Baghra believed that my lack of appetite and inability to sleep were connected to my failure to call my power. "How much harder is it to walk with your feet bound? Or to talk with a hand over your mouth?" she lectured. "Why do you waste all of your strength fighting your true nature?"

I wasn't. Or I didn't think I was. I wasn't sure of anything any more. All my life I'd been frail and weak. Every day had felt like a struggle. If Baghra was right, all that would change when I finally mastered my Grisha talent. Assuming I ever did. Until then, I was stuck.

I knew that the other Grisha were whispering about me. The Etherealki liked to practise by the lakeside together, experimenting with new ways to use wind and water and fire. I couldn't risk them discovering that I couldn't even call my own power, so I made excuses not to join them, and eventually they stopped inviting me.

In the evenings, they sat around the domed hall, sipping tea or *kvas*, planning weekend excursions into Balakirev or one of the other villages near Os Alta. But because the Darkling was still concerned about assassination attempts, I had to remain behind. I was glad for the excuse. The more time I spent with the Summoners, the greater the chance that I would be found out.

I rarely saw the Darkling, and when I did it was from a distance, coming or going, deep in conversation with Ivan or the King's military advisers. I learned from the other Grisha that he wasn't often at the Little Palace, but spent most of his time travelling between the Fold and the northern border, or south to where Shu Han raiding parties were attacking settlements before winter set in. Hundreds of Grisha were stationed throughout Ravka, and he was responsible for all of them.

He never said a word to me, rarely even glanced my way. I was sure it was because he knew that I was showing no improvement, that his Sun Summoner might turn out to be a complete failure after all.

When I wasn't suffering at the hands of Baghra or Botkin, I was sitting in the library, wading through books on Grisha theory. I thought I understood the basics of what Grisha did. (*Of what* we *did*, I amended.) Everything in the world could be broken down into the same small parts. What looked like magic was really the Grisha manipulating matter at its most fundamental levels.

Marie didn't make fire. She summoned combustible elements in the air around us, and she still needed a flint to make the spark that would burn that fuel. Grisha steel wasn't endowed with magic, but by the skill of

Fabrikators, who did not need heat or crude tools to manipulate metal.

But if I understood what we did, I was less sure of how we did it. The grounding principle of the Small Science was "like calls to like", but then it got complicated. *Odinakovost* was the "thisness" of a thing that made it the same as everything else. *Etovost* was the "thatness" of a thing that made it different from everything else. *Odinakovost* connected Grisha to the world, but it was *etovost* that gave them an affinity for something like air, or blood, or in my case, light. Around then, my head started swimming.

One thing did stand out to me: the word the philosophers used to describe people born without Grisha gifts, *otkazat'sya*, "the abandoned". It was another word for orphan.

Late one afternoon, I was plodding through a passage describing Grisha assistance with trade routes when I felt someone's presence beside me. I looked up and cringed back in my chair. The Apparat was looming above me, his flat black pupils lit with peculiar intensity.

I glanced around the library. It was empty except for us, and despite the sun pouring through the glass ceiling, I felt a chill creep over me.

He sat down in the chair beside me with a gust of musty robes, and the damp smell of tombs enveloped me. I tried to breathe through my mouth.

"Are you enjoying your studies, Alina Starkov?"

"Very much," I lied.

"I'm so glad," he said. "But I hope you will remember to feed the soul as well as the mind. I am the spiritual adviser to all those within the palace walls. Should you find yourself worried or in distress, I hope you will not hesitate to come to me."

"I will," I said. "Absolutely."

"Good, good." He smiled, revealing a mouth of crowded, yellowing teeth, his gums black like a wolf's. "I want us to be friends. It is so important that we are friends."

"Of course."

"I would be pleased if you would accept a gift from me," he said, reaching into the folds of his brown robes and removing a small book bound in red leather.

How could someone offering you a present sound so creepy?

Reluctantly, I leaned forward and took the book from his long, blue-veined hand. The title was embossed in gold on the cover: *Istorii Sankt'ya.*

"The Lives of Saints?"

He nodded. "There was a time when all Grisha children were given this book when they came to school at the Little Palace."

"Thank you," I said, perplexed.

"Peasants love their Saints. They hunger for the miraculous. And yet they do not love the Grisha. Why do you think that is?"

"I hadn't thought about it," I said. I opened the book. Someone had written my name inside the cover. I flipped a few pages. *Sankt Petyr of Brevno. Sankt Ilya in Chains. Sankta Lizabeta.* Each chapter began with a full-page illustration, beautifully rendered in brightly coloured inks.

"I think it is because the Grisha do not suffer the way the Saints suffer, the way the people suffer."

"Maybe," I said absently.

"But you have suffered, haven't you, Alina Starkov? And I think . . . yes. I think you will suffer more."

My head jerked up. I thought he might be threatening me, but his eyes were full of a strange sympathy that was even more terrifying.

I glanced back down at the book in my lap. My finger had stopped on an illustration of *Sankta Lizabeta* as she had died, drawn and quartered in a field of roses. Her blood made a river through the petals. I snapped the book closed and sprang to my feet. "I should go."

The Apparat rose, and for a moment I thought he would try to stop me. "You do not like your gift."

"No, no. It's very nice. Thank you. I don't want to be late," I babbled.

I bolted past him through the library doors, and I didn't take an easy breath until I was safe in my room. I tossed the book of Saints into the bottom drawer of my dressing table and slammed it shut.

What did the Apparat want from me? Had his words been meant as a threat? Or as some kind of warning?

I took a deep breath, a tide of fatigue and confusion washing over me. I missed the easy rhythm of the Documents Tent, the comforting monotony of my life as a cartographer, when nothing more was expected of me than a few drawings and a tidy worktable. I missed the familiar smell of inks and paper. Mostly, I missed Mal.

I'd written to him every week, care of our regiment, but I hadn't heard anything in reply. I knew the post could be unreliable and that his unit might have moved on from the Fold or might even be in West Ravka, but I still hoped that I would hear from him soon. I'd given up on the idea of him visiting me at the Little Palace. As much as I missed him, I couldn't bear the thought of him knowing that I fitted into my new life about as well as I'd fitted into my old one.

Every night, as I climbed the stairs to my room after another pointless, painful day, I would imagine the letter that might be waiting for me on my dressing table, and my steps would quicken. But the days passed, and no letter came.

Today was no different. I ran my hand over the empty surface of the table.

"Where are you, Mal?" I whispered. But there was no one there to answer.

Chapter 11

When I thought things couldn't get any worse, they did.

I was sitting at breakfast in the domed hall when the main doors blew open and a group of unfamiliar Grisha entered. I didn't pay them much attention. Grisha in the Darkling's service were always coming and going at the Little Palace, sometimes to recover from injuries received at the northern or southern front, sometimes on leave from other assignments.

Then Nadia gasped.

"Oh no," groaned Marie.

I looked up and my stomach lurched as I recognised the raven-haired girl who had found Mal so fascinating back in Kribirsk.

"Who is she?" I whispered, watching the girl glide among the other Grisha, saying her hellos, her high laugh echoing off the golden dome.

"Zoya," muttered Marie. "She was a year ahead of us at school and she's horrible."

"Thinks she's better than everyone," added Nadia.

I raised my eyebrows. If Zoya's sin was snobbery, then Marie and Nadia had no business making judgments.

Marie sighed. "The worst part is that she's kind of

right. She's an incredibly powerful Squaller, a great fighter, and look at her."

I took in the silver embroidery on Zoya's cuffs, the glossy perfection of her black hair, the big blue eyes fringed by impossibly dark lashes. She was almost as beautiful as Genya. I thought of Mal and felt a pang of pure jealousy shoot through me. Then I remembered that Zoya had been stationed at the Fold. If she and Mal had . . . well, she might know if he was there, if he was all right. I pushed my plate away. The prospect of asking Zoya about Mal made me a little nauseated.

As if she could feel my stare, Zoya turned from where she was chatting to some awestruck Corporalki and swept over to the Summoners' table.

"Marie! Nadia! How are you?"

They stood to hug her, their faces plastered with huge, fake smiles.

"You look amazing, Zoya! How are you?" gushed Marie.

"We missed you so much!" squealed Nadia.

"I missed you too," Zoya said. "It's *so* good to be back at the Little Palace. You can't imagine how busy the Darkling's kept me. But I'm being rude. I don't think I've met your friend."

"Oh!" Marie exclaimed. "I'm so sorry. This is Alina Starkov. The Sun Summoner," she said with a little pride.

I stood up awkwardly.

Zoya swept me into an embrace. "It's *such* an honour to finally meet the Sun Summoner," she said loudly. But as she hugged me she whispered, "You stink of Keramzin."

I stiffened. She released me, a smile playing on her perfect lips.

"I'll see you all later," she said with a wave. "I'm frantic for a bath." And with that she sailed from the domed hall and through the double doors to the dormitories.

I stood there, stunned, my cheeks blazing. I felt as if everyone must be gaping at me, but no one else seemed to have heard what Zoya had said.

Her words stayed with me for the rest of the day, through another botched lesson with Baghra and an interminable lunch during which Zoya held forth about the journey from Kribirsk, the state of the towns bordering the Fold, and the exquisite *lubok* woodcuts she'd seen in one of the peasant villages. It might have been my imagination, but it seemed as though every time she said "peasant" she looked directly at me. As she spoke, light glinted off the heavy silver bracelet gleaming at her wrist. It was studded with pieces of bone. *An amplifier*, I realised.

Things went from bad to dreadful when Zoya showed up at our combat lesson. Botkin hugged her, kissed both of her cheeks, and then proceeded to chatter with her in Shu. Was there anything this girl couldn't do?

She'd brought along her friend with the chestnut curls, whom I remembered from the Grisha tent. They proceeded to giggle and whisper as I stumbled through the drills with which Botkin began every class. When we separated to spar, I wasn't even surprised when Botkin paired me with Zoya.

"Is star pupil," he said, grinning proudly. "Will help little girl."

"Surely the Sun Summoner doesn't need my help," Zoya said with a smug smile.

I watched her warily. I wasn't sure why this girl hated me so much, but I'd had just about enough for one day.

We took our fighting stances, and Botkin gave the signal to start.

I actually managed to block Zoya's first jab, but not the second. It caught me hard on the jaw and my head snapped back. I tried to shake it off.

She danced forward and aimed a punch at my ribs. But some of Botkin's training must have sunk in over the last few weeks. I dodged right and the blow glanced off me.

She flexed her shoulders and circled. Out of the corner of my eye, I could see that the other Summoners had left off sparring and were watching us.

I shouldn't have let myself get distracted. I took Zoya's next punch hard to the gut. As I gasped for breath, she followed with an elbow. I managed to avoid it more by luck than skill.

She pressed her advantage and lunged forward. That was her mistake. I was weak and I was slow, but Botkin had taught me to make use of my opponent's strength.

I stepped to the side, and as she came in close, I hooked my leg around her ankle. Zoya went down hard.

The other Summoners broke into applause. But before I had a chance to even register my victory, Zoya sat up, her expression furious, her arm slashing through the air. I felt myself lifted off my feet as I flew backwards and slammed into the training room's wooden wall. I heard something crack, and all the breath went out of my body as I slid to the ground.

"Zoya!" Botkin roared. "You do not use power. Not in these rooms. Never in these rooms!"

Dimly, I was aware of the other Summoners gathering around, of Botkin calling for a Healer.

"I'm fine," I tried to say, but I couldn't gather enough breath. I lay in the dirt, panting shallowly. Every time I tried to breathe, pain tore through my left side. A group of servants arrived, but when they lifted me onto the stretcher, I fainted.

Marie and Nadia told me the rest when they came to visit me in the infirmary. A Healer had slowed my heart rate until I fell into a deep sleep, then mended my broken rib and the bruises Zoya had left on me.

"Botkin was furious!" Marie exclaimed. "I've never seen him so angry. He threw Zoya out of the training rooms. I thought he might hit her himself."

"Ivo says he saw Ivan take her through the domed hall to the Darkling's council rooms, and when she came out, she was crying."

Good, I thought with satisfaction. But when I thought of myself lying in a heap in the dirt, I felt a burning wave of embarrassment.

"Why did she do it?" I asked as I tried to sit up. I'd had plenty of people ignore me or look down on me. But Zoya actually seemed to hate me.

Marie and Nadia gaped at me as if I'd taken a crack to the skull instead of the ribs.

"Because she's jealous!" said Nadia.

"Of me?" I said incredulously.

Marie rolled her eyes. "She can't bear the idea of anyone being the Darkling's favourite."

I laughed and then winced at the stab of pain in my side. "I'm hardly his favourite."

"Of course you are. Zoya's powerful, but she's just another Squaller. You're the Sun Summoner."

Nadia's cheeks flushed when she said this, and I knew

I wasn't imagining the tinge of envy in her voice. Just how deep did that envy go? Marie and Nadia talked as though they hated Zoya, but they smiled to her face. *What do they say about me when I'm not around?* I wondered.

"Maybe he'll demote her!" squealed Marie.

"Maybe he'll send her to Tsibeya!" crowed Nadia.

A Healer appeared from the shadows to shush them and send them on their way. They promised to visit again the next day.

I must have fallen back to sleep because, when I woke a few hours later, the infirmary was dark. The room was eerily quiet, the other beds unoccupied, the only sound the soft ticking of a clock.

I pushed myself up. I still felt a little sore, but it was hard to believe that I'd had a broken rib just a few hours before.

My mouth was dry, and I had the beginning of a headache. I dragged myself out of bed and poured a glass of water from the pitcher at my bedside. Then I pushed open the window and took a deep breath of night air.

"Alina Starkov."

I jumped and whirled.

"Who's there?" I gasped.

The Apparat emerged from the long shadows by the door.

"Did I startle you?" he asked.

"A bit," I admitted. How long had he been standing there? Had he been watching me sleep?

He seemed to glide silently across the room, his ragged robes slithering over the infirmary floor. I took an involuntary step backwards.

"I was very sorry to hear of your injury," he said. "The Darkling should be more watchful of his charges."

"I'm fine."

"Are you?" he said, regarding me in the moonlight. "You do not look well, Alina Starkov. It's essential that you stay well."

"I'm just a little tired."

He stepped closer. His peculiar smell wafted over me, that strange mix of incense and mildew, and the scent of turned earth. I thought of the graveyard at Keramzin, the crooked headstones, the peasant women keening over new graves. I was suddenly very aware of the emptiness of the infirmary. Was the Corporalki Healer still nearby? Or had he gone somewhere to find a glass of *kvas* and a warm bed?

"Did you know that in some of the border villages, they are making altars to you?" murmured the Apparat.

"What?"

"Oh yes. The people are hungry for hope, and the icon painters are doing a booming business thanks to you."

"But I'm not a Saint!"

"It is a blessing, Alina Starkov. A benediction." He stepped even closer. I could see the dark and matted hairs of his beard, the stained jumble of his teeth. "You are becoming dangerous, and you will become more dangerous still."

"Me?" I whispered. "To whom?"

"There is something more powerful than any army. Something strong enough to topple kings, and even Darklings. Do you know what that thing is?"

I shook my head, inching away from him.

"Faith," he breathed, his black eyes wild. "Faith."

He reached for me. I groped for my bedside table and knocked the glass of water to the floor. It shattered loudly. Hurried footsteps pounded down the hall towards us. The Apparat stepped back, melting into the shadows.

The door burst open and a Healer entered, his red *kefta* flapping behind him. "Are you all right?"

Before I could answer, the Apparat slid soundlessly from the room.

"I . . . I'm sorry," I said. "I broke a glass."

The Healer called a servant to clean up the mess. He settled me back into bed and suggested that I try to rest. But as soon as he was gone, I sat up and lit the lamp by my bed.

My hands were shaking. I wanted to dismiss the Apparat's ramblings as nonsense, but I couldn't. Not if people were really praying to the Sun Summoner, not if they were expecting me to save them. I remembered the Darkling's dire words beneath the broken roof of the barn. *The age of Grisha power is coming to an end.* I thought of the volcra, of the lives being lost on the Shadow Fold. *A divided Ravka won't survive the new age.* I wasn't just failing the Darkling or Baghra or myself. I was failing all of Ravka.

When Genya came by the next morning, I told her about the Apparat's visit, but she didn't seem concerned by what he'd said or his strange behaviour.

"He's creepy," she admitted. "But harmless."

"He is not harmless. You should have seen him. He looked completely mad."

"He's just a priest."

"But why was he even here?"

Genya shrugged. "Maybe the King asked him to pray for you."

"I'm not staying in this place again tonight. I want to sleep in my room. With a door that locks."

Genya sniffed and looked around the spare infirmary. "Well, that, at least, I can agree with. I wouldn't want to stay here either." Then she peered at me. "You look dreadful," she said with her usual tact. "Why don't you let me fix you up a bit?"

"No."

"Just let me get rid of the dark circles."

"No!" I said stubbornly. "But I do need a favour."

"Should I get my kit?" she asked eagerly.

I scowled at her. "Not that kind of favour. A friend of mine was injured on the Fold. I . . . I've written to him, but I'm not sure my letters are getting through." I felt my cheeks flush and hurried on. "Could you find out if he's okay and where he's been stationed? I don't know who else to ask, and since you're always at the Grand Palace, I thought you might be able to help."

"Of course, but . . . well, have you been checking the casualty lists?"

I nodded, a lump in my throat. Genya left to find paper and pen so I could write down Mal's name for her.

I sighed and rubbed my eyes. I didn't know what to make of Mal's silence. I checked the casualty lists every single week, my heart pounding, my stomach in knots, terrified that I would see his name. And each week, I gave thanks to all the Saints that Mal was safe and alive, even if he couldn't be bothered to write.

Was that the truth of it? My heart gave a painful twist. Maybe Mal was glad I was gone, glad to be free of old friendships and obligations. *Or maybe he's lying in a hospital bed somewhere and you're being a petty little brat*, I chided myself.

Genya returned, and I wrote out Mal's name, regiment, and unit number. She folded the paper and slipped it into the sleeve of her *kefta*.

"Thanks," I said hoarsely.

"I'm sure he's fine," she said, and gave my hand a gentle squeeze. "Now lie back so I can fix those dark circles."

"Genya!"

"Lie back or you can forget about your little favour."

My jaw dropped. "You are rotten."

"I am marvellous."

I glared at her, then flopped down on the pillows.

After Genya left, I made arrangements to return to my own quarters. The Healer wasn't happy about it, but I insisted. I was barely even sore any more, and there was no way I was spending another night in that empty infirmary.

When I got back to my room, I took a bath and tried to read one of my theory books. I couldn't concentrate. I was dreading returning to classes the next day, dreading another futile lesson with Baghra.

The stares and gossip about me had died down a bit since I'd arrived at the Little Palace. But I had no doubt that my fight with Zoya would bring that all back.

As I rose and stretched, I caught a glimpse of myself in the mirror above my dressing table. I crossed the room and scrutinised my face in the glass.

The dark shadows beneath my eyes were gone, but I knew they would be back in a few days. And it made little difference. I looked the way I always had: tired, scrawny, sick. Nothing like a real Grisha. The power was there, somewhere inside me, but I couldn't reach it, and I didn't know why. Why was I different? Why had it taken so long for my power to reveal itself? And why couldn't I access it on my own?

Reflected in the mirror I could see the thick golden curtains at the windows, the brilliantly painted walls, the firelight glittering off the tiles in the grate. Zoya was awful, but she was also right. I didn't belong in this beautiful world, and if I didn't find a way to use my power, I never would.

Chapter 12

The next morning wasn't as bad as I'd expected. Zoya was already in the domed hall when I entered. She sat by herself at the end of the Summoners' table, eating her breakfast in silence. She didn't look up as Marie and Nadia called their greetings to me, and I did my best to ignore her too.

I savoured every step of my walk down to the lake. The sun was bright, the air cold on my cheeks, and I wasn't looking forward to the stuffy, windowless confines of Baghra's hut. But when I climbed the steps to her door, I heard raised voices.

I hesitated and then knocked softly. The voices quieted abruptly, and after a moment, I pushed the door open and peeked inside. The Darkling was standing by Baghra's tile oven, his face furious.

"Sorry," I said, and began to back out of the door.

But Baghra just snapped, "In, girl. Don't let the heat out."

When I entered and shut the door, the Darkling gave me a small bow. "How are you, Alina?"

"I'm fine," I managed.

"She's fine!" hooted Baghra. "She's fine! She cannot light a hallway, but she's fine."

I winced and wished I could disappear into my boots.

To my surprise, the Darkling said, "Leave her be."

Baghra's eyes narrowed. "You'd like that, wouldn't you?"

The Darkling sighed and ran his hands through his dark hair in exasperation. When he looked at me, there was a rueful smile on his lips, and his hair was going every which way. "Baghra has her own way of doing things," he said.

"Don't patronise me, boy!" Her voice split the air like the crack of a whip. To my amazement, I saw the Darkling stand up straighter and then scowl as if he'd caught himself.

"Don't chide me, old woman," he said in a low, dangerous voice.

Angry energy crackled through the room. What had I walked into? I was thinking about slipping away and leaving them to finish whatever argument I'd interrupted when Baghra's voice lashed out again.

"The boy thinks to get you an amplifier," she said. "What do you think of that, girl?"

It was so strange to hear the Darkling called "boy" that it took me a moment to understand her meaning. When I did, hope and relief rushed through me. An amplifier! Why hadn't I thought of it before? Why hadn't *they* thought of it before? Baghra and the Darkling were able to help me call my power because they were living amplifiers, so why not an amplifier of my own like Ivan's bear claws or the seal tooth I'd seen hanging around Marie's neck?

"I think it's brilliant!" I exclaimed more loudly than I'd intended.

Baghra made a disgusted sound.

The Darkling gave her a sharp glance, but then he turned to me. "Alina, have you ever heard of Morozova's herd?"

"Of course she has. She's also heard of unicorns and the Shu Han dragons," Baghra said mockingly.

An angry look passed over the Darkling's features, but then he seemed to master himself. "May I have a word with you, Alina?" he asked politely.

"Of . . . of course," I stammered.

Baghra snorted again. The Darkling ignored her and took me by the elbow to lead me out of the cottage, shutting the door firmly behind us. When we had walked a short distance down the path, he heaved a huge sigh and ran his hands through his hair again. "That woman," he muttered.

It was hard not to laugh.

"What?" he said warily.

"I've just never seen you so . . . ruffled."

"Baghra has that effect on people."

"Was she your teacher too?"

A shadow crossed his face. "Yes," he said. "So what do you know about Morozova's herd?"

I bit my lip. "Just, well, you know . . ."

He sighed. "Just children's stories?"

I shrugged apologetically.

"It's all right," he said. "What do you remember from the stories?"

I thought back, remembering Ana Kuya's voice in the dormitories late at night. "They were white deer, magical creatures that appeared only at twilight."

"They're no more magical than we are. But they are ancient and very powerful."

"They're real?" I asked incredulously. I didn't mention that I certainly hadn't been feeling very magical *or* powerful lately.

"I think so."

"But Baghra doesn't."

"She usually finds my ideas ridiculous. What else do you remember?"

"Well," I said with a laugh. "In Ana Kuya's stories, they could talk, and if a hunter captured them and spared their lives, they granted wishes."

He laughed then. It was the first time I'd ever heard his laugh, a lovely dark sound that rippled through the air. "Well, that part definitely isn't true."

"But the rest is?"

"Kings and Darklings have been searching for Morozova's herd for centuries. My hunters claim they've seen signs of them, though never the creatures themselves."

"And you believe them?"

His slate-coloured gaze was cool and steady. "My men don't lie to me."

I felt a chill skitter up my spine. Knowing what the Darkling could do, I wouldn't be keen on lying to him either. "All right," I said uneasily.

"If Morozova's stag can be taken, its antlers can be made into an amplifier." He reached out and tapped my collarbone – even that brief contact was enough to send a jolt of power through me.

"A necklace?" I asked, trying to picture it, still feeling the tap of his fingers at the base of my throat.

He nodded. "The most powerful amplifier ever known."

My jaw dropped. "And you want to give it to me?"

He nodded again.

"Wouldn't it just be easier for me to get a claw or a fang or, I don't know, pretty much anything else?"

He shook his head. "If we have any hope of destroying the Fold, we need the stag's power."

"But maybe if I had one to practise with—"

"You know it doesn't work that way."

"I do?"

He frowned. "Haven't you been reading your theory?"

I gave him a look and said, "There's a lot of theory."

He surprised me by smiling. "I forget that you're new to this."

"Well, I don't," I muttered.

"Is it that bad?"

To my embarrassment, I felt a lump well up in my throat. I swallowed it down. "Baghra must have told you I can't summon a single sunbeam on my own."

"It will happen, Alina. I'm not worried."

"You're not?"

"No. And even if I were, once we have the stag, it won't matter."

I felt a surge of frustration. If an amplifier could make it possible for me to be a real Grisha, then I didn't want to wait for some mythical antler. I wanted a real one. Now.

"If no one's found Morozova's herd in all this time, what makes you think you'll find it now?" I asked.

"Because this was meant to be. The stag was meant for you, Alina. I can feel it." He looked at me. His hair was still a mess, and in the bright morning sunlight, he looked more handsome and more human than I'd ever seen him. "I guess I'm asking you to trust me," he said.

What was I supposed to say? I didn't really have a choice. If the Darkling wanted me to be patient, I would have to be patient. "Okay," I said finally. "But hurry it up."

He laughed again, and I felt a pleased flush creep up my cheeks. Then his expression became serious. "I've been waiting for you a long time, Alina," he said. "You and I are going to change the world."

I laughed nervously. "I'm not the world-changing type."

"Just wait," he said softly, and when he looked at me with those grey eyes, my heart gave a little thump. I thought he was going to say something more, but abruptly he stepped back, a troubled look on his face. "Good luck with your lessons," he said. He gave a short bow and turned on his heel to walk up the path to the lake shore. He'd only gone a few steps before he turned back to me. "Alina," he said. "About the stag?"

"Yes?"

"Please keep it to yourself. Most people think it's just a children's story, and I'd hate to look a fool."

"I won't say anything," I promised.

He nodded once and, without another word, strode away. I stared after him. I felt a little dazed, and I wasn't sure why.

When I looked up, Baghra was standing on the porch of her cottage, watching me. For no reason at all, I blushed.

"Hmph," she snorted, and then she turned her back on me too.

After my conversation with the Darkling, I took my first opportunity to visit the library. There was no mention of the stag in any of my theory books, but I did find a reference to Ilya Morozova, one of the first and most powerful Grisha.

There was also plenty about amplifiers. The books were very clear on the fact that a Grisha could have only one amplifier in his or her lifetime and that once a Grisha owned an amplifier, it could be possessed by no one else: *"The Grisha claims the amplifier, but the amplifier claims the Grisha, as well. Once it is done, there can be no other. Like calls to like, and the bond is made."*

The reason for this wasn't entirely clear to me, but it seemed to have something to do with a check on Grisha power.

"The horse has speed. The bear has strength. The bird has wings. No creature has all of these gifts, and so the world is held in balance. Amplifiers are part of this balance, not a means of subverting it, and each Grisha would do well to remember this or risk the consequences."

Another philosopher wrote, *"Why can a Grisha possess but one amplifier? I will answer this question instead: What is infinite? The universe and the greed of men."*

Sitting beneath the library's glass dome, I thought of the Black Heretic. The Darkling had said that the Shadow Fold was the result of his ancestor's greed. Was that what the philosophers meant by consequences? For the first time, it occurred to me that the Fold was the one place where the Darkling was helpless, where his powers meant nothing. The Black Heretic's descendants had suffered for his ambition. Still, I couldn't help but think that it was Ravka that had been made to pay in blood.

Autumn turned to winter, and cold winds stripped the branches in the palace gardens bare. Our table was still laden with fresh fruit and flowers furnished from the Grisha hothouses, where they made their own weather. But even juicy plums and purple grapes did little to improve my appetite.

Somehow I'd thought that my conversation with the Darkling might change something in me. I wanted to believe the things he'd said, and standing by the lake shore, I almost had. But nothing changed. I still couldn't summon without Baghra's help. I still wasn't truly a Grisha.

All the same, I felt a bit less miserable about it. The Darkling had asked me to trust him, and if he believed that the stag was the answer, then all I could do was hope he was right. I still avoided practising with the other Summoners, but I let Marie and Nadia drag me to the *banya* a couple of times and to one of the ballets at the Grand Palace. I even let Genya put a little colour in my cheeks.

My new attitude infuriated Baghra.

"You're not even trying any more!" she shouted. "You're waiting for some magical deer to come and save you? For your pretty necklace? You might as well wait for a unicorn to put its head in your lap, you stupid thing."

When she started railing at me, I just shrugged. She

was right. I was tired of trying and failing. I wasn't like the other Grisha, and it was time I accepted that. Besides, some rebellious part of me enjoyed driving her mad.

I didn't know what punishment Zoya had received, but she continued to ignore me. She'd been barred from the training rooms, and I'd heard she would be returning to Kribirsk after the winter fete. Occasionally, I caught her glaring at me or giggling behind her hand with her little group of Summoner friends, but I tried not to let it get to me.

Yet I couldn't shake the sense of my own failure. When the first snow came, I woke to find a new *kefta* waiting for me on my door. It was made of heavy midnight blue wool and had a hood lined in thick golden fur. I put it on, but it was hard not to feel like a fraud.

After picking at my breakfast, I made the familiar walk to Baghra's cottage. The gravel paths, cleared of snow by Inferni, sparkled beneath the weak winter sun. I was almost all the way to the lake when a servant caught up with me.

She handed me a folded piece of paper and bobbed a curtsey before scurrying back up the path. I recognised Genya's handwriting.

Malyen Oretsev's unit has been stationed at the Chernast outpost in northern Tsibeya for six weeks. He is listed as healthy. You can write to him care of his regiment.

The Kerch ambassadors are showering the Queen with gifts. Oysters and sandpipers packed in dry ice (vile) and almond candies! I'll bring some by tonight.

Mal was in Tsibeya. He was safe, alive, far from the fighting, probably hunting winter game.

I should be grateful. I should be glad.

You can write to him care of his regiment. I'd been writing to him care of his regiment for months.

I thought of the last letter I'd sent.

Dear Mal, I'd written. *I haven't heard from you, so I assume you've met and married a volcra and that you're living comfortably on the Shadow Fold, where you have neither light nor paper with which to write. Or, possibly, your new bride has eaten both your hands.*

I'd filled the letter with descriptions of Botkin, the Queen's snuffling dog, and the Grisha's curious fascination with peasant customs. I'd told him about beautiful Genya and the pavilions by the lake and the marvellous glass dome in the library. I'd told him about mysterious Baghra and the orchids in the hothouse and the birds painted above my bed. But I hadn't told him about Morozova's stag or the fact that I was such a disaster as a Grisha or that I still missed him every single day.

When I was done, I'd hesitated and then hastily scrawled at the bottom, *I don't know if you got my other letters. This place is more beautiful than I can describe, but I would trade it all to spend an afternoon skipping stones with you at Trivka's pond. Please write.*

But he had got my letters. What had he done with all of them? Had he even bothered to open them? Had he sighed with embarrassment when the fifth and the sixth and the seventh arrived?

I cringed. Please write, Mal. Please don't forget me, Mal.

Pathetic, I thought, brushing angry tears away.

I stared out at the lake. It was starting to freeze. I thought of the creek that ran through Duke Keramsov's estate. Every winter, Mal and I had waited for that creek to freeze so we could skate on it.

I crumpled Genya's note in my fist. I didn't want to think about Mal any more. I wished I could blot out every memory of Keramzin. Mostly I wished I could run back to my room and have a good cry. But I couldn't. I had to spend another pointless, miserable morning with Baghra.

I took my time making my way down the lake path, then stomped up the steps to Baghra's hut and banged open the door.

As usual, she was sitting by the fire, warming her bony body by the flames. I plunked myself down in the chair opposite her and waited.

Baghra let out a short bark of laughter. "So you're angry today, girl? What do you have to be angry about? Are you tired of waiting for your magical white deer?"

I crossed my arms and said nothing.

"Speak up, girl."

On any other day, I would have lied, told her I was fine, said that I was tired. But I guess I'd reached my breaking point, because I snapped. "I'm sick of all of this," I said angrily. "I'm sick of eating rye and herring for breakfast. I'm sick of wearing this stupid *kefta*. I'm sick of being pummelled by Botkin, and I'm sick of you."

I thought she would be furious, but instead she just peered at me. With her head cocked to one side and her eyes glittering black in the firelight, she looked like a very mean sparrow.

"No," she said slowly. "No. It's not that. There's something else. What is it? Is the poor little girl homesick?"

I snorted. "Homesick for what?"

"You tell me, girl. What's so bad about your life here? New clothes, a soft bed, hot food at every meal, the chance to be the Darkling's pet."

"I'm not his pet."

"But you want to be," she jeered. "Don't bother lying to me. You're the same as all the rest. I saw the way you looked at him."

My cheeks burned, and I thought about hitting Bahgra over the head with her own stick.

"A thousand girls would sell their own mothers to be in your shoes, and yet here you are, miserable and sulking like a child. So tell me, girl. What is your sad little heart pining for?"

She was right, of course. I knew very well that I was homesick for my best friend. But I wasn't about to tell her that.

I stood up, knocking my chair back with a clatter. "This is a waste of time."

"Is it? What else do you have to do with your days? Make maps? Fetch inks for some old cartographer?"

"There's nothing wrong with being a mapmaker."

"Of course not. And there's nothing wrong with being a lizard either. Unless you were born to be a hawk."

"I've had enough of this," I snarled, and turned my back on her. I was close to tears and I refused to cry in front of this spiteful old woman.

"Where are you going?" she called after me, her voice mocking. "What's waiting for you out there?"

"Nothing!" I shouted at her. "No one!"

As soon as I said it, the truth of the words hit me so

hard that it left me breathless. I gripped the door handle, feeling suddenly dizzy.

In that moment, the memory of the Grisha Examiners came rushing back to me.

I am in the sitting room at Keramzin. A fire is burning in the grate. The heavyset man in blue is pulling me away from Mal.

I feel Mal's fingers slip as his hand is torn from mine.

The young man in purple picks Mal up and drags him into the library, slamming the door behind him. I kick and thrash. I can hear Mal shouting my name.

The other man holds me. The woman in red slides her hand around my wrist. I feel a sudden rush of pure certainty wash over me.

I stop struggling. A call rings through me. Something within me rises up to answer.

I can't breathe. It's as if I'm kicking up from the bottom of a lake, about to break the surface, my lungs aching for air.

The woman in red watches me closely, her eyes narrowed.

I hear Mal's voice through the library door. Alina, Alina.

I know then. I know that we are different from one another. Terribly, irrevocably different.

Alina. Alina!

I make my choice. I grab hold of the thing inside me and push it back down.

"Mal!" I shout, and begin to struggle once more.

The woman in red tries to keep hold of my wrist, but I wriggle and wail until finally she lets me go.

I leaned against the door to Baghra's hut, trembling. The woman in red had been an amplifier. That was why the Darkling's call had felt familiar. But somehow I'd managed to resist her.

At last, I understood.

Before Mal, Keramzin had been a place of terrors, long nights spent crying in the dark, older children who ignored me, cold and empty rooms. But then Mal had arrived and all of that had changed. The dark hallways became places to hide and play. The lonely woods became places to explore. Keramzin became our palace, our kingdom, and I wasn't afraid any more.

But the Grisha Examiners would have taken me from Keramzin. They would have taken me away from Mal, and he had been the only good thing in my world. So I'd made my choice. I'd pushed my power down and held it there each day, with all my energy and will, without ever realising it. I'd used up every bit of myself to keep that secret.

I remembered standing at the window with Mal, watching the Grisha depart in their troika, how tired I'd felt. The next morning, I'd woken to find dark circles beneath my eyes. They'd been with me ever since.

And now? I asked myself, pressing my forehead against the cool wood of the door, my whole body shaking.

Now Mal had left me behind.

The only person in the world who truly knew me had decided I wasn't worth the effort of a few words. But I was holding on still. Despite all the luxuries of the Little Palace, despite my newfound powers, despite Mal's silence, I held on.

Baghra was right. I'd thought I was making such an effort, but deep down, some part of me just wanted to go home to Mal. Some part of me hoped that this had all been a mistake, that the Darkling would realise his error and send me back to the regiment, that Mal would realise how much he'd missed me, that we'd grow old together in our meadow. Mal had moved on, but I was still standing frightened before those three mysterious figures, holding tight to his hand.

It was time to let go. That day on the Shadow Fold, Mal had saved my life, and I had saved his. Maybe that was meant to be the end of us.

The thought filled me with grief, grief for the dreams we'd shared, for the love I'd felt, for the hopeful girl I would never be again. That grief flooded through me, dissolving a knot that I hadn't even known was there. I closed my eyes, feeling tears slide down my cheeks, and I reached out to the thing within me that I'd kept hidden for so long. *I'm sorry*, I whispered to it.

I'm sorry I left you so long in the dark.

I'm sorry, but I'm ready now.

I called and the light answered. I felt it rushing towards me from every direction, skimming over the lake, skittering over the golden domes of the Little Palace, under the door and through the walls of Baghra's cottage. I felt it everywhere. I opened my hands and the light bloomed right through me, filling the room, illuminating the stone walls, the old tile oven, and every angle of Baghra's strange face. It surrounded me, blazing with heat, more powerful and more pure than ever before because it was all mine. I wanted to laugh, to sing, to shout. At last, there was something that belonged wholly and completely to me.

"Good," said Baghra, squinting in the sunlight. "Now we work."

Chapter 13

That very afternoon, I joined the other Etherealki by the lake and called my power for them for the first time. I sent a sheet of light shimmering out over the water, letting it roll over the waves that Ivo had summoned. I didn't have the others' control yet, but I managed. In fact, it was easy.

Suddenly, lots of things seemed easy. I wasn't tired all the time or winded when I climbed the stairs. I slept deeply and dreamlessly every night and woke refreshed. Food was a revelation: bowls of porridge heaped with sugar and cream, plates of skate fried in butter, fat plums and hothouse peaches, the clear and bitter taste of *kvas*. It was as if that moment in Baghra's cottage was my first full breath and I had awakened into a new life.

Since none of the other Grisha knew that I'd had so much trouble summoning, they were all a little baffled by the change in me. I didn't offer any explanations, and Genya let me in on some of the more hilarious rumours.

"Marie and Ivo were speculating that the Fjerdans had infected you with a disease."

"I thought Grisha didn't get sick."

"Exactly!" she said. "That's why it was so very sinister. But apparently the Darkling cured you by feeding you his own blood and an extract of diamonds."

"That's disgusting," I said, laughing.

"Oh that's nothing. Zoya actually tried to put it around that you were possessed."

I laughed even harder.

My lessons with Baghra were still difficult and I never actually enjoyed them. But I did relish any chance to use my power, and I knew I was making progress. At first, I'd been frightened every time I got ready to call the light, afraid that it just wouldn't be there and I'd be back to where I'd started.

"It isn't something separate from you," Baghra snapped. "It isn't an animal that shies away from you or chooses whether or not to come when you call it. Do you ask your heart to beat or your lungs to breathe? Your power serves you because that is its purpose, because *it cannot help but serve you.*"

Sometimes I felt as if there was a shadow in Baghra's words, a second meaning she wanted me to understand. But the work I was doing was hard enough without guessing at the secrets of a bitter old woman.

She drove me hard, pushing me to expand my reach and my control. She taught me to focus my power in short bright bursts, piercing beams that burned with heat, and long sustained cascades. She forced me to call the light again, and again, and again, until I barely had to reach for it. She made me trek to her cottage at night to practise when it was nearly impossible for me to find any light to summon. When I finally, proudly, produced a weak thread of sunlight, she slammed her cane down on the ground and shouted, "Not good enough!"

"I'm doing my best," I muttered in exasperation.

"Pah!" she spat. "Do you think the world cares if you

do your best? Do it again and do it right."

My lessons with Botkin were the real surprise. As a little girl, I had run and played with Mal in the woods and fields, but I'd never been able to keep up with him. I'd always been too sickly and frail, too easy to tire. But as I ate and slept regularly for the first time in my life, all of that changed. Botkin put me through brutal combat drills and seemingly endless runs through the palace grounds, but I found myself enjoying some of the challenges. I liked learning what this new, stronger body could do.

I doubted I'd ever be able to outspar the old mercenary, but the Fabrikators had helped even the field. They'd produced a pair of fingerless leather gloves for me that were lined with little mirrors – the mysterious glass discs David had shown me on that first day in the workshops. With a flick of the wrist, I could slide a mirror between my fingers and, with Botkin's permission, I practised bouncing flashes of light off them and into my opponent's eyes. I worked with them until they felt almost natural in my hands, like extensions of my own fingers.

Botkin remained gruff and critical, and took every opportunity to call me useless, but once in a while I thought I glimpsed a hint of approval on his weathered features.

Late in winter, he took me aside after a long lesson in which I'd actually managed to land a blow to his ribs (and been thanked for it with a hard cuff across my jaw).

"Here," he said, handing me a heavy knife in a steel and leather sheath. "Always keep with you."

With a jolt, I saw that it was no ordinary knife. It was Grisha steel. "Thank you," I managed.

"Not 'thank you', " he said. He tapped the ugly scar at his throat. "Steel is earned."

Winter looked different to me than it ever had before. I spent sunny afternoons skating on the lake or sledding on the palace grounds with the other Summoners. Snowy evenings were passed in the domed hall, gathered around the tile ovens, drinking *kvas* and gorging ourselves on sweets. We celebrated the feast of *Sankt Nikolai* with huge bowls of dumpling soup and *kutya* made with honey and poppy seeds. Some of the other Grisha left the palace to go on sleigh rides and dogsledding excursions in the snow-blanketed countryside surrounding Os Alta, but for security reasons, I was still confined to the palace grounds.

I didn't mind. I felt more comfortable with the Summoners now, but I doubted I'd ever really enjoy being around Marie and Nadia. I was much happier sitting in my room with Genya, drinking tea and gossiping by the fire. I loved to hear all the court gossip, and even better were the tales of the opulent parties at the Grand Palace. My favourite was the story of the massive pie that a count had presented to the King, and the dwarf who had burst out of it to hand the *tsaritsa* a bouquet of forget-me-nots.

At the end of the season, the King and the Queen would host a final winter fete attended by all the Grisha. Genya claimed it would be the most lavish party of all. Every noble family and high court officer would be there, along with military heroes, foreign dignitaries, and the *tsarevitch*, the King's eldest son and heir to the throne. I'd once seen the Crown Prince riding around the palace grounds on a white gelding that was roughly the size of a house. He was almost handsome, but he had the King's weak chin and eyes so heavy-lidded that it was hard to tell if he was tired or just supremely bored.

"Probably drunk," said Genya, stirring her tea. "He devotes all of his time to hunting, horses and imbibing. Drives the Queen mad."

"Well, Ravka is at war. He should probably be more concerned with matters of state."

"Oh she doesn't care about that. She just wants him to find a bride instead of gallivanting around the world spending mounds of gold buying up ponies."

"What about the other one?" I asked. I knew the King and Queen had a younger son, but I'd never actually seen him.

"*Sobachka?*"

"You can't call a royal prince 'puppy'," I said, laughing.

"That's what everyone calls him." She lowered her voice. "And there are rumours that he isn't strictly royal."

I nearly choked on my tea. "No!"

"Only the Queen knows for sure. He's a bit of a black sheep anyway. He insisted on doing his military service in the infantry, then he apprenticed to a gunsmith."

"And he's never at court?"

"Not in years. I think he's off studying shipbuilding or something equally dull. He'd probably get along well with David," she added sourly.

"What do you two talk about, anyway?" I asked curiously. I still didn't quite understand Genya's fascination with the Fabrikator.

She sighed. "The usual. Life. Love. The melting point of iron ore." She wound a curl of bright red hair around her finger, and her cheeks flushed a pretty pink. "He's actually quite funny when he lets himself be."

"Really?"

Genya shrugged. "*I* think so."

I patted her hand reassuringly. "He'll come around. He's just shy."

"Maybe I should lie down on a table in the workroom and wait to see if he welds something to me."

"I think that's the way most great love stories begin."

She laughed, and I felt a sudden niggle of guilt. Genya talked so easily about David, but I'd never confided in her about Mal.

That's because there's nothing to confide, I reminded myself harshly and added more sugar to my tea.

One quiet afternoon when the other Grisha had ventured out of Os Alta, Genya convinced me to sneak into the Grand Palace, and we spent hours looking through the clothes and shoes in the Queen's dressing room. Genya insisted that I try on a pale pink silk gown studded with riverpearls, and when she laced me up in it and stuck me in front of one of the giant golden mirrors, I had to look twice.

I'd learned to avoid mirrors. They never seemed to show me what I wanted to see. But the girl standing next to Genya in the glass was a stranger. She had rosy cheeks and shiny hair and . . . a shape. I could have stared at her for hours. I suddenly wished good old Mikhael could see me. "*Sticks*" *indeed*, I thought smugly.

Genya caught my eye in the mirror and grinned.

"Is this why you dragged me in here?" I asked suspiciously.

"Whatever do you mean?"

"You know what I mean."

"I just thought you might want to get a good look at yourself, that's all."

I swallowed the embarrassing lump in my throat and gave her an impulsive hug. "Thanks," I whispered. Then I gave her a little shove. "Now get out of the way. It's impossible to feel pretty with you standing next to me."

We spent the rest of the afternoon trying on dresses and goggling at ourselves in the mirror – two activities I never would have expected to enjoy. We lost track of time, and Genya had to help me scramble out of an aquamarine ball gown and back into my *kefta* so that I could hurry down to the lake for my evening lesson with Baghra. I ran all the way but I was still late, and she was furious.

The evening sessions with Baghra were always the hardest, and she was particularly tough on me that night.

"Control!" she snapped as the weak wave of sunlight that I'd summoned flickered on the lake shore. "Where is your focus?"

At dinner, I thought but didn't say. Genya and I had been so caught up in the distractions of the Queen's wardrobe that we'd forgotten to eat, and my stomach was growling.

I centred myself and the light bloomed brighter, reaching out over the frozen lake.

"Better," she said. "Let the light do the work for you. Like calls to like."

I tried to relax and let the light call to itself. To my

surprise, it surged across the ice, illuminating the little island in the middle of the lake.

"More!" Baghra demanded. "What's stopping you?"

I dug deeper and the circle of light swelled past the island, bathing the whole lake and the school on the opposite shore in gleaming sunlight. Though there was snow on the ground, the air around us shone bright and heavy with summer heat. My body thrummed with power. It was exhilarating, but I could feel myself tiring, bumping up against the limits of my abilities.

"More!" Baghra shouted.

"I can't!" I protested.

"More!" she said again, and there was an urgency in her voice that sounded an alarm inside of me and caused my focus to falter. The light wavered and slipped from my grasp. I scrambled for it but it rushed away from me, plunging the school, then the island, and then the lake shore back into darkness.

"It's not enough." His voice made me jump. The Darkling emerged from the shadows onto the lamplit path.

"It might be," said Baghra. "You see how strong she is. I wasn't even helping her. Give her an amplifier and see what she can do."

The Darkling shook his head. "She'll have the stag."

Baghra scowled. "You're a fool."

"I've been called worse. Often by you."

"This is folly. You must reconsider."

The Darkling's face went cold. "I *must*? You don't give me orders any more, old woman. I know what has to be done."

"I might surprise you," I piped up. The Darkling and

Baghra turned to stare at me. It was almost as if they'd forgotten I was there. "Baghra's right. I know I can do better. I can work harder."

"You've been on the Shadow Fold, Alina. You know what we're up against."

I felt suddenly stubborn. "I'm getting stronger every day. If you give me a chance—"

Again, the Darkling shook his head. "I can't take that kind of a chance. Not with Ravka's future at stake."

"I understand," I said numbly.

"Do you?"

"Yes," I said. "Without Morozova's stag, I'm pretty much useless."

"Ah, so she's not as stupid as she looks," cackled Baghra.

"Leave us," said the Darkling with surprising ferocity.

"We'll all suffer for your pride, boy."

"I won't ask you again."

Baghra gave him a disgusted glower, then turned on her heel and marched back up the path to her cottage.

When her door slammed shut, the Darkling regarded me in the lamplight. "You look well," he said.

"Thanks," I mumbled, my eyes sliding away. Maybe Genya could teach me to take a compliment.

"If you're returning to the Little Palace, I'll walk with you," he said.

For a while, we strolled in silence along the lake shore, past the deserted stone pavilions. Across the ice, I could see the lights of the school.

Finally, I had to ask. "Has there been any word? Of the stag?"

He pressed his lips together. "No," he said. "My men think that the herd may have crossed into Fjerda."

"Oh," I said, trying to hide my disappointment.

He stopped abruptly. "I don't think you're useless, Alina."

"I know," I said to the tops of my boots. "Not useless. Just not exactly useful."

"No Grisha is powerful enough to face the Fold. Not even me."

"I get it."

"But you don't like it."

"Should I? If I can't help you destroy the Fold, then what exactly am I good for? Midnight picnics? Keeping your feet warm in the winter?"

His mouth quirked up in a half smile. "Midnight picnics?"

I couldn't smile back. "Botkin told me that Grisha steel is earned. It's not that I'm not grateful for all of this. I am, truly. But I don't feel I've earned any of it."

He sighed. "I'm sorry, Alina. I asked you to trust me and I haven't delivered."

He looked so weary that I felt instantly contrite. "It's not that—"

"It's true." He took another deep breath and ran a hand over his neck. "Maybe Baghra's right, as much as I hate to admit it."

I cocked my head to one side. "You never seem fazed by anything. Why do you let her bother you so much?"

"I don't know."

"Well, I think she's good for you."

He started in surprise. "Why?"

"Because she's the only one around here who isn't

scared of you or constantly trying to impress you."

"Are you trying to impress me?"

"Of course," I laughed.

"Do you always say exactly what you're thinking?"

"Not even half the time."

Then he laughed too, and I remembered how much I liked the sound. "Then I guess I should count myself lucky," he said.

"What's Baghra's power, anyway?" I asked, the thought occurring to me for the first time. She was an amplifier like the Darkling, but he had his own power too.

"I'm not sure," he said. "I think she was a Tidemaker. No one around here is old enough to remember." He looked down at me. The cold air had put a flush in his cheeks, and the lamplight shone in his eyes. "Alina, if I tell you that I still believe we can find the stag, would you think I'm mad?"

"Why would you care what I think?"

He looked genuinely baffled. "I don't know," he said. "But I do."

And then he kissed me.

It happened so suddenly that I barely had time to react. One moment, I was staring into his slate-coloured eyes, and the next, his lips were pressed to mine. I felt that familiar sense of surety melt through me as my body sang with sudden heat and my heart jumped into a skittery dance. Then, just as suddenly, he stepped back. He looked as surprised as I felt.

"I didn't mean . . . " he said.

At that moment, we heard footsteps and Ivan rounded the corner. He bowed to the Darkling and then to me, but I caught a little smirk playing on his lips.

"The Apparat is getting impatient," he said.

"One of his less appealing traits," replied the Darkling smoothly. The look of surprise had vanished from his face. He bowed to me, completely composed, and without another glance, he and Ivan left me alone in the snow.

I stood there for a long moment and then made my way back to the Little Palace in a daze. *What just happened?* I touched my fingers to my lips. *Did the Darkling really just kiss me?* I avoided the domed hall and went straight to my room, but once I was there, I didn't know what to do with myself. I rang for a dinner tray and then sat picking at my food. I was desperate to talk to Genya, but she slept at the Grand Palace every night, and I didn't have the courage to go and try to find her. Finally, I gave up and decided to go down to the domed hall after all.

Marie and Nadia had returned from their sleighing excursion and were sitting by the fire, drinking tea. I was shocked to see Sergei sitting next to Marie, his arm looped through hers. *Maybe there's something in the air*, I thought in amazement.

I sat sipping tea with them, asking about their day and their trip to the countryside, but I had trouble keeping my mind on the conversation. My thoughts kept wandering back to the feel of the Darkling's lips on mine and the way he'd looked standing in the lamplight, his breath a white cloud in the cold night air, that stunned expression on his face.

I knew I wouldn't be able to sleep, so when Marie suggested going to the *banya*, I decided to join them. Ana

Kuya had always told us that the *banya* was barbaric, an excuse for peasants to drink *kvas* and engage in wanton behavior. But I was beginning to realise that old Ana had been a bit of a snob.

I sat in the steam for as long as I could bear the heat and then plunged, squealing, into the snow with the others, before running inside to do it all over again. I stayed until long past midnight, laughing and gasping, trying to clear my head.

When I stumbled back to my room, I fell into bed, my skin damp and pink, my hair in wet tangles. I felt flushed and boneless, but my mind was still whirring. I focused and summoned a warm wash of sunlight, making it dance in slivers across the painted ceiling, letting the rush of power soothe my nerves. Then the memory of the Darkling's kiss blew through me and rattled my concentration, scattering my thoughts and making my heart swoop and dive like a bird borne aloft by uncertain currents.

The light shattered, leaving me in darkness.

Chapter 14

As winter drew to a close, talk turned to the King and Queen's fete at the Grand Palace. The Grisha Summoners were expected to put on a demonstration of their powers to entertain the nobles, and much time was spent discussing who would perform and what would make the most impressive showing.

"Just don't call it 'performing'," Genya warned. "The Darkling can't stand it. He thinks the winter fete is a giant waste of Grisha time."

I thought he might have a point. The Materialki workshops buzzed morning and night with orders from the palace for cloth and gems and fireworks. The Summoners spent hours at the stone pavilions honing their "demonstrations". Given that Ravka was at war and had been for over a hundred years, it all seemed a little frivolous. Still, I hadn't been to many parties, and it was hard not to get caught up in the talk of silks and dances and flowers.

Baghra had no patience with me. If I lost focus for even a moment, she'd smack me with her stick and say, "Dreaming of dancing with your dark prince?"

I ignored her but, too often, she was right. Despite my best efforts, I was thinking of the Darkling. He'd disappeared once again, and Genya told me that he'd left for the north. The other Grisha speculated that he would have to put in an appearance at the winter fete, though no one could be sure. Again and again, I found myself on the verge of telling Genya about the kiss, but I always stopped just as the words were on my lips.

You're being ridiculous, I told myself sternly. *It didn't mean anything. He probably kisses a lot of Grisha girls. And why would the Darkling have any interest in you when there are people like Genya and Zoya around?* But if those things were true, I didn't want to know. As long as I kept my mouth shut, the kiss was a secret that the Darkling and I shared, and I wanted it to stay that way. All the same, some days it took everything in me not to stand up in the middle of breakfast and shout, "The Darkling kissed me!"

If Baghra was disappointed in me, it was nothing compared to my disappointment in myself. As hard as I pushed, my limitations were becoming obvious. At the end of every lesson, I kept hearing the Darkling say, "It's not enough," and I knew he was right. He wanted to destroy the very fabric of the Fold, to turn back the black tide of the Unsea, and I simply wasn't strong enough to manage that. I'd read enough to understand that this was the way of things. All Grisha had limits to their power, even the Darkling. But he'd said I was going to change the world, and it was hard to accept that I might not be up to the task.

The Darkling had vanished, but the Apparat seemed to be everywhere. He lurked in hallways and by the path to the lake. I thought he might be trying to trap me alone again, but I didn't want to listen to him rant about faith and suffering. I was careful never to let him catch me by myself.

On the day of the winter fete, I was excused from my classes, but I went to see Botkin anyway. I was too anxious about my part in the demonstration and the prospect of seeing the Darkling again to just sit in my room. Being around the other Grisha didn't help. Marie and Nadia talked constantly about their new silk *kefta* and what jewels they intended to wear, and David and the other Fabrikators kept accosting me to talk over the details of the demonstration. So I avoided the domed hall and went out to the training rooms by the stables.

Botkin put me through my paces and made me drill using my mirrors. Without them, I was still pretty helpless against him. But with my gloves on, I could almost hold my own. Or so I thought. When the lesson was over, Botkin admitted that he'd been pulling his punches.

"Should not hit girl in face when she is going to party," he said with a shrug. "Botkin will be fairer tomorrow."

I groaned at the prospect.

I had a quick dinner in the domed hall and then, before anyone could corner me, I hurried up to my room, already thinking of my beautiful sunken bath. The *banya* was fun, but I'd had my share of communal bathing in the army, and privacy was still a novelty to me.

When I'd had a long, luxurious soak, I sat down by the windows to dry my hair and watch night fall over the lake. Soon, the lamps lining the long drive to the palace would be lit as nobles arrived in their lavish coaches, each more ornate than the last. I felt a prickle of excitement. A few months ago, I would have dreaded a night like this: a performance, playing dress-up with hundreds of beautiful people in their beautiful clothes. I was still nervous, but I thought it all might actually be . . . fun.

I looked at the little clock on the mantel and frowned. A servant was supposed to be delivering my new silk *kefta*. If she didn't arrive soon, I was going to have to wear my old wool one or borrow something from Marie.

Even as I had the thought, a knock sounded at the door. But it was Genya, her tall frame swathed in cream silk heavily embroidered in gold, her red hair piled high on her head to better display the massive diamonds dangling from her ears and the graceful turn of her neck.

"Well?" she said, turning this way and that.

"I loathe you," I said with a smile.

"I do look remarkable," she said, admiring herself in the mirror over the basin.

"You'd look even better with a little humility."

"I doubt that. Why aren't you dressed?" she asked, taking a break from marvelling at her own reflection to notice I was still in my robe.

"My *kefta* hasn't arrived."

"Oh, well, the Fabrikators have been a bit overwhelmed with the Queen's requests. I'm sure it will get here. Now, sit down in front of the mirror so I can do your hair."

I practically squealed with excitement, but I managed to restrain myself. I'd been hoping Genya would offer to do my hair, but I hadn't wanted to ask. "I thought you would be helping the Queen," I said as Genya set her clever hands to work.

She rolled her amber eyes. "I can only do so much. Her Highness has decided she doesn't feel up to attending the ball tonight. She has a headache. Ha! I'm the one who spent an hour removing her crow's feet."

"So she's not going?"

"Of course she's going! She just wants her ladies to fuss over her so she can feel even more important. This is the biggest event of the season. She wouldn't miss it for the world."

The biggest event of the season. I let out a shaky breath.

"Nervous?" asked Genya.

"A little. I don't know why."

"Maybe because a few hundred nobles are waiting to get their first look at you."

"Thanks. That really helps."

"You're very welcome," she said, giving my hair a hard tug. "You should be used to being gawked at by now."

"And yet I'm not."

"Well, if it gets too bad, give me a signal, and I'll get up on the banquet table, toss my skirt over my head, and do a dance. That way no one will be looking at you."

I laughed and felt myself relax a bit. After a moment, trying to keep my voice casual, I asked, "Has the Darkling arrived?"

"Oh yes. He arrived yesterday. I saw his coach."

My heart sank a little. He had been in the palace for an entire day and he hadn't come to see me or called for me.

"I imagine he's very busy," said Genya.

"Of course."

After a moment, she said softly, "We all feel it, you know."

"Feel what?"

"The pull. Towards the Darkling. But he's not like us, Alina."

I tensed. Genya kept her gaze studiously focused on the coils of my hair.

"What do you mean?" I asked. Even to my own ears, my voice sounded unnaturally high.

"His kind of power, the way he looks. You'd have to be mad or blind not to notice it."

I didn't want to ask, but I couldn't help myself. "Has he ever . . . ? I mean, have you and he ever . . . ?"

"No! Never!" A mischievous smile twitched on her lips. "But I would."

"Really?"

"Who wouldn't?" Her eyes met mine in the mirror. "But I'd never let my heart get involved."

I gave what I hoped was an indifferent shrug. "Of course not."

Genya raised her flawless brows and tugged hard on my hair.

"Ouch!" I yelped. "Will David be there tonight?"

Genya sighed. "No, he doesn't like parties. But I did just happen to drop by the workrooms so he could get a peek at what he was missing. He barely looked at me."

"I doubt that," I said comfortingly.

Genya twisted a final piece of my hair into place and secured it with a golden hairpin.

"There!" she said triumphantly. She handed me my little mirror and turned me around so that I could see her handiwork. Genya had piled half of my hair into an elaborate knot. The rest cascaded around my shoulders in shining waves. I beamed and gave her a quick hug.

"Thank you!" I said. "You're spectacular."

"A lot of good it does me," she grumbled.

How was it that Genya had fallen so hard for

someone so serious and so quiet and so seemingly oblivious to her gorgeousness? Or was that exactly why she had fallen for David?

A knock at the door pulled me from my thoughts. I ran to open it. I felt a rush of relief when I saw two servants standing in the doorway, each carrying several boxes. Until that moment, I hadn't realised how worried I'd been about my *kefta* arriving. I laid the largest box on the bed and pulled off the lid.

Genya squeaked, and I just stood there gaping at the contents. When I didn't move, she reached into the box and pulled out yards of rippling black silk. The sleeves and neckline were delicately embroidered in gold and glittered with tiny jet beads.

"Black," Genya whispered.

His colour. What did it mean?

"Look!" she gasped.

The neckline of the gown was laced with a black velvet ribbon, and from it hung a small golden charm: the sun in eclipse, the Darkling's symbol.

I bit my lip. This time, the Darkling had chosen to set me apart, and there was nothing I could do about it. I felt a little jab of resentment, but it was drowned by excitement. Had he chosen these colours for me before or after the night by the lake? Would he regret seeing me in them tonight?

I couldn't think about that now. Unless I wanted to go to the ball naked, I didn't have a lot of options. I stepped behind the screen and slipped into the new *kefta*. The silk felt cool on my skin as I fumbled with the tiny buttons. When I emerged, Genya broke into a huge grin.

"Ooh, I knew you'd look good in black." She grabbed my arm. "Come on!"

"I don't even have my shoes on!"

"Just come on!"

She pulled me down the hall, then threw open a door without knocking.

Zoya shrieked. She was standing in the middle of her room in a *kefta* of midnight blue silk, a brush in her hand.

"Excuse us!" announced Genya. "But we have need of this chamber. Darkling's orders!"

Zoya's beautiful blue eyes slitted dangerously. "If you think—" she began and then she caught sight of me. Her jaw dropped, and the blood drained from her face.

"Out!" commanded Genya.

Zoya snapped her mouth shut, but to my amazement, she left the room without another word. Genya slammed the door behind her.

"What are you doing?" I asked dubiously.

"I thought it was important that you see yourself in a proper mirror, not that useless sliver of glass on your dressing table," she said. "But mostly I wanted to see the look on that bitch's face when she saw you in the Darkling's colour."

I couldn't restrain my grin. "That was pretty wonderful."

"Wasn't it?" Genya said dreamily.

I turned to the mirror, but Genya grabbed me and sat me at Zoya's dressing table. She started rooting around in the drawers.

"Genya!"

"Just wait . . . aha! I knew she was darkening her lashes!" Genya pulled a little pot of black antimony from

Zoya's drawer. "Can you summon a little light for me to work with?"

I called a nice warm glow to help Genya see better and tried to be patient as she made me look up, down, left, right.

"Perfect!" she said when she was done. "Oh, Alina, you look quite the temptress."

"Right," I said, and snatched the mirror from her. But then I had to smile. The sad, sickly girl with hollowed-out cheeks and bony shoulders was gone. In her place was a Grisha with sparkling eyes and shimmering waves of bronze hair. The black silk clung to my new form, shifting and sliding like sewn-together shadows. And Genya had done something marvellous to my eyes so that they looked dark and almost cat-like.

"Jewellery!" shouted Genya, and we ran back to my room, passing Zoya, who was seething in the hallway.

"Are you finished?" she snapped.

"For the moment," I said airily, and Genya gave a very unladylike snort.

In the other boxes on my bed, we found golden silk slippers, glittering jet and gold earrings, and a thick fur muff. When I was ready, I examined myself in the little mirror above the basin. I felt exotic and mysterious, as if I was wearing some other, far more glamorous girl's clothes.

I looked up to see Genya watching me with a troubled expression.

"What's wrong?" I said, suddenly self-conscious again.

"Nothing," she said with a smile. "You look beautiful. Truly. But . . ." Her smile faltered. She reached out and lifted the little golden charm at my neckline.

"Alina, the Darkling doesn't notice most of us. We're moments he'll forget in his long life. And I'm not sure that's such a bad thing. Just . . . be careful."

I stared at her, baffled. "Of what?"

"Of powerful men."

"Genya," I asked before I could lose my nerve, "what happened between you and the King?"

She examined the toes of her satin slippers. "The King has his way with lots of servants," she said. Then she shrugged. "At least I got a few jewels out if it."

"You don't mean that."

"No. I don't." She fiddled with one of her earrings. "The worst part is that everyone knows."

I put my arm around her. "They don't matter. You're worth all of them put together."

She gave a weak imitation of her confident smile. "Oh, I know that."

"The Darkling should have done something," I said. "He should have protected you."

"He has, Alina. More than you know. Besides, he's as much a slave to the whims of the King as the rest of us. At least for now."

"For now?"

She gave me a quick squeeze. "Let's not dwell on depressing things tonight. Come on," she said, her gorgeous face breaking into a dazzling grin. "I'm in desperate need of champagne!"

And with that, she glided serenely from the room. I wanted to say more to her. I wanted to ask her what she meant about the Darkling. I wanted to take a hammer to the King's head. But she was right. There would be plenty of time for trouble tomorrow. I took a last peek in the little mirror and hurried out into the hall, leaving my worries and Genya's warnings behind me.

My black kefta caused quite a stir in the domed hall as Marie and Nadia and a group of other Etherealki dressed in blue velvets and silks swarmed around me and Genya. Genya made to slip away as she usually did, but I held fast to her arm. If I was wearing the Darkling's colour, then I intended to take full advantage of it and have my friend by my side.

"You know I can't go into the ballroom with you. The Queen would have a fit," she whispered in my ear.

"Okay, but you can still walk over with me."

Genya beamed.

As we walked down the gravel path and into the wooded tunnel, I noticed that Sergei and several other Heartrenders were keeping pace with us, and I realised with a start that they were guarding us – or probably me. I supposed it made sense with all of the strangers on the palace grounds for the fete, but it was still disconcerting, a reminder that there were a lot of people in the world who wanted me dead.

The grounds surrounding the Grand Palace had been lit up to showcase tableaus of actors and troupes of acrobats performing for wandering guests. Masked musicians strolled the paths. A man with a monkey on his shoulder ambled past, and two men covered from head to toe in gold leaf rode by on zebras, throwing jewelled flowers to everyone they passed. Costumed choirs sang in the trees.

A trio of redheaded dancers splashed around in the double-eagle fountain, wearing little more than seashells and coral and holding up platters full of oysters to guests.

We had just started to climb the marble steps when a servant appeared with a message for Genya. She read the note and sighed.

"The Queen's headache has miraculously disappeared, and she has decided to attend the ball after all." She gave me a hug, promised to find me before the demonstration, and then slipped away.

Spring had barely begun to show itself, but it was impossible to tell that in the Grand Palace. Music floated down the marble hallways. The air felt curiously warm and was perfumed with the scent of thousands of white flowers, grown in Grisha hothouses. They covered tables and trailed down balustrades in thick clusters.

Marie, Nadia and I drifted through groups of nobles, who pretended to ignore us but whispered as we passed by with our Corporalki guard. I held my head high and even smiled at one of the young noblemen standing by the entrance to the ballroom. I was surprised to see him blush and look down at his shoes. I glanced at Marie and Nadia to see if they had noticed, but they were gabbling about some of the dishes served to the nobles at dinner – roasted lynx, salted peaches, burnt swan with saffron. I was glad that we'd eaten earlier.

The ballroom was larger and grander than even the throne room had been, lit by row after row of sparkling chandeliers, and full of masses of people drinking and dancing to the sounds of a masked orchestra seated along the far wall. The gowns, the jewels, the crystals dripping from the chandeliers, even the floor beneath our feet seemed to sparkle, and I wondered how much of it was Fabrikator craft.

The Grisha themselves mingled and danced, but they were easy to pick out in their bold colours: purple, red, and midnight blue, glowing beneath the chandeliers like exotic flowers that had sprung up in some pale garden.

The next hour passed in a blur. I was introduced to countless noblemen and their wives, high-ranking military officers, courtiers, and even some Grisha from noble households who had come as guests to the ball. I quickly gave up trying to remember names and simply smiled and nodded and bowed. And tried to keep myself from scanning the crowd for the Darkling's black-clad form. I also had my first taste of champagne, which I found I liked much better than *kvas*.

At one point, I discovered myself face-to-face with a tired-looking nobleman leaning on a cane.

"Duke Keramsov!" I exclaimed. He was wearing his old officer's uniform, his many medals pinned to his broad chest.

The old man looked at me with a flicker of interest, clearly startled that I knew his name.

"It's me," I said. "Alina Starkov?"

"Yes . . . yes. Of course!" he said with a faint smile.

I looked into his eyes. He didn't remember me at all.

And why should he? I was just another orphan, and a very forgettable one at that. Still, I was surprised at how much it hurt.

I made polite conversation for as long as I had to and then took the first opportunity to escape.

I leaned against a pillar and grabbed another glass of champagne from a passing servant. The room felt uncomfortably warm. As I looked around, I suddenly felt very alone. I thought of Mal, and for the first time in weeks, my heart gave that old familiar twist. I wished he could be here to see this place. I wished he could see me in my silk *kefta* with gold in my hair. Mostly I just wished that he was standing beside me. I pushed the thought away and took a big gulp of champagne. What difference did it make if some drunk old man didn't know me? I was glad he didn't recognise the scrawny, miserable little girl I'd been.

I saw Genya gliding through the crowd towards me. Counts and dukes and wealthy merchants turned to stare at her as she passed, but she ignored them all. *Don't waste your time*, I wanted to tell them. *Her heart belongs to a gangly Fabrikator who doesn't like parties.*

"Time for the show – I mean, the demonstration," she said when she reached me. "Why are you all by yourself?"

"I just needed to take a little break."

"Too much champagne?"

"Maybe."

"Silly girl," she said, looping her arm through mine. "There's no such thing as too much champagne. Though your head will try to tell you otherwise tomorrow."

She steered me through the crowd, gracefully dodging people who wanted to meet me or leer at her, until we'd made our way behind the stage that had been set up along the far wall of the ballroom. We stood by the orchestra and watched as a man dressed in an elaborate silver ensemble took to the stage to introduce the Grisha.

The orchestra struck a dramatic chord, and the guests were soon gasping and applauding as Inferni sent arcs of flame shooting over the crowd and Squallers sent spires of glitter whirling about the room. They were joined by a large group of Tidemakers who, with the Squallers' help, brought a massive wave crashing over the balcony to hover inches above the audience's heads. I saw hands reach up to touch the shining sheet of water. Then the Inferni raised their arms and, with a hiss, the wave exploded into a swirling mass of mist. Hidden by the side of the stage, I had a sudden inspiration and sent light cascading through the mist, creating a rainbow that shimmered briefly in the air.

"Alina."

I jumped. The light faltered and the rainbow disappeared. The Darkling was standing next to me. As usual, he wore a black *kefta*, though this one was made of raw silk and velvet. The candlelight gleamed off his dark hair. I swallowed and glanced around, but Genya had disappeared.

"Hello," I managed.

"Are you ready?"

I nodded, and he led me to the base of the steps leading to the platform. As the crowd applauded and the Grisha left the stage, Ivo punched my arm. "Nice touch, Alina! That rainbow was perfect." I thanked him and then turned my attention to the crowd, feeling suddenly nervous. I saw eager faces, the Queen surrounded by her ladies, looking bored. Beside her, the King swayed on his throne, clearly well in his cups, the Apparat at his side. If the royal princes had bothered to show up, they were nowhere to be seen. With a start, I realised the Apparat was staring directly at me, and I looked quickly away.

We waited as the orchestra began to play an ominous, escalating thrum and the man in silver bounded onto the stage once again to introduce us.

Suddenly, Ivan was with us saying something in the Darkling's ear. I heard the Darkling reply, "Take them to the war room. I'll be there shortly."

Ivan darted away, ignoring me completely. When the Darkling turned to me, he was smiling, his eyes alive with excitement. Whatever news he'd received had been good.

A burst of applause signalled that it was time for us to take the stage. He took my arm and said, "Let's give the people what they want."

I nodded, my throat dry as he led me up the steps and to the centre of the stage. I heard eager buzzing from the crowd, looked out at their expectant faces. The Darkling gave me a short nod. With little preamble, he slammed his hands together and thunder boomed through the room as a wave of darkness fell over the party.

He waited, letting the crowd's anticipation grow. The Darkling might not have liked the Grisha performing, but he certainly knew how to put on a show. Only when the room was practically vibrating with tension did he lean into me and whisper, so softly that only I could hear, "Now."

Heart clattering, I extended my arm, palm up. I took a deep breath and called up that feeling of surety, the feeling of light rushing towards me and through me, and focused it in my hand. A bright column of light shot upwards from my palm, gleaming in the darkness of the ballroom. The crowd gasped, and I heard someone shout, "It's true!"

I turned my hand slightly, angling at what I hoped

was the right spot on the balcony that David had described to me earlier.

"Just make sure you aim high enough, and we'll find you," he'd said.

I knew I'd got it right when the beam from my palm shot out from the balcony, zigging and zagging across the room as the light bounced from one large Fabrikator-made mirror to the next until the dark ballroom was a pattern of crisscrossing streams of gleaming sunlight.

The crowd murmured in excitement.

I closed my palm, and the beam disappeared, then in a flash I let the light bloom around me and the Darkling, wrapping us in a glowing sphere that surrounded us like a flowing, golden halo.

He looked at me and held out his hand, sending black ribbons of darkness climbing through the sphere, twisting and turning. I grew the light wider and brighter, feeling the pleasure of the power move through me, letting it play through my fingertips as he sent inky tendrils of darkness shooting through the light, making them dance.

The crowd applauded and the Darkling murmured softly, "Now, *show them.*"

I grinned and did as I had been taught, throwing my arms wide and feeling my whole self open, then I slammed my hands together and a loud rumble shook the ballroom. Brilliant white light exploded through the crowd with a *whoosh* as the guests released a collective "Ahhhh!" and closed their eyes, flinging their hands up against the brightness.

I held it for a few long seconds and then unclasped my hands, letting the light fade. The crowd burst into wild applause, clapping furiously and stomping their feet.

We took our bows as the orchestra began to play and the applause gave way to excited chatter. The Darkling pulled me to the side of the stage and whispered, "Do you hear them? See them dancing and embracing? They know now that the rumours are true, that everything is about to change."

My elation ebbed slightly as I felt uncertainty creep in. "But aren't we giving these people false hope?" I asked.

"No, Alina. I told you that you were my answer. And you are."

"But after what happened by the lake . . ." I blushed furiously and hurried to clarify. "I mean, you said I wasn't strong enough."

The Darkling's mouth quirked in the suggestion of a grin but his eyes were serious. "Did you really think I'd finished with you?"

A little tremor quaked through me. He watched me, his half smile fading. Then, abruptly, he took me by the arm and pulled me from the stage into the crowd. People offered their congratulations, reached their hands out to touch us, but he cast a rippling pool of darkness that snaked through the crowd and vanished as soon as we had passed. It was almost like being invisible. I could hear snatches of conversation as we slipped between groups of people.

"I didn't believe it . . ."

". . . a miracle!"

". . . never trusted him but . . ."

"It's over! It's over!"

I heard people laughing and crying. That feeling of

disquiet twisted through me again. These people believed that I could save them. What would they think when they learned I was good for nothing but parlour tricks? But these thoughts were only dim flickers. It was hard to think of anything other than the fact that, after weeks of ignoring me, the Darkling was gripping my hand, pulling me through a narrow door, and down an empty corridor.

A giddy laugh escaped me as we slipped inside an empty room lit only by the moonlight pouring in through the windows. I barely had time to register that it was the sitting room where I had once been brought to meet the Queen, because as soon as the door closed, he was kissing me and I could think of nothing else.

I'd been kissed before, drunken mistakes, awkward fumblings. This was nothing like that. It was sure and powerful. My whole body was suddenly awake. I could feel my racing heart, the press of silk against my skin, the strength of his arms around me, one hand buried deep in my hair, the other at my back, pulling me closer. The moment his lips met mine, the connection between us opened and I felt his power flood through me. I could feel how much he wanted me – but behind that desire, I could feel something else, something that felt like anger.

I drew back, startled. "You don't want to be doing this."

"This is the only thing I want to be doing," he growled, and I could hear the bitterness and desire all tangled up in his voice.

"And you hate that," I said with a sudden flash of comprehension.

He sighed and leaned against me, brushing my hair back from my neck. "Maybe I do," he murmured, his lips grazing my ear, my throat, my collarbone.

I shivered, letting my head fall back, but I had to ask. "Why?"

"Why?" he repeated, his lips still brushing over my skin, his fingers sliding over the ribbons at my neckline. "Alina, do you know what Ivan told me before we took to the stage? Tonight, we received word that my men have spotted Morozova's herd. The key to the Shadow Fold is finally within our grasp, and right now, I should be in the war room, hearing their report. I should be planning our trip north. But I'm not, am I?"

My mind had shut down, given itself over to the pleasure coursing through me and the anticipation of where his next kiss would land.

"Am I?" he repeated and he nipped at my neck. I gasped and shook my head, unable to think. He had me pushed up against the door now, his hips hard against mine. "The problem with wanting," he whispered, his mouth trailing along my jaw until it hovered over my lips, "is that it makes us weak." And then, at last, when I thought I couldn't bear it any longer, he brought his mouth down on mine.

His kiss was harder this time, laced with the anger I could feel lingering inside him. I didn't care. I didn't care that he'd ignored me or that he confused me or about any of Genya's vague warnings. He'd found the stag. He'd been right about me. He'd been right about everything.

His hand slid down to my hip. I felt a little trill of panic as my skirt slid higher and his fingers closed on my bare thigh, but instead of pulling away, I pushed closer to him.

I don't know what might have happened next – at that moment we heard a loud clamour of voices from the hallway. A group of very noisy, very drunk people were careening down the corridor, and someone bumped heavily into the door, rattling the handle. We froze. The Darkling shoved his shoulder against the door so that it wouldn't open, and the group moved on, shouting and laughing.

In the silence that followed, we stared at each other. Then he sighed and dropped his hand, letting the silk of my skirts fall back into place.

"I should go," he murmured. "Ivan and the others are waiting for me."

I nodded, not trusting myself to speak.

He stepped away from me. I moved aside, and he opened the door a crack, glancing down the hallway to make sure it was empty.

"I won't return to the party," he said. "But you should, at least for a while."

I nodded again. I was suddenly acutely aware of the fact that I was standing in a dark room with a near stranger and that only a few moments before I'd nearly had my skirts around my waist. Ana Kuya's stern face appeared in my mind, lecturing me about the foolish mistakes of peasant girls, and I flushed with embarrassment.

The Darkling slipped through the doorway, but then he turned back to me. "Alina," he said, and I could see that he was fighting with himself, "can I come to you tonight?"

I hesitated. I knew that if I said yes, there would be no turning back. My skin still burned where he'd touched me, but the excitement of the moment was melting away, and a bit of sense was returning. I wasn't sure what I wanted. I wasn't sure of anything.

I waited too long. We heard more voices coming down the hall. The Darkling pulled the door shut, striding out into the hallway as I stepped back into the darkness. I waited nervously, trying to think of an excuse for why I might be hiding in an empty room.

The voices passed and I let out a long, shuddering breath. I hadn't had a chance to say yes or no to the Darkling. Would he come anyway? Did I want him to? My mind was whirring. I had to set myself to rights and get back to the party. The Darkling could just disappear, but I didn't have that luxury.

I peered out into the corridor and then hurried to the ballroom, stopping to check my appearance in one of the gilt mirrors. It wasn't as bad as I'd feared. My cheeks were flushed, my lips a bit bruised looking, but there was nothing I could do about that. I smoothed my hair and straightened my *kefta*. As I was about to enter the ballroom, I heard a door open at the other end of the hallway. The Apparat was hurrying towards me, his brown robes flapping behind him. *Oh please not now.*

"Alina!" he called.

"I have to get back to the ball," I said cheerily and turned away from him.

"I must speak with you! Things are moving far more quickly than—"

I slipped back into the party with what I hoped was a serene expression. Almost instantly, I was surrounded by nobles hoping to meet me and congratulate me on the demonstration. Sergei hurried over with my other

Heartrender guards, murmuring apologies for losing me in the crowd. Glancing over my shoulder, I was relieved to see the Apparat's ragged form swallowed by a tide of partygoers.

I did my best to make polite conversation and to answer the questions that the guests asked. One woman had tears in her eyes and asked me to bless her. I had no idea what to do, so I patted her hand in what I hoped was a reassuring manner. All I wanted was to be alone to think, to sort through the confused mess of emotions in my head. The champagne wasn't helping.

As one group of guests moved off to be replaced by another, I recognised the long, melancholy face of the Corporalnik who had ridden with me and Ivan in the Darkling's coach and helped to fight off the Fjerdan assassins. I scrambled to remember his name.

He came to my rescue, bowing deeply and saying, "Fedyor Kaminsky."

"Forgive me," I said. "It's been a long night."

"I can only imagine."

I hope not, I thought with a twinge of embarrassment.

"It seems the Darkling was right after all," he said with a smile.

"Pardon?" I squeaked.

"You were so certain that you couldn't possibly be Grisha."

I returned his grin. "I try to make a habit of getting things hopelessly wrong."

Fedyor barely had time to tell me of his new assignment near the southern border before he was swept away by another wave of impatient guests waiting to get their moment with the Sun Summoner. I hadn't even thanked him for protecting my life that day in the glen.

I managed to keep talking and smiling for about an hour, but as soon as I had a free moment, I told my guards that I wanted to leave, and headed for the doors.

The instant I was outside, I felt better. The night air was blessedly cold, the stars bright in the sky. I took a deep breath. I felt giddy and exhausted, and my thoughts seemed to keep bouncing from excitement to anxiety and back again. If the Darkling came to my room tonight, what would it mean? The idea of being his sent a little jolt through me. I didn't think he was in love with me and I had no idea what I felt for him, but he wanted me, and maybe that was enough.

I shook my head, trying to make sense of everything. The Darkling's men had found the stag. I should be thinking about that, about my destiny, about the fact that I would have to kill an ancient creature, about the power it would give me and the responsibility of that, but all I could think about was his hands on my hips, his lips on my neck, the lean, hard feel of him in the dark. I took another deep breath of night air. The sensible thing would be to lock my door and go to sleep. But I wasn't sure I wanted to be sensible.

When we arrived at the Little Palace, Sergei and the others left me to return to the ball. The domed hall was silent, the fires in its tile ovens banked, its lamps glowing low and golden. Just as I was about to pass through the doorway to the main staircase, the carved doors behind the Darkling's table opened. Hurriedly, I stepped into the shadows. I didn't want the Darkling to know I'd left the party early, and I wasn't ready to see him yet anyway. But it was just a group of soldiers crossing through the entry hall on their way out of the Little Palace. I wondered if they were the men who had come to report on the location of the stag. As the light from one of the lamps fell on the last soldier of the group, my heart nearly stopped.

"Mal!"

When he turned around, I thought I might dissolve from happiness at the sight of his familiar face. Somewhere in the back of my mind, I registered his grim expression, but it was lost in the sheer joy I felt. I sprinted across the hall and threw my arms around him, nearly knocking him off his feet. He steadied himself and then pulled my arms from around his neck as he glanced at the other soldiers who had stopped to watch us. I knew I'd probably embarrassed him, but I just didn't care. I was bouncing on the balls of my feet, practically dancing with happiness.

"Go on," he said to them. "I'll catch up to you."

A few eyebrows were raised, but the soldiers disappeared through the main entrance, leaving us alone.

I opened my mouth to speak, but I wasn't sure where to begin, so I settled for the first thing that came to mind. "What are you doing here?"

"Hell if I know," Mal said with a weariness that surprised me. "I had a report to make to your master."

"My . . . what?" Then it hit me, and I broke into a huge grin. "You're the one who found Morozova's herd! I should have known."

He didn't return my smile. He didn't even meet my eyes. He just looked away and said, "I should go."

I stared at him in disbelief, my elation withering. So I'd been right. Mal had stopped caring. All the anger and embarrassment I'd felt over the last few months crashed in on me. "Sorry," I said coldly. "I didn't realise I was wasting your time."

"I didn't say that."

"No, no. I understand. You can't be bothered to answer my letters. Why would you want to stand here talking to me while your real friends are waiting?"

He frowned. "I didn't get any letters."

"Right," I said angrily.

He sighed and rubbed a hand over his face. "We have to move constantly to track the herd. My unit is barely in contact with the regiment."

There was such fatigue in his voice. For the first time, I looked at him, really looked at him, and I saw how much he had changed. There were shadows beneath his blue eyes. A jagged scar ran along the line of his unshaven jaw. He was still Mal, but there was something harder about him, something cold and unfamiliar.

"You didn't get any of my letters?"

He shook his head, still wearing that same distant expression.

I didn't know what to think. Mal had never lied to me before, and for all my anger, I didn't think he was lying to me now. I hesitated.

"Mal, I . . . Can't you stay a little while longer?" I heard the pleading in my voice. I hated it, but I hated the thought of him leaving even more. "You can't imagine what it's been like here."

He gave a rough bark of laughter. "I don't need to imagine. I saw your little demonstration in the ballroom. Very impressive."

"You saw me?"

"That's right," he said harshly. "Do you know how worried I've been about you? No one knew what had happened to you, what they'd done to you. There was no way to reach you. There were even rumours you were being tortured. When the captain needed men to report back to the Darkling, like an idiot I made the trek down here just on the chance that I would find you."

"Really?" That was hard for me to believe. I'd grown so used to the idea of Mal's indifference.

"Yes," he hissed. "And here you are, safe and sound, dancing and flirting like some cosseted little princess."

"Don't sound so disappointed," I snapped. "I'm sure the Darkling can arrange for a rack or some hot coals if that would make you feel better."

Mal scowled and stepped away from me.

Tears of frustration pricked my eyes. Why were we fighting? Desperately, I reached out to lay a hand on his arm. His muscles tensed, but he didn't pull away. "Mal, I can't help the way things are here. I didn't ask for any of this."

He looked at me and then looked away. I felt some of the tension go out of him. Finally, he said, "I know you didn't."

Again, I heard that terrible weariness in his voice.

"What happened to you, Mal?" I whispered.

He said nothing, just stared into the darkness of the hall.

I raised my hand and rested it on his stubbly cheek, gently turning his face to mine. "Tell me."

He closed his eyes. "I can't."

I let my fingertips trail over the raised skin of the scar on his jaw. "Genya could fix this. She can—"

Instantly, I knew I'd said the wrong thing. His eyes flew open.

"I don't need fixing," he snapped.

"I didn't mean—"

He snatched my hand from his face, holding it tightly, his blue eyes searching mine. "Are you happy here, Alina?"

The question took me by surprise.

"I . . . I don't know. Sometimes."

"Are you happy here *with him?*"

I didn't have to ask who Mal meant. I opened my mouth to answer, but I had no idea what to say.

"You're wearing his symbol," he observed, glancing at the little gold charm that hung from my neckline. "His symbol and his colour."

"They're just clothes."

Mal's lips twisted in a cynical smile, a smile so different from the one I knew and loved that I almost flinched. "You don't really believe that."

"What difference does it make what I wear?"

"The clothes, the jewels, even the way you look. *He's all over you.*"

The words hit me like a slap. In the dark of the hall, I felt an ugly flush creeping up my cheeks. I snatched my hand from his, crossing my arms over my chest.

"It's not like that," I whispered, but I didn't meet his gaze. It was as if Mal could see right through me, as if he could pluck every fevered thought I'd ever had of the Darkling right out of my head. But on the heels of that shame came anger. So what if he did know? What right did he have to judge me? How many girls had Mal held in the dark?

"I saw how he looked at you," he said.

"I *like* how he looks at me!" I practically shouted.

He shook his head, that bitter smile still playing on his lips. I wanted to smack it right off his face.

"Just admit it," he sneered. "He owns you."

"He owns you too, Mal," I lashed back. "He owns us all."

That wiped away his smile.

"No he doesn't," Mal said fiercely. "Not me. Not ever."

"Oh really? Don't you have somewhere to be, Mal? Don't you have orders to follow?"

Mal stood up straight, his face cold. "Yes," he said. "Yes, I do."

He turned sharply and walked out of the door.

For a moment, I stood there, quivering with anger, and then I ran to the doorway. I got all the way down the steps before I stopped myself. The tears that had been threatening to overflow finally did, coursing down my cheeks. I wanted to run after him, to take back what I'd said, to beg him to stay, but I'd spent my life running after Mal. Instead, I stood in silence and let him go.

Chapter 15

Only when I was in my room, the door closed securely behind me, did I let my sobs overtake me. I slid to the floor, my back pressed against the bed, my arms around my knees, trying to hold myself together.

By now, Mal would be leaving the palace, travelling back to Tsibeya to join the other trackers hunting Morozova's herd. The distance widening between us felt like a palpable thing. I felt further from him than I had in all the lonely months that had gone before.

I rubbed my thumb over the scar on my palm. "Come back," I whispered, my body shaking with fresh sobs. "Come back." But he wouldn't. I'd as good as ordered him to leave. I knew I would probably never see him again, and I ached with it.

I don't know how long I sat there in the dark. At some point I became aware of a soft knocking at my door. I sat up straight, trying to stifle my sniffling. What if it was the Darkling? I couldn't bear to see him now, to explain my tears to him, but I had to do something. I dragged myself to my feet and opened the door.

A bony hand snaked around my wrist, seizing me in an iron grip.

"Baghra?" I asked, peering at the woman standing at my door.

"Come," she said, pulling at my arm and glancing over her shoulder.

"Leave me alone, Baghra." I tried to pull away from her, but she was surprisingly strong.

"You come with me now, girl," she spat. "Now!"

Maybe it was the intensity of her gaze or the shock of seeing fear in her eyes, or maybe I was just used to doing what Baghra said, but I followed her out of the door.

She closed it behind us, keeping hold of my wrist.

"What is this? Where are we going?"

"Quiet."

Instead of turning right and heading towards the main staircase, she dragged me in the opposite direction to the other end of the hall. She pressed a panel in the wall, and a hidden door swung open. She gave me a shove. I didn't have the will to fight her, so I stumbled down the narrow spiral staircase. Every time I looked back at her, she gave me another little push. When we reached the bottom, Baghra stepped in front of me and led me along a cramped hallway with bare stone floors and plain wooden walls. It looked almost naked compared to the rest of the Little Palace, and I thought we might be in the servants' quarters.

Baghra grabbed my wrist again and tugged me into a dark, empty chamber. She lit a single candle, locked and bolted the door, then crossed the room and reached up on her tiptoes to draw closed the curtain on the tiny basement window. The room was sparsely furnished with a narrow bed, a simple chair and a washbasin.

"Here," she said, shoving a pile of clothes at me. "Put these on."

"I'm too tired for lessons, Baghra."

"No more lessons. You must leave this place. Tonight."

I blinked. "What are you talking about?"

"I'm trying to keep you from spending the rest of your life as a slave. Now get changed."

"Baghra, what's going on? Why did you bring me down here?"

"We don't have much time. The Darkling is close to finding Morozova's herd. Soon he will have the stag."

"I know," I said, thinking of Mal. My heart ached, but I also couldn't resist feeling a little smug. "I thought you didn't believe in Morozova's stag."

She waved her arm as if brushing away my words. "That's what I told him. I hoped that he might give up the stag's pursuit if he thought it was nothing but a peasant tale. But once he has it, nothing will be able to stop him."

I threw up my hands in exasperation. "Stop him from doing what?"

"Using the Fold as a weapon."

"I see," I said. "Does he also plan to build a summer home there?"

Baghra seized hold of my arm, "This isn't a joke!"

There was a desperate, unfamiliar edge to her voice, and her grip on my arm was nearly painful. What was wrong with her?

"Baghra, maybe we should go to the infirmary—"

"I'm not sick and I'm not insane," she spat. "You must listen to me."

"Then talk sense," I said. "How could anyone use the Shadow Fold as a weapon?"

She leaned into me, her fingers digging into my flesh. "By expanding it."

"Right," I said slowly, trying to extricate myself from her grasp.

"The land that the Unsea covers was once green and good, fertile and rich. Now it is dead and barren, crawling with abominations. The Darkling will push its boundaries north into Fjerda, south to the Shu Han. Those who do not bow to him will see their kingdoms turned to desolate wasteland and their people devoured by ravening volcra."

I gaped at her in horror, shocked by the images she had conjured. The old woman had clearly lost her mind.

"Baghra," I said gently, "I think you have some kind of fever." *Or you've gone completely senile.* "Finding the stag is a good thing. It means I can help the Darkling destroy the Fold."

"No!" she cried, and it was almost a howl. "He never intended to destroy it. The Fold is his creation."

I sighed. Why had Baghra picked tonight to lose all touch with reality? "The Fold was created hundreds of years ago by the Black Heretic. The Darkling—"

"He *is* the Black Heretic," she said furiously, her face mere inches from mine.

"Of course he is." With some effort, I pried her fingers loose and stepped past her to the door. "I'm going to go find you a Healer and then I'm going to bed."

"Look at me, girl."

I took a deep breath and turned around, my patience at an end. I felt sorry for her, but this was just too much. "Baghra—"

The words died on my lips.

Darkness was pooling in Baghra's palms, the skeins of inky blackness floating into the air.

"You do not know him, Alina." It was the first time she had ever used my name. "But I do."

I stood there watching dark spirals unfurl around her, trying to comprehend what I was seeing. Searching Baghra's strange features, I saw the explanation clearly written there. I saw the ghost of what must have once been a beautiful woman, a beautiful woman who gave birth to a beautiful son.

"You're his mother," I whispered numbly.

She nodded. "I am not mad. I am the only person who knows what he truly is, what he truly intends. And I am telling you that you must run."

The Darkling had claimed he didn't know what Baghra's power was. Had he lied to me?

I shook my head, trying to clear my thoughts, trying to make sense of what Baghra was telling me. "It's not possible," I said. "The Black Heretic lived hundreds of years ago."

"He has served countless kings, faked countless deaths, bided his time, waiting for you. Once he takes control of the Fold, no one will be able to stand against him."

A shiver went through me. "No," I said. "He told me the Fold was a mistake. He called the Black Heretic evil."

"The Fold was no mistake." Baghra dropped her hands and the swirling darkness around her melted away. "The only mistake was the volcra. He did not anticipate them, did not think to wonder what power of that magnitude might do to mere men."

My stomach turned. "The volcra were men?"

"Oh yes. Generations ago. Farmers and their wives, their children. I warned him that there would be a price, but he didn't listen. He was blinded by his hunger for power. Just as he is blinded now."

"You're wrong," I said, rubbing my arms, trying to shake the bone-deep cold stealing through me. "You're lying."

"Only the volcra have kept the Darkling from using the Fold against his enemies. They are his punishment, a living testimony to his arrogance. But you will change all that. The monsters cannot abide sunlight. Once the Darkling has used your power to subdue the volcra, he will be able to enter the Fold safely. He will finally have what he wants. There will be no limit to his power."

I shook my head. "He wouldn't do that. He would never do that." I remembered the night he'd spoken to me by the fire in the broken-down barn, the shame and sorrow in his voice. *I've spent my life searching for a way to make things right. You're the first glimmer of hope I've had in a long time.* "He said he wants to make Ravka whole again. He said that—"

"Stop telling me what he said!" she snarled. "He is *ancient*. He's had plenty of time to master lying to a lonely, naive girl." She advanced on me, her black eyes burning. "Think, Alina. If Ravka is made whole, the Second Army will no longer be vital to its survival. The Darkling will be nothing but another servant of the King. Is that his dream of the future?"

I was starting to shake. "Please stop."

"But with the Fold in his power, he will spread destruction before him. He will lay waste to the world, and he will never have to kneel to another King again."

"No."

"All because of you."

"No!" I shouted at her. "I wouldn't do that! Even if what you're saying is true, I would never help him do that."

"You won't have a choice. The stag's power belongs to whoever slays it."

"But he can't use an amplifier," I protested weakly.

"He can use *you*," Baghra said softly. "Morozova's stag is no ordinary amplifier. He will hunt it. He will kill it. He will take its antlers, and once he places them around your neck, you will belong to him completely. You will be the most powerful Grisha who has ever lived, and all that newfound power will be his to command. You will be bound to him forever, and you will be powerless to resist."

It was the pity in her voice that undid me. Pity from the woman who'd never allowed me a moment's weakness, a moment's rest.

My legs gave way, and I slid to the floor. I covered my head with my hands, trying to block out Baghra's voice. But I couldn't stop the Darkling's words from echoing through my mind.

We all serve someone.

The King is a child.

You and I are going to change the world.

He had lied to me about Baghra. He had lied about the Black Heretic. Had he lied about the stag too?

I'm asking you to trust me.

Baghra had begged him to give me another amplifier, but he'd insisted it had to be the stag's antlers. A necklace – no, a collar – of bone. And when I'd pushed him, he'd kissed me and I'd forgotten all about the stag and amplifiers and everything else. I remembered his perfect face in the lamplight, his stunned expression, his rumpled hair.

Had it all been deliberate? The kiss by the lake shore, the flash of hurt that had played across his face that night in the barn, every human gesture, every whispered confidence – even what had happened between us tonight?

I cringed at the thought. I could still feel his warm breath on my neck, hear his whisper in my ear. *The problem with wanting is that it makes us weak.*

How right he was. I'd wanted so badly to belong somewhere, anywhere. I'd been so eager to please him, so proud to keep his secrets. I'd never bothered to question what he might really want, what his true motives might be. I'd been too busy imagining myself by his side, the saviour of Ravka, most treasured, most desired, like some kind of queen. I'd made it so easy for him.

You and I are going to change the world. Just wait.

Put on your pretty clothes and wait for the next kiss, the next kind word. Wait for the stag. Wait for the collar. Wait to be made into a murderer and a slave.

He had warned me that the age of Grisha power was coming to an end. I should have known he would never let that happen.

I took a shaky breath and tried to still my trembling. I thought of poor Alexei and all the others who had been left to die in the black reaches of the Fold. I thought of the ashen sands that had once been soft brown earth. I thought of the volcra, the first victims of the Black Heretic's greed.

Did you really think I'd finished with you?

The Darkling wanted to use me. He wanted to take away the one thing that had ever really belonged to me, the only power I'd ever had.

I got to my feet. I wasn't going to make it easy for him any more.

"All right," I said, reaching for the pile of clothes Baghra had brought me. "What do I do?"

Chapter 16

Baghra's relief was unmistakable, but she wasted no time. "You can slip out with the performers tonight. Head west. When you get to Os Kervo, find the *Verloren*. It's a Kerch trader. Your passage has been paid."

My fingers froze on the buttons of my *kefta*. "You want me to go to West Ravka? To cross the Fold alone?"

"I want you to disappear, girl. You're strong enough to travel the Fold on your own now. It should be easy work. Why do you think I've spent so much time training you?"

Another thing I hadn't bothered to question. The Darkling had told Baghra to leave me be. I'd thought he was defending me, but maybe he'd just wanted to keep me weak.

I shrugged off the *kefta* and pulled a rough wool tunic over my head. "You knew what he intended all along. Why tell me now?" I asked her. "Why tonight?"

"We've run out of time. I never truly believed he'd find Morozova's herd. They're elusive creatures, part of the oldest science, the making at the heart of the world. But I underestimated his men."

No, I thought as I yanked on leather breeches and boots. *You underestimated Mal.* Mal, who could hunt and track like no other. Mal who could make rabbits out of rocks. Mal who would find the stag and deliver me, deliver us all into the Darkling's power without ever knowing it.

Baghra passed me a thick brown travelling coat lined in fur, a heavy fur hat, and a broad belt. As I looped it around my waist, I found a money bag attached to it, along with my knife and a pouch that held my leather gloves, the mirrors tucked safely inside.

She led me out of a small door and handed me a leather travelling pack that I slung across my shoulders. She pointed across the grounds to where the lights from the Grand Palace flickered in the distance. I could hear music playing. With a start, I realised that the party was still in full swing. It seemed as though years had passed since I'd left the ballroom, but it couldn't have been much more than an hour.

"Go to the hedge maze and turn left. Stay off the lighted paths. Some of the entertainers are already leaving. Find one of the departing wagons. They're only searched on their way into the palace, so you should be safe."

"Should be?"

Baghra ignored me. "When you get out of Os Alta, try to avoid the main roads." She handed me a sealed envelope. "You're a serf woodworker on your way to West Ravka to meet your new master. Do you understand?"

"Yes." I nodded, my heart already starting to race in my chest. "You could stop him," I said suddenly, almost desperately. "You're older, stronger—"

"I won't murder my own son."

"But you'd betray him?"

"I would save him," she said. For a moment, she stood straight-backed and silent in the shadow of the Little Palace. Then she turned to me, and I took a startled step back, because I saw it, as clearly as if I had been standing at its edge: the abyss. Ceaseless, black, and yawning, the unending emptiness of a life lived too long.

"All those years ago," she said softly. "Before he'd ever dreamed of a Second Army, before he gave up his name and became the Darkling, he was just a brilliant, talented boy. I gave him his ambition. I gave him his pride. When the time came, I should have been the one to stop him." She smiled then, a small smile of such aching sadness that it was hard to look at. "You think I don't love my son," she said. "But I do. It is because I love him that I will not let him put himself beyond redemption."

She glanced back at the Little Palace. "I will post a servant at your door tomorrow morning to claim that you are ill. I'll try to buy you as much time as I can."

I bit my lip. "Tonight. You'll have to post the servant tonight. The Darkling might . . . might come to my room."

I expected Baghra to laugh at me again, but instead she just shook her head and said softly, "Foolish girl." Her contempt would have been easier to bear.

Looking out at the grounds, I thought of what lay ahead of me. Was I really going to do this? I had to choke back my panic. "Thank you, Baghra," I gulped. "For everything."

"Hmph," she said. "Go now, girl. Be quick and take care."

I turned my back on her and ran.

Endless days of training with Botkin meant I knew

the grounds well. I was grateful for every sweaty hour as I jogged over lawns and between trees. Baghra sent thin coils of blackness to either side of me, cloaking me in darkness as I drew closer to the back of the Grand Palace. Were Marie and Nadia still dancing inside? Was Genya wondering where I'd gone? I pushed those thoughts from my mind. I was afraid to think too hard about what I was doing, about everything I was leaving behind.

A theatrical troupe was loading up a wagon with props and racks of costumes, their driver already gripping the reins and shouting at them to hurry things along. One of them climbed up beside him, and the others crowded into a little pony cart that departed with a jingle of bells. I darted into the back of the wagon and wiggled my way between pieces of scenery, covering myself with a burlap drop cloth.

As we rumbled down the long gravel drive and through the palace gates, I held my breath. I was sure that, at any moment, someone would raise the alarm and we would be stopped. I would be pulled from the wagon in disgrace. But then the wheels jounced forward and we were rattling over the cobblestone streets of Os Alta.

I tried to remember the route that I had taken with the Darkling when he had brought me through the city those many months ago, but I'd been so tired and overwhelmed that my memory was a useless blur of mansions and misty streets. I couldn't see much from my hiding place, and I didn't dare peek out. With my luck, someone would be passing at just that instant and catch sight of me.

My only hope was to put as much distance as possible between myself and the palace before my absence was noticed. I didn't know how long Baghra would be able to stall, and I willed the wagon's driver to move faster. When we crossed over the bridge and into the market town, I allowed myself a tiny sigh of relief.

Cold air crept through the cart's wooden slats, and I was grateful for the thick coat Baghra had provided. I was weary and uncomfortable, but mostly I was just frightened. I was running from the most powerful man in Ravka. The Grisha, the First Army, maybe even Mal and his trackers would be unleashed to find me. What chance did I have of making it to the Fold on my own? And if I did make it to West Ravka and onto the *Verloren*, then what? I would be alone in a strange land where I didn't speak the language and I knew no one. Tears stung my eyes and I brushed them furiously away. If I started crying, I didn't think I'd be able to stop.

We travelled through the early hours of the morning, past the stone streets of Os Alta and onto the wide dirt swath of the Vy. Dawn came and went. Occasionally, I dozed, but my fear and discomfort kept me awake for most of the ride. When the sun was high in the sky and I'd begun to sweat in my thick coat, the wagon rolled to a stop.

I risked taking a look over the side of the cart. We were behind what looked like a tavern or an inn.

I stretched my legs. Both of my feet had fallen asleep, and I winced as the blood rushed painfully back to my toes. I waited until the driver and the other members of the troupe had gone inside before I slid out from my hiding place.

I figured I would attract more attention if I looked like I was sneaking around, so I stood up straight and walked briskly around the building, joining the bustle of carts and people on the village's main street.

It took a little eavesdropping, but I soon realised I was in Balakirev. It was a small town almost directly west of Os Alta. I'd been lucky; I was heading in the right direction.

During the ride, I'd counted the money Baghra had given me and tried to make a plan. I knew the fastest way to travel would be on horseback, but I also knew that a girl on her own with enough coin to buy a mount would attract attention. What I really needed to do was to steal a horse – but I had no idea how to go about that, so I decided to just keep moving.

On the way out of town, I stopped at a market stall to buy a supply of hard cheese, bread and dried meat.

"Hungry, are you?" asked the toothless old vendor, looking at me a little too closely as I shoved the food into my pack.

"My brother is. He eats like a pig," I said, and pretended to wave at someone in the crowd. "Coming!" I shouted, and hurried off. All I could hope was that he would remember a girl travelling with her family or, better yet, that he wouldn't remember me at all.

I spent that night sleeping in the tidy hayloft of a dairy farm just off the Vy. It was a long way from my beautiful bed at the Little Palace, but I was grateful for the shelter and for the sounds of animals around me. The soft lowing and rustle of the cows made me feel less alone as I curled on my side, using my pack and fur hat as a makeshift pillow.

What if Baghra was wrong? I worried as I lay there. What if she'd lied? Or what if she was just mistaken? I could go back to the Little Palace. I could sleep in my own bed and take my lessons with Botkin and chat with Genya. It was such a tempting thought. If I went back, would the Darkling forgive me?

Forgive me? What was wrong with me? He was the one who wanted to put a collar around my neck and make me a slave, and I was fretting over his forgiveness? I rolled onto my other side, furious with myself.

In my heart, I knew that Baghra was right. I remembered my own words to Mal: *He owns us all.* I'd said it angrily, without thinking, because I'd wanted to hurt Mal's pride. But I'd spoken the truth just as surely as Baghra. I knew the Darkling was ruthless and dangerous, but I'd ignored all that, happy to believe in my supposedly great destiny, thrilled to think that I was the one he wanted.

Why don't you just admit that you wanted to belong to him? said a voice in my head. *Why don't you admit that part of you still does?*

I thrust the thought away. I tried to think of what the next day might bring, of what might be the safest route west. I tried to think of anything but the stormcloud colour of his eyes.

I let myself spend the next day and night travelling on the Vy, blending in with the traffic that came and went on the way to Os Alta. But I knew that Baghra's stalling would only buy me so much time, and the main roads were just too risky. From then on, I kept to the woods and fields, using hunters' trails and farm tracks. It was slow going on foot. My legs ached, and I had blisters on the tops of my toes, but I kept heading west, following the trajectory of the sun in the sky.

At night, I pulled my fur hat low over my ears and huddled shivering in my coat, listening to my belly grumble and making myself picture maps in my head, the maps I had worked on so long ago in the comfort of the Documents Tent. I pictured my own slow progress from Os Alta to Balakirev, skirting the little villages of Chernitsyn, Kerskii, and Polvost, and tried not to give up hope. I had a long way to go to the Fold, but all I could do was keep moving and hope that my luck held.

"You're still alive," I whispered to myself in the dark. "You're still free."

Occasionally, I encountered farmers or other travellers. I wore my gloves and kept my hand on my knife in case of trouble, but they took little notice of me. I was constantly hungry. I had always been a rotten hunter, so I subsisted on the meagre supplies I'd bought back in Balakirev, on water from streams, and the occasional egg or apple stolen from a lonely farm.

I had no idea what the future held or what waited for me at the end of this gruelling journey and yet, somehow, I wasn't miserable. I'd been lonely my whole life, but I'd never been truly alone before, and it wasn't nearly as scary as I'd imagined.

All the same, when I came upon a tiny whitewashed church one morning, I couldn't resist slipping inside to hear the priest say Mass. When he'd finished, he offered prayers for the congregation: for a woman's son who had been wounded in battle, for an infant who was ill with fever, and for the health of Alina Starkov. I flinched.

"Let the Saints protect the Sun Summoner," intoned the priest, "she who was sent to deliver us from the evils of the Shadow Fold and make this nation whole again."

I swallowed hard and ducked quickly out of the church. *They pray for you now*, I thought bleakly. *But if the Darkling has his way, they'll come to hate you.* And maybe they should. Wasn't I abandoning Ravka and all the people who believed in me? Only my power could destroy the Fold, and I was running away.

I shook my head. I couldn't afford to think about any of that right now. I was a traitor and a fugitive. Once I was free of the Darkling, I could worry about Ravka's future.

I set a fast pace along the trail and into the woods, chased up the hillside by the ringing of church bells.

As I pictured the map in my head, I realised I would soon reach Ryevost, and that meant making a decision about the best way to reach the Shadow Fold. I could follow the river route or head into the Petrazoi, the stony mountains that loomed to the north-west. The river would be easier going, but it would mean passing through heavily populated areas. The mountains were a more direct route, but would be much tougher to traverse.

I debated with myself until I came to the crossroads at Shura, then chose the mountain route. I would have to stop in Ryevost before I headed into the foothills. It was the largest of the river cities, and I knew I was taking a risk, but I also knew I wouldn't make it through the Petrazoi without more food and some kind of tent or bedroll.

After so many days on my own, the noise and bustle of Ryevost's crowded streets and canals felt strange to me. I kept my head down and my hat pulled low, sure that I would find posters of my face on every lamp post and shop window. But the deeper I got into the city, the more I began to relax. Maybe word of my disappearance hadn't spread as far or as fast as I'd expected.

My mouth watered at the smells of roasting lamb and fresh bread, and I treated myself to an apple as I refreshed my supplies of hard cheese and dried meat.

I was tying my new bedroll to my travelling pack and trying to figure out how I was going to carry all the extra weight up the mountainside when I rounded a corner and nearly ran straight into a group of soldiers.

My heart slammed into a gallop at the sight of their long olive coats and the rifles on their backs. I wanted to turn on my heel and sprint in the opposite direction, but I kept my head low and forced myself to keep walking at a normal pace. Once I'd passed them, I risked a glance back. They weren't looking after me suspiciously. In fact, they didn't seem to be doing much of anything. They were talking and joking, one of them catcalling at a girl hanging out the washing.

I stepped into a side street and waited for my heartbeat to return to normal. What was going on? I'd escaped from the Little Palace well over a week ago. The alarm must have been raised by now. I'd been sure the Darkling would send riders to every regiment in every town. Every member of the First and Second Armies should be looking for me by now.

As I headed out of Ryevost, I saw other soldiers. Some were on leave, others on duty, but none of them seemed to be looking for me. I didn't know what to make of it. I wondered if I had Baghra to thank. Maybe she'd managed to convince the Darkling that I'd been kidnapped or even killed by Fjerdans. Or maybe he just thought that I'd already made it further west. I decided not to press my luck and hurried to find my way out of town.

It took me longer than I'd expected, and I didn't reach the western outskirts of the city until well past nightfall. The streets were dark and empty except for a few disreputable-looking taverns and an old drunk leaning up against a building, singing softly to himself. As I hurried past a noisy inn, the door burst open and a heavyset man toppled out into the street on a burst of light and music.

He grabbed hold of my coat and pulled me close. "Hello, pretty! Have you come to keep me warm?"

I tried to pull away.

"You're strong for such a little thing." I could smell the stink of stale beer on his hot breath.

"Let go of me," I said in a low voice.

"Don't be like that, *lapushka*," he crooned. "We could have fun, you and me."

"I said let go of me!" I pushed against his chest.

"Not for a bit yet," he chuckled, pulling me into the shadows of the alley beside the tavern. "I want to show you something."

I flicked my wrist and felt the comforting weight of the mirror slide between my fingers. My hand shot out and light flared into his eyes in a single quick flash.

He grunted as the light blinded him, throwing his hands up and letting go of me. I did as Botkin had instructed. I stomped down hard on the arch of his foot and then hooked my leg behind his ankle. His legs flew out from under him, and he hit the ground with a thud.

At that moment, the side door to the tavern flew

open. A uniformed soldier emerged, a bottle of *kvas* in one hand and a scantily clad woman clutched in the other. With a wave of dread, I saw that he was dressed in the charcoal uniform of the Darkling's guard. His bleary glance took in the scene: the man on the ground and me standing over him.

"What's all this?" he slurred. The girl on his arm tittered.

"I'm blind!" wailed the man on the ground. "She blinded me!"

The *oprichnik* looked at him and then peered at me. His eyes met mine, and recognition spread across his face. My luck had run out. Even if no one else was looking for me, the Darkling's guards were.

"You . . . " he whispered.

I ran.

I bolted down an alleyway and into a maze of narrow streets, my heart pounding in my chest. As soon as I'd cleared the last few dingy buildings of Ryevost, I hurtled off the road and into the underbrush. Branches stung my cheeks and forehead as I stumbled deeper into the woods.

Behind me rose the sounds of pursuit: men shouting to one another, heavy footfalls through the wood. I wanted to run blindly, but I made myself stop and listen.

They were to the east of me, searching near the road. I couldn't tell how many there were.

I quieted my breathing and realised I could hear rushing water. There must be a stream nearby, a tributary of the river. If I could make it to the water I could hide my tracks, and they would be hard-pressed to find me in the darkness.

I made for the sounds of the stream, stopping

periodically to correct my course. I struggled up a hill so steep I was almost crawling, using branches and exposed tree roots to pull myself higher.

"There!" The voice called out from below me, and looking over my shoulder, I saw lights moving through the woods towards the base of the hill. I clawed my way higher, the earth slipping beneath my hands, each breath burning in my lungs. When I got to the top, I dragged myself over the edge and looked down. I felt a surge of hope as I spotted moonlight glimmering off the surface of the stream.

I slid down the steep hill, leaning back to try to keep my balance, moving as fast as I dared. I heard shouts, and when I looked behind me, I saw the shapes of my pursuers silhouetted against the night sky. They had reached the top of the hill.

Panic got the better of me, and I started to run down the slope, sending showers of pebbles clattering down the hill to the stream below. The grade was too steep. I lost my footing and fell forward, scraping both hands as I hit the ground hard and, unable to stop my momentum, somersaulted down the hill and plunged into the freezing water.

For a moment, I thought my heart had stopped. The cold was like a hand, gripping my body in a relentless, icy grip as I tumbled through the water. Then my head broke the surface and I gasped, drawing in precious air before the current grabbed me and pulled me under again. I don't know how far the water took me. All I could think about was my next breath and the growing numbness in my limbs.

Finally, when I thought I couldn't fight my way to the

surface again, the current drove me into a slow, silent pool. I grabbed hold of a rock and pulled myself into the shallows, dragging myself to my feet, my boots slipping on the smooth river stones as I stumbled under the weight of my sodden coat.

I don't know how I did it, but I pushed my way into the woods and burrowed under a thick copse of bushes before I let myself collapse, shivering in the cold and still coughing river water.

It was easily the worst night of my life. My coat was soaked through. My feet were numb in my boots. I started at any sound, sure that I'd been found. My fur hat, my pack full of food, and my new bedroll had all been lost somewhere upstream, so my disastrous excursion into Ryevost had been for nothing. My money pouch was gone. At least my knife was still safely sheathed at my hip.

Some time near dawn, I let myself summon a little sunlight to dry my boots and warm my clammy hands. I dozed and dreamed of Baghra holding my own knife to my throat, her laugh a dry rattle in my ear.

I awoke to the pounding of my heart and the sounds of movement in the woods around me. I had fallen asleep slumped against the base of a tree, hidden – I hoped – behind the copse of bushes. From where I sat, I could see no one, but I could hear voices in the distance. I hesitated, frozen in place, unsure what to do. If I moved, I risked giving away my position, but if I stayed quiet, it would only be a matter of time before they found me.

My heart began to race as the sounds grew closer. Through the leaves, I glimpsed a stocky, bearded soldier. He had a rifle in his hands, but I knew there was no chance that they would kill me. I was too valuable. It gave me an advantage, if I was willing to die.

They're not going to take me. The thought came to me with sure and sudden clarity. *I won't go back.*

I flicked my wrist and a mirror slid into my left hand. With my other hand I pulled out my knife, feeling the weight of Grisha steel in my palm. Silently, I drew myself into a crouch and waited, listening. I was frightened, but I was surprised to find that some part of me felt eager.

I watched the bearded soldier through the leaves, circling closer until he was just feet from me. I could see a bead of sweat trickling down his neck, the morning light gleaming off his rifle barrel, and for a moment, I thought he might be looking right at me. A call sounded from deep in the woods. The soldier shouted back to them. "*Nichyevo!*" Nothing.

And then, to my amazement, he turned and walked away from me.

I listened as the sounds faded, the voices growing more distant, the footfalls more faint. Could I possibly be so lucky? Had they somehow mistaken an animal's trail or another traveller's for mine? Or was it some kind of trick? I waited, my body trembling, until all I could hear was the relative quiet of the wood, the calls of insects and birds, the rustle of the wind in the trees.

At last, I slid the mirror back into my glove and took a deep, shuddering breath. I returned my knife to its sheath and slowly rose out of my crouch. I reached for my still-damp coat lying in a crumpled heap on the ground and froze at the unmistakable sound of a soft step behind me.

I spun on my heel, my heart in my throat, and saw a figure partially hidden by branches, only a few feet from me. I'd been so focused on the bearded soldier that I hadn't realised there was someone behind me. In an instant, the knife was back in my hand, the mirror held high as the figure emerged silently from the trees. I stared, sure I must be hallucinating.

Mal.

I opened my mouth to speak, but he put his finger to his lips in warning, his gaze locked onto mine. He waited a moment, listening, then gestured to me to follow and melted back into the woods. I grabbed my coat and hurried after him, doing my best to keep up. It was no easy task. He moved silently, slipping like a shadow through the branches, as if he could see paths invisible to others' eyes.

He led me back to the stream, to a shallow bend where we were able to slog across. I cringed as the icy water poured into my boots again. When we emerged on the other side, he circled back to cover our tracks.

I was bursting with questions, and my mind kept jumping from one thought to the next. How had Mal found me? Had he been tracking me with the other soldiers? What did it mean that he was helping me? I wanted to reach out and touch him to make sure he was real. I wanted to throw my arms around him in gratitude. I wanted to punch him in the eye for the things he'd said to me that night at the Little Palace.

We walked for hours in complete silence. Periodically, he would gesture for me to stop, and I would wait as he disappeared into the underbrush to hide our tracks. Some time in the afternoon, we began climbing a rocky path. I wasn't sure where the stream had deposited me, but I felt fairly certain that he must be leading me into the Petrazoi.

Each step was agony. My boots were still wet, and

fresh blisters formed on my heels and toes. My miserable night in the woods had left me with a pulsing headache, and I was dizzy from lack of food, but I wasn't about to complain. I kept quiet as he led me up the mountain and then off the trail, scrabbling over rocks until my legs were shaking with fatigue and my throat burned with thirst. When Mal finally stopped, we were high up the mountain, hidden from view by an enormous outcropping of rock and a few scraggly pines.

"Here," he said, dropping his pack. He slid sure-footed back down the mountain, and I knew he was going to try to cover the traces of my clumsy progress over the rocks.

Gratefully, I sank to the ground and closed my eyes. My feet were throbbing, but I was worried that if I took my boots off, I would never get them back on again. My head drooped, but I couldn't let myself sleep. Not yet. I had a thousand questions, but only one couldn't wait until morning.

Dusk was falling by the time Mal returned, moving silently over the terrain. He sat down across from me and pulled a canteen from his pack. After taking a swig, he swiped his hand over his mouth and passed the water to me. I drank deeply.

"Slow down," he said. "That has to last us through tomorrow."

"Sorry." I handed the canteen back to him.

"We can't risk a fire tonight," he said, gazing out into the gathering dark. "Maybe tomorrow."

I nodded. My coat had dried during our trek up the mountain, though the sleeves were still a little damp. I felt rumpled, dirty and cold. Mostly, I was just reeling from the miracle that was sitting in front of me. That would have to wait. I was terrified of the answer, but I had to ask.

"Mal." I waited for him to look at me. "Did you find the herd? Did you capture Morozova's stag?"

He tapped his hand on his knee. "Why is it so important?"

"It's a long story. I need to know, does he have the stag?"

"No."

"They're close, though?"

He nodded. "But . . ."

"But what?"

Mal hesitated. In the remnants of the afternoon light, I saw a ghost of the cocky smile I knew so well playing on his lips. "I don't think they'll find it without me."

I raised my eyebrows. "Because you're just that good?"

"No," he said, serious again. "Maybe. Don't get me wrong. They're good trackers, the best in the First Army, but . . . you have to have a feel for tracking the herd. They aren't ordinary animals."

And you're no ordinary tracker, I thought but didn't say. I watched him, thinking of what the Darkling had once said about not understanding our own gifts. Could there be more to Mal's talent than just luck or practice? He'd certainly never suffered from a lack of confidence, but I didn't think this was about conceit.

"I hope you're right," I murmured.

"Now you answer a question for me," he said, and there was a harsh edge to his voice. "Why did you run?"

For the first time, I realised that Mal had no idea why I'd fled the Little Palace, why the Darkling was searching for me. The last time I'd seen him, I'd essentially ordered him out of my sight, but still he'd left everything behind and come for me. He deserved an explanation, but I had no idea where to begin. I sighed and rubbed a hand over my face. What had I got us into?

"If I told you that I'm trying to save the world, would you believe me?"

He stared at me, his eyes hard. "So this isn't some kind of lovers' quarrel where you turn around and go running back to him?"

"No!" I exclaimed in shock. "It's not . . . we're not . . ." I was at a loss for words and then I just had to laugh. "I wish it were something like that."

Mal was quiet for a long time. Then, as if he'd reached some kind of decision, he said, "All right." He stood up, stretched, and slung his rifle over his shoulder. Then he drew a thick wool blanket from his pack and tossed it to me.

"Get some rest," he said. "I'll take the first watch." He turned his back on me, looking out at the moon rising high over the valley we had left behind.

I curled up on the hard ground, pulling the blanket tight around me for warmth. Despite my discomfort, my eyelids felt heavy and I could feel exhaustion dragging me under.

"Mal," I whispered into the night.

"What?"

"Thanks for finding me."

I wasn't sure if I was dreaming, but somewhere in the dark, I thought I heard him whisper, "Always."

I let sleep take me.

Chapter 17

Mal took both watches and let me sleep through the night. In the morning, he handed me a strip of dried meat and said simply, "Talk."

I wasn't sure where to begin, so I started with the worst of it. "The Darkling plans to use the Shadow Fold as a weapon."

Mal didn't even blink. "How?"

"He'll expand it, spread it through Ravka and Fjerda and anywhere else he meets resistance. But he can't do it without me to keep the volcra at bay. How much do you know about Morozova's stag?"

"Not much. Just that it's valuable." He looked out over the valley. "And that it was intended for you. We were supposed to locate the herd and capture or corner the stag, but not harm it."

I nodded and tried to explain the little bit I knew about the way amplifiers worked, how Ivan had to slay the Sherborn bear, and Marie had to kill the northern seal. "A Grisha has to earn an amplifier," I finished. "The same thing is true for the stag, but it was never meant for me."

"Let's walk," Mal said abruptly. "You can tell me the rest while we're moving. I want to get us deeper into the mountains."

He shoved the blanket into his pack and did his best to hide any signs that we'd ever made camp there. Then he led us up a steep and rocky trail. His bow was tied to his pack. He kept his rifle at the ready.

My feet protested every step, but I followed and did my best to tell the rest of the story. I told him everything that Baghra had told me, about the origins of the Fold, about the collar that the Darkling intended to fashion so that he could use my power, and finally about the ship waiting in Os Kervo.

When I'd finished, Mal said, "You shouldn't have listened to Baghra."

"How can you say that?" I demanded.

He turned suddenly, and I almost ran right into him. "What do you think will happen if you make it to the Fold? If you make it onto that ship? Do you think his power stops at the shore of the True Sea?"

"No, but—"

"It's just a question of time before he finds you and slaps that collar around your neck."

He turned on his heel and marched up the trail, leaving me standing, dazed, behind him. I made my legs move and hurried to catch up.

Maybe Baghra's plan was a weak one, but what choice had either of us had? I remembered her fierce grip, the fear in her feverish eyes. She'd never expected the Darkling would really locate Morozova's herd. The night of the winter fete, she'd been genuinely panicked, but she'd tried to help me. If she'd been as ruthless as her son, she might have dispensed with risk and slit my throat instead. *And maybe we all would have been better off*, I thought dismally.

We walked in silence for a long time, moving up the mountain in slow switchbacks. In some spots, the trail was so narrow that I could do little more than cling to the mountainside, take tiny, shuffling steps, and hope the Saints were kind. Around noon, we descended the first slope and started up the second, which was, to my misery, even steeper and taller than the first.

I stared at the trail in front of me, putting one foot in front of the other, trying to shake my sense of hopelessness. The more I thought about it, the more I worried that Mal might be right. I couldn't lose the feeling that I'd doomed both of us. The Darkling needed me alive, but what might he do to Mal? I'd been so focused on my own fear and my own future that I hadn't given much thought to what Mal had done or what he'd chosen to give up. He could never go back to the army, to his friends, to being a decorated tracker. Worse, he was guilty of desertion, maybe of treason, and the penalty for that was death.

By dusk, we'd climbed high enough that the few scraggling trees had all but disappeared and winter frost still lay on the ground in places. We ate a meagre dinner of hard cheese and stringy dried beef. Mal still didn't think it was safe to build a fire, so we huddled beneath the blanket in silence, shivering against the howling wind, our shoulders barely touching.

I had almost dozed off when Mal suddenly said, "I'm taking us north tomorrow."

My eyes flew open. "North?"

"To Tsibeya."

"You want to go after the stag?" I said in disbelief.

"I know I can find it."

"If the Darkling hasn't found it already!"

"No," he said, and I felt him shake his head. "He's still out there. I can feel it."

His words reminded me eerily of what the Darkling had said on the path to Baghra's cottage. *The stag was meant for you, Alina. I can feel it.*

"And what if the Darkling finds us first?" I asked.

"You can't spend the rest of your life running, Alina. You said the stag could make you powerful. Powerful enough to fight him?"

"Maybe."

"Then we have to do it."

"If he catches us, he'll kill you."

"I know."

"All Saints, Mal. Why did you come after me? What were you thinking?"

He sighed and ran a hand over his short hair. "I didn't think. We were halfway back to Tsibeya when we got orders to turn back around and hunt *you*. So that's what I did. The hard part was leading the others away from you, especially after you basically announced yourself in Ryevost."

"And now you're a deserter."

"Yes."

"Because of me."

"Yes."

My throat ached with unshed tears, but I managed to keep my voice from shaking. "I didn't mean for any of this to happen."

"I'm not afraid to die, Alina," he said in that cold, steady voice that seemed so alien to me. "But I'd like to give us a fighting chance. We have to go after the stag."

I thought about what he said for a long while. At last, I whispered, "Okay."

All I got back was a snore. Mal was already asleep.

Over the next few days, he drove us mercilessly through the mountains, but my pride, and maybe my fear, wouldn't let me ask him to slow down. We saw an occasional goat skittering down the slopes above us and spent one night camped by a brilliant blue lake, but those were rare breaks in the monotony of leaden rock and sullen sky.

Mal's grim silences didn't help. I wanted to know how he'd ended up tracking the stag for the Darkling and what his life had been like for the last five months, but my questions were met with terse one-word replies, and sometimes he ignored me completely. When I was feeling particularly tired or hungry, I'd glare resentfully at his back and think about giving him a good whack over the head to get his attention. Most of the time, I just worried. I worried that Mal regretted his decision to come after me. I worried about the impossibility of finding the stag in the vastness of Tsibeya. But more than anything I worried about what the Darkling might do to Mal if we were captured.

When we finally began the north-west descent out of the Petrazoi, I was thrilled to leave the barren mountains and their cold winds behind. My heart lifted as we descended below the tree line and into a welcoming wood. After days of scrabbling over hard ground, it was a pleasure to walk on soft beds of pine needles, to hear the rustle of animals in the underbrush and breathe air dense with the smell of sap.

We camped by a burbling creek, and when Mal began

gathering twigs for a fire, I nearly broke out in song. I summoned a tiny, concentrated shaft of light to start the flames, but Mal didn't seem particularly impressed. He disappeared into the woods and brought back a rabbit that we cleaned and roasted for dinner. With a bemused expression, he watched as I gobbled down my portion and then sighed, still hungry.

"You'd be a lot easier to feed if you hadn't developed an appetite," he groused, finishing his food and stretching out on his back, his head pillowed on his arm.

I ignored him. I was warm for the first time since I'd left the Little Palace, and nothing could spoil that bliss. Not even Mal's snores.

We needed to restock our supplies before we headed further north into Tsibeya, but it took us another day and a half to find a hunting trail that led us to one of the villages on the north-west side of the Petrazoi. The closer we got to civilisation, the more nervous Mal became. He would disappear for long stretches, scouting ahead, keeping us moving parallel to the town's main road. Early in the afternoon, he appeared wearing an ugly brown coat and a brown squirrel hat.

"Where did you find those?" I asked.

"I grabbed them from an unlocked house," he said guiltily. "But I left a few coins. It's eerie, though – the houses are all empty. I didn't see anyone on the road either."

"Maybe it's Sunday," I said. I had lost track of the days since I'd left the Little Palace. "They could all be at church."

"Maybe," he conceded. But he looked troubled as he buried his old army coat and hat beside a tree.

We were half a mile from the village when we heard the drums. They got louder as we crept closer to the road, and soon we heard bells and fiddles, clapping and cheering. Mal climbed a tree to get a better view, and when he came down, some of the worry had gone from his face.

"There are people everywhere. There must be hundreds walking the road, and I can see the *dom* cart."

"It's butter week!" I exclaimed.

In the week before the spring fast, every nobleman was expected to ride out among his people in a *dom* cart, a cart laden with sweets and cheeses and baked breads. The parade would pass from the village church all the way back to the noble's estate, where the public rooms would be thrown open to peasants and serfs, who were fed on tea and *blini*. The local girls wore red *sarafan* and flowers in their hair to celebrate the coming of spring.

Butter week had been the best time at the orphanage, when classes were cut short so that we could clean the house and help with the baking. Duke Keramsov had always timed his return from Os Alta to coincide with it. We would all ride out in the *dom* cart, and he would stop at every farm to drink *kvas* and pass out cakes and sweets. Sitting beside the Duke, waving to the cheering villagers, we'd felt almost like nobility ourselves.

"Can we go and look, Mal?" I asked eagerly.

He frowned, and I knew his caution was wrestling with some of our happiest memories from Keramzin. Then a smile tugged at the corner of his mouth. "All right. There are certainly enough people for us to blend in."

We joined the crowds parading down the road, slipping in with the fiddlers and drummers, the little girls clutching branches tied with bright ribbons. As we passed through the village's main street, shopkeepers stood in their doorways ringing bells and clapping their hands with the musicians. Mal stopped to buy furs and stock up on supplies, but when I saw him shove a wedge of hard cheese into his pack, I stuck out my tongue. If I never saw another piece of hard cheese again, it would be too soon.

Before Mal could tell me not to, I darted into the crowd, snaking between people trailing behind the *dom* cart where a red-cheeked man sat with a bottle of *kvas* in one chubby hand as he swayed from side to side, singing and tossing bread to the peasants crowding around the cart. I reached out and snatched a warm golden roll.

"For you, pretty girl!" the man shouted, practically toppling over.

The sweet roll smelled divine, and I thanked him, prancing my way back to Mal and feeling quite pleased with myself.

He grabbed my arm and pulled me down a muddy walkway between two houses. "What do you think you're doing?"

"Nobody saw me. He just thought I was another peasant girl."

"We can't take risks like that."

"So you don't want a bite?"

He hesitated. "I didn't say that."

"I was going to give you a bite, but since you don't want one, I'll just have to eat the whole thing myself."

Mal grabbed for the roll, but I danced out of reach, dodging left and right, away from his hands. I could see his surprise, and I loved it. I wasn't the same clumsy girl he remembered.

"You are a brat," he growled and took another swipe.

"Ah, but I'm a brat with a sweet roll."

I don't know which of us heard it first, but we both stood up straight, suddenly aware that we had company. Two men had snuck up behind us in the empty alleyway. Before Mal could even turn around, one of the men was holding a dirty-looking knife to his throat, and the other had clapped his filthy hand over my mouth.

"Quiet now," rasped the man with the knife. "Or I'll open both your throats." He had greasy hair and a comically long face.

I eyed the blade at Mal's neck and nodded slightly. The other man's hand slid away from my mouth, but he kept a firm grip on my arm.

"Coin," said Longface.

"You're robbing us?" I burst out.

"That's right," hissed the man holding me, giving me a shake.

I couldn't help it. I was so relieved and surprised that we weren't being captured that a little giggle bubbled out of me.

The thieves and Mal both looked at me as if I was crazy.

"A bit simple, is she?" asked the man holding me.

"Yeah," Mal said, glaring at me with eyes that clearly said, *Shut up.* "A bit."

"Money," said Longface. "Now."

Mal reached carefully into his coat and pulled out his money bag, handing it over to Longface, who grunted and frowned at its light weight.

"That it? What's in the pack?"

"Not much, some furs and food," Mal replied.

"Show me."

Slowly, Mal unshouldered his pack and opened the top, giving the thieves a view of the contents. His rifle, wrapped in a wool blanket, was clearly visible at the top.

"Ah," said Longface. "Now, that's a nice rifle. Isn't it, Lev?"

The man holding me kept one thick hand tight around my wrist and fished out the rifle with the other. "Very nice," he grunted. "And the pack looks like military issue." My heart sank.

"So?" asked Longface.

"So Rikov says a soldier from the outpost at Chernast has gone missing. Word is he went south and never came back. Could be we caught ourselves a deserter."

Longface studied Mal speculatively, and I knew he was already thinking of the reward that awaited him. He had no idea.

"What do you say, boy? You wouldn't be on the run, would you?"

"The pack belongs to my brother," Mal said easily.

"Maybe. And maybe we'll let the captain at Chernast take a look at it and take a look at you."

Mal shrugged. "Good. I'd be happy to let him know you tried to rob us."

Lev didn't seem to like that idea. "Let's just take the money and go."

"Nah," said Longface, still squinting at Mal. "He's gone deserter or he took that off some other grunt. Either way, the captain'll pay good money to hear about it."

"What about her?" Lev gave me another shake.

"She can't be up to anything good if she's travelling with this lot. Could be she's done a runner too. And if not, she'll be good for a bit of fun. Won't you, sweet?"

"Don't touch her," spat Mal, stepping forward.

With one swift movement, Longface brought the handle of his knife down hard on Mal's head. Mal stumbled, one knee buckling, blood pouring from his temple.

"No!" I shouted. The man holding me clamped his hand back around my mouth, releasing my arm. That was all I needed. I flicked my wrist and the mirror slid between my fingers.

Longface loomed over Mal, the knife in his hand. "Could be the captain'll pay whether he's alive or dead."

He lunged. I twisted the mirror, and bright light shot into Longface's eyes. He hesitated, throwing his hand up to block the glare. Mal seized his chance. He leapt to his feet and grabbed hold of Longface, throwing him hard against the wall.

Lev loosened his grip on me to raise Mal's rifle, but I whirled on him, bringing the mirror up, blinding him.

"What the—" he grunted, squinting. Before he could recover, I slammed a knee into his groin. As he bent double, I put my hands on the back of his head and brought my knee up hard. There was a disgusting *crunch*, and I stepped backwards as he fell to the ground clutching his nose, blood spurting between his fingers.

"I did it!" I exclaimed. Oh, if only Botkin could see me now.

"Come on!" Mal said, distracting me from my jubilation. I turned and saw Longface lying unconscious in the dirt.

Mal snatched up his pack and ran towards the opposite end of the alley, away from the noise of the parade. Lev was moaning, but he still had a grip on the rifle. I gave him a good hard kick in the gut and sprinted after Mal.

We darted past empty shops and houses and back across the muddy main road, then plunged into the woods and the safety of the trees. Mal set a furious pace, leading us through a little creek and then over a ridge, on and on for what felt miles. Personally, I didn't think the thieves were in any condition to come chasing after us, but I was also too out of breath to argue the point. Finally, Mal slowed and stopped, bending double, hands on knees, his breath coming in gasps.

I collapsed to the ground, my heart thudding against my ribs, and flopped onto my back. I lay there with the blood rushing in my ears, drinking in the afternoon light that slanted through the tops of the trees and trying to catch my breath. When I felt I could talk, I pushed myself up on my elbows and said, "Are you okay?"

Gingerly, Mal touched the wound on his head. It had stopped bleeding, but he winced. "Fine."

"Do you think they'll say anything?"

"Of course. They'll see if they can get some coin for the information."

"Saints," I swore.

"There's nothing we can do about it now." Then, to my surprise, he cracked a smile. "Where did you learn to fight like that?"

"Grisha training," I whispered dramatically. "Ancient secrets of the groin kick."

"Whatever works."

I laughed. "That's what Botkin always says. 'Not showy, just to make pain,'" I said, imitating the mercenary's heavy accent.

"Smart guy."

"The Darkling doesn't think Grisha should rely on their powers for defence." I was instantly sorry I'd said it. Mal's smile disappeared.

"Another smart guy," he said coldly, staring out into the wood. After a minute, he said, "He'll know that you didn't head straight to the Fold. He'll know we're hunting the stag." He sat down heavily beside me, his face grim. We'd had very few advantages in this fight, and now we'd lost one of them.

"I shouldn't have taken us into town," he said bleakly.

I gave him a light punch on the arm. "We couldn't know someone was going to try to rob us. I mean, whose luck is actually that bad?"

"It was a stupid risk. I should know better." He picked up a twig from the forest floor and threw it away angrily.

"I still have the roll," I offered lamely, pulling the squashed, lint-covered lump from my pocket. It had been baked into the shape of a bird to celebrate the spring flocks, but now it looked more like a rolled-up sock.

Mal dropped his head, covering it with his hands, his elbows resting on his knees. His shoulders began to shake, and for a horrible moment, I thought he might be crying, but then I realised he was laughing silently. His whole body rocked, his breath coming in hitches, tears starting to leak from his eyes. "That'd better be one hell of a roll," he gasped.

I stared at him for a second, afraid he might have gone completely mad, and then I started laughing too. I covered my mouth to stop the sound, which only made me laugh harder. It was as if all the tension and the fear of the last few days had just become too much.

Mal put a finger to his lips in an exaggerated, "Shhhh!" and I collapsed in a fresh wave of giggles.

"I think you broke that guy's nose," he snorted.

"That's not nice. I'm not nice."

"No, you're not," he agreed, and then we were laughing again.

"Do you remember when that farmer's son broke your nose at Keramzin?" I gasped between fits. "And you didn't tell anyone, and you bled all over Ana Kuya's favourite tablecloth?"

"You are making that up."

"I am not!"

"Yes you are! You break noses, and you lie."

We laughed until we couldn't breathe, until our sides ached and our heads spun with it. I couldn't remember the last time I had laughed like that.

We did actually eat the roll. It was dusted with sugar and tasted just like the sweet rolls we'd eaten as children. When we'd finished, Mal said, "That *was* a really good roll," and we burst into another fit of laughter.

Eventually, he sighed and stood, offering a hand to help me up.

We walked until dusk and then made camp by the ruins of a cottage. Given our close call, he didn't think we should risk a fire that night, so we ate from the supplies we'd picked up in the village. As we chewed on dried beef and that miserable hard cheese, he asked about Botkin and the other teachers at the Little Palace. I didn't realise how much I'd been longing to share my stories with him until I started talking. He didn't laugh as easily as he once had. But when he did, some of that grim coolness lifted from him and he seemed a bit more like the Mal I used to know. It gave me hope that he might not be lost forever.

When it was time to bed down for the night, Mal walked the perimeter of the camp, making sure we were safe, while I repacked the food. There was plenty of room in the pack now that we'd lost Mal's rifle and wool blanket. I was just grateful that he still had his bow.

I bunched the squirrel-fur hat up under my head and left the pack for Mal to use as a pillow. Then I pulled my coat close around me and huddled beneath the new furs. I was nodding off when I heard Mal return and settle himself beside me, his back pressed comfortably against mine.

As I drifted into sleep, I felt as though I could still taste the sugar from that sweet roll on my tongue, feel the pleasure of laughter gusting through me. We'd been robbed. We'd almost been killed. We were being hunted by the most powerful man in Ravka. But we were friends again, and sleep came more easily than it had in a long time.

At some point during the night, I woke to Mal's snoring. I jabbed him in the back with my elbow. He rolled onto his side, muttered something in his sleep, and threw his arm over me. A minute later he started snoring again, but this time I didn't wake him.

Chapter 18

We saw shoots of new grasses and even a few wildflowers, but there were fewer signs of spring as we headed north to Tsibeya and into the wild reaches where Mal believed we would find the stag. The dense pines gave way to sparse birchwood forests and then to long stretches of grazing land.

Though Mal regretted our trip into the village, he soon had to admit that it had been a necessity. The nights grew colder as we travelled north, and cookfires weren't an option as we drew closer to the outpost at Chernast. We also didn't want to waste time hunting or trapping food every day, so we relied on our supplies and nervously watched them dwindle.

Something between us seemed to have thawed, and instead of the stony silence of the Petrazoi, we talked as we walked. He seemed curious to hear about life in the Little Palace, the strange ways of the court, and even Grisha theory.

He wasn't at all shocked to hear of the contempt with which most Grisha regarded the King. Apparently, the trackers had been grumbling more and more loudly among themselves about the King's incompetence.

"The Fjerdans have a breech-loading rifle that can fire twenty-eight rounds per minute. Our soldiers should have them too. If the King could be bothered to take an interest in the First Army, we wouldn't be so dependent on the Grisha. But it'll never happen," he told me. Then he muttered, "We all know who's running the country."

I said nothing. I tried to avoid talking about the Darkling as much as possible.

When I asked about the time Mal had spent tracking the stag, he always seemed to find a way to bring the conversation back to me. I didn't press him. I knew that Mal's unit had crossed the border into Fjerda. I suspected that they'd had to fight their way out and that was where Mal had acquired the scar on his jaw, but he refused to say more.

As we were walking through a band of dessicated willows, the frost crunching beneath our boots, Mal pointed out a sparrowhawk nest, and I found myself wishing that we could just keep walking forever. As much as I longed for a hot meal and a warm bed, I was afraid of what the end of our journey might bring. What if we found the stag, and I claimed the antlers? How might an amplifier that powerful change me? Would it be enough to free us from the Darkling? If only we could stay this way, walking side by side, sleeping huddled beneath the stars. Maybe these empty plains and quiet groves could shelter us as they had sheltered Morozova's herd and keep us safe from the men who sought us.

They were foolish thoughts. Tsibeya was an inhospitable place, a wild and empty world of bitter winters and gruelling summers. And we weren't strange and ancient creatures who roamed the earth at twilight. We were just Mal and Alina, and we could not stay ahead of our pursuers forever. A dark thought that had flitted through my head for days now finally settled. I sighed, knowing that I had put off talking to Mal about this problem for too long. It was irresponsible, and given how much we'd both risked, I couldn't let it continue.

That night, Mal was almost asleep, his breathing deep and even, before I worked up the courage to speak.

"Mal," I began. Instantly, he was awake, tension flooding through his body, as he sat up and reached for his knife. "No," I said, laying a hand on his arm. "Everything's all right. But I need to talk to you."

"Now?" he grumbled, flopping down and throwing his arm back around me.

I sighed. I wanted to just lie there in the dark, listening to the rustle of the wind in the grass, warm in this feeling of safety, however illusory. But I knew I couldn't. "I need you to do something for me."

He snorted. "You mean other than deserting the army, scaling mountains and freezing my ass off on the cold ground every night?"

"Yes."

"Hmmph," he grumbled noncommittally, his breath already returning to the deep, even rhythm of sleep.

"Mal," I said clearly, "if we don't make it . . . if they catch up to us before we find the stag, you can't let him take me."

He went perfectly still. I could actually feel his heart beating. He was quiet for so long that I began to think he'd fallen back to sleep.

Then he said, "You can't ask that of me."

"I have to."

He sat up, pushing away from me, rubbing a hand over his face. I sat up too, drawing the furs tighter around my shoulders, watching him in the moonlight.

"No."

"You can't just say no, Mal."

"You asked, I answered. No."

He stood up and walked a few steps away.

"If he puts that collar on me, you know what it will mean, how many people will die because of me. I can't let that happen. I can't be responsible for that."

"No."

"You had to know this was a possibility when we headed north, Mal."

He turned and strode back, dropping into a crouch in front of me so that he could look into my eyes.

"I won't kill you, Alina."

"You may have to."

"No," he repeated, shaking his head, looking away from me. "No, no, no."

I took his face in my cold hands, turning his head until he had to meet my gaze.

"Yes."

"I can't, Alina. *I can't.*"

"Mal, that night at the Little Palace, you said the Darkling owned me."

He winced slightly. "I was angry. I didn't mean—"

"If he gets that collar, he really will own me. Completely. And he'll turn me into a monster. Please, Mal. I need to know you won't let that happen to me."

"How can you ask me to do this?"

"Who else could I ask?"

He looked at me, his face full of desperation and anger and something else I couldn't read. Finally, he nodded once.

"Promise me, Mal." His mouth set in a grim line, and a muscle twitched in his jaw. I hated doing this to him, but I had to be sure. "Promise me."

"I promise," he said hoarsely.

I breathed a long sigh, feeling relief flood through me. I leaned forward, resting my forehead against his, closing my eyes. "Thank you."

We stayed like that for a long moment, then he leaned back. When I opened my eyes, he was looking at me. His face was inches from mine, near enough that I could feel his warm breath. I dropped my hands from his stubbled cheeks, suddenly aware of just how close we were. He stared at me for a moment and then stood abruptly and walked into the dark.

I stayed awake for a long time, cold and miserable, gazing into the night. I knew he was out there, moving silently through the new grass, carrying the weight of the burden I had placed on him. I was sorry for it, but I was glad that it was done. I waited for him to return, but finally I fell asleep, alone beneath the stars.

We spent the next few days in the areas surrounding Chernast, scouring miles of terrain for signs of Morozova's herd, drawing as close to the outpost as we dared. With every passing day, Mal's mood darkened. He tossed in his sleep and barely ate. Sometimes I woke to him thrashing about under the furs mumbling, "Where are you? Where are you?"

He saw signs of other people – broken branches, displaced rocks, patterns that were invisible to me until he pointed them out – but no signs of the stag.

Then one morning, he shook me awake before dawn.

"Get up," he said. "They're close, I can feel it." He was already pulling the furs off me and shoving them into his pack.

"Hey!" I complained, trying to keep back the covers to no avail. "What about breakfast?"

He tossed me a piece of hard tack. "Eat and walk. I want to try the western trails today. I have a feeling."

"But yesterday you thought we should head east."

"That was yesterday," he said, already shouldering his pack and striding into the tall grass. "Get moving. We need to find that stag so I don't have to chop your head off."

"I never said you had to chop my head off," I grumbled, rubbing the sleep from my eyes and stumbling after him.

"Run you through with a sword, then? Firing squad?"

"I was thinking something quieter, like maybe a nice poison."

"All you said was that I had to kill you. You didn't say how."

I stuck my tongue out at his back, but I was glad to see him so energised, and I supposed it was a good thing that he could joke about it all. At least, I hoped he was joking.

The western trails took us through groves of squat larches and past meadows clustered with fireweed and red lichen. Mal moved with purpose, his step light as always.

The air felt cool and damp, and a few times I caught him glancing nervously up at the overcast sky, but he drove onwards. Late in the afternoon, we reached a low hill that sloped gently down into a broad plateau covered in pale grass. Mal paced along the top of the slope, ranging west and then east. He walked down the hill and up the hill, and down it again, until I thought I would scream. At last, he led us to the leeward side of a large cluster of boulders, slid his pack off his shoulders, and said, "Here."

I shook a fur out on the cold ground and sat down to wait, watching Mal pace uneasily. Finally, he sat down beside me, eyes trained on the plateau, one hand resting lightly on his bow. I knew that he was imagining them there, picturing the herd emerging from the horizon, white bodies glowing in the gathering dusk, breath pluming in the cold. Maybe he was willing them to appear. This seemed like the right place for the stag – fresh with new grass and spotted with tiny blue lakes that shone like coins in the setting sun.

The sun melted away and we watched the plateau turn blue in the twilight. We waited, listening to the sound of our own breath and the wind moaning over the vastness of Tsibeya. But as the light faded, the plateau stayed empty.

The moon rose, obscured by clouds. Mal didn't move. He sat still as stone, staring out into the reaches of the plateau, his blue eyes distant. I pulled the other fur from the pack and wrapped it around his shoulders and mine. Here, in the lee of the rock, we were protected from the worst of the wind, but it wasn't much for shelter.

Then he sighed deeply and squinted up at the night sky. "It's going to snow. I should have taken us into the woods, but I thought . . ." He shook his head. "I was so sure."

"It's okay," I said, leaning my head against his shoulder. "Maybe tomorrow."

"Our supplies won't last forever, and every day we're out here is another chance for us to get caught."

"Tomorrow," I said again.

"For all we know, he's found the herd already. He's killed the stag and now they're just hunting us."

"I don't believe that."

Mal said nothing. I pulled the fur up higher and I let the tiniest bit of light blossom from my hand.

"What are you doing?"

"I'm cold."

"It isn't safe," he said, drawing the fur up to hide the light that shone warm and golden on his face.

"We haven't seen another living soul for over a week. And staying hidden won't do us much good if we freeze to death."

He frowned but then he reached out, letting his fingers play in the light, and said, "That's really something."

"Thanks," I said, smiling.

"Mikhael is dead."

The light sputtered in my hand. "What?"

"He's dead. He was killed in Fjerda. Dubrov too."

I sat frozen in shock. I'd never liked Mikhael or Dubrov, but none of that mattered now. "I didn't realise..." I hesitated. "How did it happen?"

For a moment, I didn't know if he would answer or even if I should have asked. He stared at the light that still glimmered from my hand, his thoughts far away.

"We were way up north near the permafrost, far past the outpost at Chernast," he said quietly. "We had hunted the stag almost all the way into Fjerda. The captain came up with this idea that a few of us should cross the border disguised as Fjerdans and keep tracking the herd. It was stupid, ridiculous really. Even if we managed to get through the border country undiscovered, what were we supposed to do if we caught up with the herd? We had orders not to kill the stag, so we'd have to capture it and then somehow get it back over the border into Ravka. It was insane."

I nodded. It did sound crazy.

"So that night, Mikhael and Dubrov and I laughed about it, talked about how it was a suicide mission and how the captain was a complete idiot, and we toasted the poor bastards who got stuck with the job. And the next morning I volunteered."

"Why?" I said, startled.

Mal was silent again. At last, he said, "You saved my life on the Shadow Fold, Alina."

"And you saved mine," I countered, unsure what any of that had to do with a suicide mission into Fjerda. But Mal didn't seem to hear me.

"You saved my life and then in the Grisha tent, when they led you away, I didn't do anything. I stood there and let him take you."

"What were you supposed to do, Mal?"

"Something. Anything."

"Mal—"

He ran a hand through his hair in frustration. "I know it doesn't make sense. But it's how I felt. I couldn't eat. I couldn't sleep. I kept seeing you walk away, seeing you disappear."

I thought of all the nights I had lain awake in the Little Palace, remembering my last glimpse of Mal's face vanishing into the crowd as the Darkling's guards led me away, wondering if I would ever see him again. I had missed him so terribly, but I had never really believed that Mal might be missing me just as much.

"I knew we were hunting the stag for the Darkling," Mal continued. "I thought . . . I had this idea that if I found the herd, I could help you. I could help to make things right." He glanced at me and the knowledge of how very wrong he had been passed between us. "Mikhael didn't know any of that. But he was my friend, so like an idiot, he volunteered too. And then, of course, Dubrov had to sign on. I told them not to, but Mikhael just laughed and said he wasn't going to let me get all the glory."

"What happened?"

"Nine of us crossed the border, six soldiers and three trackers. Two of us came back."

His words hung in the air, cold and final. Seven men dead in pursuit of the stag. And how many others that I didn't know about? But even as I thought it, a disturbing idea entered my mind: *How many lives could the stag's power save?* Mal and I were refugees, born to the wars that had raged at Ravka's borders for so long. What if the Darkling and the terrible power of the Shadow Fold could stop all that? Could silence Ravka's enemies and make us safe forever?

Not just Ravka's enemies, I reminded myself. *Anyone who stands against the Darkling, anyone who dares oppose him.* The Darkling would make the world a wasteland before he ceded one bit of power.

Mal rubbed a hand over his tired face. "It was all for nothing anyway. The herd crossed back into Ravka when the weather turned. We could have just waited for the stag to come to us."

I looked at Mal, at his distant eyes and the hard set of his scarred jaw. He looked nothing like the boy I'd known. He'd been trying to help me when he went after the stag. That meant that I was partially responsible for the change in him, and it broke my heart to think of it.

"I'm sorry, Mal. I'm so sorry."

"It's not your fault, Alina. I made my own choices. But those choices got my friends killed."

I wanted to throw my arms around him and hug him close. But I couldn't, not with this new Mal. Maybe not with the old one either, I admitted to myself. We weren't children any more. The ease of our closeness was a thing of the past. I reached out and laid a hand on his arm.

"If it's not my fault, then it's not yours either, Mal. Mikhael and Dubrov made their own choices too. Mikhael wanted to be a good friend to you. And for all you know, he had his own reasons for wanting to track the stag. He wasn't a child, and he wouldn't want to be remembered as one."

Mal didn't look at me, but after a moment he laid his hand over mine. We were still sitting that way when the first flakes of snow began to fall.

Chapter 19

My light kept us warm through the night in the lee of the rock. Sometimes I dozed off and Mal had to nudge me awake so that I could pull sun across the dark and starlit stretches of Tsibeya to warm us beneath the furs.

When we emerged the next morning, the sun shone brightly over a world blanketed in white. This far north, snow was common well into spring, but it was hard not to feel that the weather was just another part of our bad luck. Mal took one look at the pristine expanse of the meadow and gave a disgusted shake of his head. I didn't have to ask what he was thinking. If the herd had been close by, any sign they had left would have been covered by the snow. But we would leave plenty of tracks for anyone else to follow.

Without a word, we shook out the furs and stowed them away. Mal tied his bow to his pack, and we began the trek across the plateau. It was slow going. Mal did what he could to disguise our tracks, but it was clear that we were in serious trouble.

I knew Mal blamed himself for not being able to find the stag, but I didn't know how to fix that. Tsibeya felt somehow bigger than it had the previous day. Or maybe I just felt smaller.

Eventually, the meadow gave way to groves of thin silver birches and dense clusters of pines, their branches laden with snow. Mal's pace slowed. He looked exhausted, dark shadows lingering beneath his blue eyes. On an impulse, I slid my gloved hand into his. I thought he might pull away, but instead, he squeezed my fingers. We walked on that way, hand in hand through the late afternoon, the pine boughs clustered in a canopy high above us as we moved deeper into the dark heart of the woods.

Around sunset, we emerged from the trees into a little glade where the snow lay in heavy, perfect drifts that glittered in the fading light. We slipped into the stillness, our footfalls muffled by the snow. It was late. I knew we should be making camp, finding shelter. Instead, we stood there in silence, hands clasped, watching the day disappear.

"Alina?" he said quietly. "I'm sorry. For what I said that night, at the Little Palace."

I glanced at him, surprised. Somehow, that all felt such a long time ago. "I'm sorry too," I said.

"And I'm sorry for everything else."

I squeezed his hand. "I knew we didn't have much chance of finding the stag."

"No," he said, looking away from me. "No, not for that. I . . . When I came after you, I thought I was doing it because you saved my life, because I owed you something."

My heart gave a little twist. The idea that Mal had come after me to pay off some kind of imagined debt was more painful than I'd expected. "And now?"

"Now I don't know what to think. I just know everything is different."

My heart gave another miserable twist. "I know," I whispered.

"Do you? That night at the palace when I saw you on that stage with him, you looked so happy. Like you belonged with him. I can't get that picture out of my head."

"I was happy," I admitted. "In that moment, I was happy. I'm not like you, Mal. I never really fitted in the way that you did. I never really belonged anywhere."

"You belonged with me," he said quietly.

"No, Mal. Not really. Not for a long time."

He looked at me then, and his eyes were deep blue in the twilight. "Did you miss me, Alina? Did you miss me when you were gone?"

"Every day," I said honestly.

"I missed you every hour. And do you know what the worst part was? It caught me completely by surprise. I'd catch myself walking around to find you, not for any reason, just out of habit, because I'd seen something that I wanted to tell you about or because I wanted to hear your voice. And then I'd realise that you weren't there any more, and every time, *every single time*, it was like having the wind knocked out of me. I've risked my life for you. I've walked half the length of Ravka for you, and I'd do it again and again and again just to be with you, just to starve with you and freeze with you and hear you complain about hard cheese every day. So don't tell me we don't belong together," he said fiercely. He was very close now, and my heart was suddenly hammering in my chest. "I'm sorry it took me so long to see you, Alina. But I see you now."

He lowered his head, and I felt his lips on mine. The

world seemed to go silent and all I knew was the feel of his hand in mine as he drew me closer, and the warm press of his mouth.

I thought that I'd given up on Mal. I thought the love I'd had for him belonged to the past, to the foolish, lonely girl I never wanted to be again. I'd tried to bury that girl and the love she'd felt, just as I'd tried to bury my power. I wouldn't make that mistake again. Whatever burned between us was just as bright, just as undeniable. The moment our lips met, I knew with pure and piercing certainty that I would have waited for him forever.

He pulled away from me, and my eyes fluttered open. He raised a gloved hand to cup my face, his gaze searching mine. Then, from the corner of my eye, I caught a flickering movement.

"Mal," I breathed softly, gazing over his shoulder, "look."

Several white bodies emerged from the trees, their graceful necks bent to nibble at the grasses on the edge of the snowy glade. In the middle of Morozova's herd stood a massive white stag. He looked at us with great dark eyes, his silvery antlers gleaming in the half-light.

In one swift movement, Mal drew his bow from the side of his pack. "I'll bring it down, Alina. You have to make the kill," he said.

"Wait," I whispered, placing a hand on his arm.

The stag walked slowly forward and stopped just a few yards from us. I could see his sides rising and falling, the flare of his nostrils, the fog of his breath in the chill air.

He watched us with eyes dark and liquid. I walked towards him.

"Alina!" Mal whispered.

The stag didn't move as I approached him, not even when I reached out my hand and laid it on his warm muzzle. His ears twitched slightly, his hide glowing milky white in the deepening gloom. I thought of everything Mal and I had given up, the risks we'd taken. I thought about the weeks we had spent tracking the herd, the cold nights, the miserable days of endless walking, and I was glad of it all. Glad to be here and alive on this chilly night. Glad that Mal was beside me. I looked into the stag's dark eyes and knew the feel of the earth beneath his steady hooves, the smell of pine in his nostrils, the powerful beat of his heart. I knew I could not be the one to end his life.

"Alina," Mal murmured urgently, "we don't have much time. You know what you have to do."

I shook my head. I could not break the stag's gaze. "No, Mal. We'll find another way."

The sound was like a soft whistle on the air followed by a dull thunk as the arrow found its target. The stag bellowed and reared up, an arrow blooming from his chest, and then crumpled to his forelegs. I staggered backwards as the rest of the herd took flight, scattering into the forest. Mal was at my side in an instant, his bow at the ready, as the clearing filled with charcoal-clad *oprichniki* and Grisha cloaked in blue and red.

"You should have listened to him, Alina." The voice came clear and cold out of the shadows, and the Darkling stepped into the glade, a grim smile playing on his lips, his black *kefta* flowing behind him like an ebony stain.

The stag had fallen on his side and lay in the snow, breathing heavily, his black eyes wide and panicked.

I felt Mal move before I saw him. He turned his bow

on the stag and let fly, but a blue-robed Squaller stepped forward, his hand arcing through the air. The arrow swerved left, falling harmlessly into the snow.

Mal reached for another arrow and at the same moment the Darkling threw his hand out, sending a black ribbon of darkness rippling towards us. I raised my hands and light shot from my fingers, shattering the darkness easily.

But it had only been a diversion. The Darkling turned on the stag, lifting his arm in a gesture I knew only too well. "No!" I screamed and, without thinking, I threw myself in front of the stag. I closed my eyes, ready to feel myself torn in half by the Cut, but the Darkling must have turned his body at the last moment. The tree behind me split open with a loud crack, tendrils of darkness spilling from the wound. He'd spared me, but he'd also spared the stag.

All humour was gone from the Darkling's face as he slammed his hands together and a huge wall of rippling darkness surged forward, engulfing us and the stag. I didn't have to think. Light bloomed in a pulsing, glowing sphere, surrounding me and Mal, keeping the darkness at bay and blinding our attackers. For a moment, we were at a stalemate. They couldn't see us and we couldn't see them. The darkness swirled around the bubble of light, pushing to get in.

"Impressive," said the Darkling, his voice coming to us as if from a great distance. "Baghra taught you far too well. But you're not strong enough for this, Alina."

I knew he was trying to distract me and I ignored him.

"You! Tracker! Are you so ready to die for her?" the Darkling called. Mal's expression didn't change. He stood, bow at the ready, arrow nocked, turning in a slow circle, searching out the Darkling's voice. "That was a very touching scene we witnessed," he sneered. "Did you tell him, Alina? Does the boy know how willing you were to give yourself to me? Did you tell him what I showed you in the dark?"

A wave of shame rushed through me and the glowing light faltered. The Darkling laughed.

I glanced at Mal. His jaw was set. He radiated the same icy anger I had seen the night of the winter fete. I felt my hold on the light slip and I scrambled for it. I tried to refocus my power. The sphere stuttered with fresh brilliance, but I could already feel my reach brushing up against the boundaries of what I could do. Darkness began to leak into the edges of the bubble like ink.

I knew what had to be done. The Darkling was right; I wasn't strong enough. And we wouldn't have another chance.

"Do it, Mal," I whispered. "You know what has to happen."

Mal looked at me, panic flaring in his eyes. He shook his head. Darkness surged against the bubble. I stumbled slightly.

"Quick, Mal! Before it's too late."

In one lightning movement, Mal dropped his bow and reached for his knife.

"Do it, Mal! Do it now!"

Mal's hand was shaking. I could feel my strength ebbing. "I can't," he whispered miserably. "I can't." He let go of the knife, letting it fall soundlessly into the snow. Darkness crashed in on us.

Mal disappeared. The clearing disappeared. I was thrown into suffocating blackness. I heard Mal cry out and reached towards his voice, but suddenly, strong arms seized hold of me from both sides. I kicked and struggled furiously.

The darkness lifted, and that quickly, I saw it was over.

Two of the Darkling's guards had me, while Mal struggled between two others.

"Be still or I'll kill you where you stand," Ivan snarled at him.

"Leave him alone!" I shouted.

"Shhhh." The Darkling approached, one finger held to his lips, which were curled into a mocking smile. "Quiet now, or I will let Ivan kill him. Slowly."

Tears spilled onto my cheeks, freezing in the cold night air.

"Torches," he said. I heard flint striking and two torches burst into flame, lighting the clearing, the soldiers, and the stag, which lay panting on the ground. The Darkling pulled a heavy knife from his belt, and the firelight glinted off Grisha steel. "We've wasted enough time here."

He strode forward and without hesitating slit the stag's throat.

Blood gushed into the snow, pooling around the stag's body. I watched as the life left his dark eyes, and a sob broke from my chest.

"Take the antlers," the Darkling said to one of the *oprichniki*. "Cut a piece from each."

The *oprichnik* stepped forward and bent over the stag's body, a serrated blade in his hand.

I turned away, my stomach heaving as a sawing sound

filled the stillness of the clearing. We stood in silence, our breath curling in the icy air, as the sound went on and on. Even when it stopped, I could still feel it vibrating through my clenched jaw.

The *oprichnik* crossed the glade and handed the two pieces of antler to the Darkling. They were almost evenly matched, both ending in double prongs of roughly the same size. The Darkling clasped the pieces in his hands, letting his thumb roll over the rough, silvery bone. Then he gestured, and I was surprised to see David emerge from the shadows in his purple *kefta*.

Of course. The Darkling would want his best Fabrikator to fashion this collar. David wouldn't meet my gaze. I wondered if Genya knew where he was and what he was doing. Maybe she would be proud. Maybe she thought of me as a traitor now too.

"David," I said softly, "don't do this."

David glanced at me and then hurriedly looked away.

"David understands the future," said the Darkling, the edge of a threat in his voice. "And he knows better than to fight it."

David came to stand behind my right shoulder. The Darkling studied me in the torchlight. For a moment, all was silence. Twilight had gone, and the moon had risen, bright and full. The glade seemed suspended in stillness.

"Open your coat," said the Darkling.

I didn't move.

The Darkling glanced at Ivan and nodded. Mal screamed, his hands clutching his chest as he crumpled to the ground.

"No!" I cried. I tried to run to Mal's side, but the guards on either side of me held tight to my arms.

"Please," I begged the Darkling. "Make him stop!"

Again, the Darkling nodded, and Mal's cries ceased. He lay in the snow, breathing hard, his gaze fixed on Ivan's arrogant sneer, his eyes full of hatred.

The Darkling watched me, waiting, his face impassive. He looked almost bored. I shrugged off the *oprichniki*. With shaking hands, I wiped the tears from my eyes and unbuttoned my coat, letting it slide over my shoulders.

Distantly, I was aware of the cold seeping through my wool tunic, of the watching eyes of the soldiers and the Grisha. My world had narrowed to the curving pieces of bone in the Darkling's hands, and I felt a sweeping sense of terror.

"Lift your hair," he murmured. I lifted the hair away from my neck with both hands.

The Darkling stepped forward and pushed the fabric of my tunic out of the way. When his fingertips brushed against my skin, I flinched. I saw a flash of anger pass over his face.

He placed the curving pieces of antler around my throat, one on each side, letting them rest on my collarbone with infinite care. He nodded at David, and I felt the Fabrikator take the antlers. In my mind's eye, I saw David standing behind me, wearing the same focused expression I'd seen that first day in the workrooms of the Little Palace. I saw the pieces of bone shift and melt together. No clasp, no hinge. This collar would be mine to wear forever.

"It's done," whispered David. He dropped the collar, and I felt the weight of it settle on my neck. I bunched my hands into fists, waiting.

Nothing happened. I felt a sudden reckless shock of hope. What if the Darkling had been wrong? What if the collar did nothing at all?

Then the Darkling closed his fingers over my shoulder and a silent command reverberated inside me: *Light*. It felt like an invisible hand reaching into my chest.

Golden light burst through me, flooding the clearing. I saw the Darkling squinting in the brightness, his features alight with triumph and exultation.

No, I thought, trying to release the light, to send it away. But as soon as the idea of resistance had formed, that invisible hand batted it away as if it was nothing.

Another command echoed through me: *More*. A fresh surge of power roared through my body, wilder and stronger than anything I had ever felt. There was no end to it. The control I'd learned, the understanding I'd gained collapsed before it – houses I'd built, fragile and imperfect, smashed to kindling in the oncoming flood that was the power of the stag. Light exploded from me in wave after shimmering wave, obliterating the night sky in a torrent of brilliance. I felt none of the exhilaration or joy that I had come to expect from using my power. It wasn't mine any more, and I was drowning, helpless, caught in that horrible, invisible grip.

The Darkling held me there, testing my new limits – for how long, I couldn't tell. I only knew when I felt the invisible hand release its grip.

Darkness fell on the clearing once again. I drew a ragged breath, trying to get my bearings, to piece myself back together. The flickering torchlight illuminated the awed expressions of the guards and Grisha, and Mal, still crumpled on the ground, his face miserable, his eyes full of regret.

When I looked at the Darkling, he was watching me closely, his eyes narrowed. He looked from me to Mal, then turned to his men. "Put him in chains."

I opened my mouth to object, but a glance from Mal made me shut it.

"We'll camp tonight and leave for the Fold at first light," said the Darkling. "Send word to the Apparat to be ready." He turned to me. "If you try to harm yourself, the tracker will suffer for it."

"What about the stag?" asked Ivan.

"Burn it."

One of the Etherealki lifted his arm to a torch, and the flame shot forward in a sweeping arc, surrounding the stag's lifeless body. As we were led from the clearing, there was no sound but our own footfalls and the crackling of the flames behind us. No rustle came from the trees, no insect buzz or nightbird call. The woods were silent in their grief.

Chapter 20

We walked in silence for over an hour. I stared numbly down at my feet, watching my boots move through the snow, thinking about the stag and the price of my weakness. Eventually, I saw firelight flickering through the trees, and we emerged into a clearing where a small camp had been made around a roaring fire. I noted several tents and a group of horses tethered amid the trees. Two *oprichniki* sat beside the fire, eating their evening meal.

Mal's guards took him to one of the tents, pushing him inside and following after. I tried to catch his eye, but he disappeared too quickly.

Ivan dragged me across the camp to another tent and gave me a shove. Inside, I saw several bedrolls laid out. He pushed me forward and gestured to the pole at the centre of the tent. "Sit," he ordered. I sat with my back to the pole, and he tethered me to it, tying my hands behind my back and binding my ankles.

"Comfortable?"

"You know what he plans to do, Ivan."

"He plans to bring us peace."

"At what price?" I asked desperately. "You know this is madness."

"Did you know I had two brothers?" Ivan asked

abruptly. The familiar smirk was gone from his handsome face. "Of course not. They weren't born Grisha. They were soldiers, and they both died fighting the King's wars. So did my father. So did my uncle."

"I'm sorry."

"Yes, everyone is sorry. The King is sorry. The Queen is sorry. I'm sorry. But only the Darkling will do something about it."

"It doesn't have to be this way, Ivan. My power could be used to destroy the Fold."

Ivan shook his head. "The Darkling knows what has to be done."

"He'll never stop! You know that. Not once he's had a taste of that kind of power. I'm the one wearing the collar now. But eventually, it will be all of you. And there won't be anyone or anything strong enough to stand in his way."

A muscle twitched in Ivan's jaw. "Keep talking treason and I'll gag you," he said, and without another word, he strode out of the tent.

A while later, a Summoner and a Heartrender ducked inside. I didn't recognise either of them. Avoiding my gaze, they silently hunched into their furs and blew out the lamp.

I sat awake in the dark, watching the flickering light of the campfire play over the canvas walls of the tent. I could feel the weight of the collar against my neck, and my bound hands itched to claw at it. I thought of Mal, just a few feet away in another tent.

I'd brought us to this. If I'd taken the stag's life, his power would have been mine. I'd known what mercy might cost us. My freedom. Mal's life. The lives of countless others. And still I'd been too weak to do what needed to be done.

That night, I dreamed of the stag. I saw the Darkling cut his throat again and again. I saw the life fading from his dark eyes. But when I looked down, it was my blood that spilled red into the snow.

With a gasp, I woke to the sounds of the camp coming to life around me. The tent flap opened and a Heartrender appeared. She cut me loose from the tent pole and dragged me to my feet. My body creaked and popped in protest, stiff from a night spent sitting in a cramped position.

The Heartrender led me to where the horses were already saddled and the Darkling stood talking quietly to Ivan and the other Grisha. I looked around for Mal and felt a sudden jab of panic when I couldn't find him, but then I saw an *oprichnik* pull him from the other tent.

"What do we do with him?" the guard asked Ivan.

"Let the traitor walk," Ivan replied. "And when he gets too tired, let the horses drag him."

I opened my mouth to protest, but before I could say a word, the Darkling spoke.

"No," he said, gracefully mounting his horse. "I want him alive when we reach the Shadow Fold."

The guard shrugged and helped Mal mount his horse, then tied his shackled hands to the saddle horn. I felt a rush of relief followed by a sharp prickle of fear. Did the Darkling intend for Mal to stand trial? Or did he have something far worse in mind for him? *He's still alive*, I told myself, *and that means there's a chance to save him.*

"Ride with her," the Darkling said to Ivan. "Make sure

she doesn't do anything stupid." He didn't spare me another glance as he kicked his horse into a trot.

We rode for hours through the forest, past the plateau where Mal and I had waited for the herd. I could just see the boulders where we'd spent the night, and I wondered if the light that had kept us alive through the snowstorm had been the very thing that led the Darkling to us.

I knew he was taking us back to Kribirsk, but I hated to think what might be waiting for me there. Who would the Darkling choose to move against first? Would he launch a fleet of sand skiffs north to Fjerda? Or did he intend to march south to drive the Fold into the Shu Han? Whose deaths would be on my hands?

It took another night and day of travel before we reached the wide roads that would lead us south to the Vy. We were met at the crossroads by a huge contingent of armed men, most of them in *oprichniki* grey. They brought fresh horses and the Darkling's coach. Ivan dumped me on the velvet cushions with little ceremony and climbed inside after me. Then, with a snap of the reins, we were moving again.

Ivan insisted we keep the curtains drawn, but I snuck a peek outside and saw that we were flanked by heavily armed riders. It was hard not to be reminded of the first trip I'd made with Ivan in this same vehicle.

The soldiers made camp at night, but I was kept in isolation, confined to the Darkling's coach. Ivan brought me my meals, clearly disgusted at having to play nursemaid. He refused to speak to me as we rode and threatened to slow my pulse enough to send me into unconsciousness if I persisted in asking about Mal.

But I asked every day anyway and kept my eyes trained on the little crack of window visible between curtain and coach, hoping to catch a glimpse of him.

I slept poorly. Every night, I dreamed of the snowy glade, and the stag's dark eyes, staring at me in the stillness, a relentless reminder of my failure and the sorrow my mercy had reaped. The stag had died anyway, and now Mal and I were doomed. Every morning, I woke with a fresh sense of guilt and shame, but also with the frustrating feeling that I had forgotten something, some message that had been clear and obvious in the dream but that hovered just outside of understanding when I woke.

I didn't see the Darkling again until we reached the outskirts of Kribirsk, when the door to the coach suddenly opened and he slid into the seat opposite me. Ivan vanished without a word.

"Where's Mal?" I asked as soon as the door had closed.

I saw the fingers of his gloved hand clench, but when he spoke, his voice was as cold and smooth as ever. "We're entering Kribirsk," he said. "When we are greeted by the other Grisha, you will not say a word about your little excursion."

My jaw dropped. "They don't know?"

"All they know is that you've been in seclusion, preparing for your crossing of the Shadow Fold with prayer and rest."

A dry bark of laughter escaped me. "I certainly look well rested."

"I'll say you've been fasting."

"That's why none of the soldiers in Ryevost were

looking for me," I said with dawning understanding. "You never told the King."

"If word of your disappearance had got out, you would have been hunted down and killed by Fjerdan assassins within days."

"And you would have had to account for losing the kingdom's only Sun Summoner."

The Darkling studied me for a long moment. "Just what kind of life do you think you could have with him, Alina? He's *otkazat'sya*. He can never hope to understand your power, and if he did, he'd only come to fear you. There is no ordinary life for people like you and me."

"I'm nothing like you," I said flatly.

His lips curled in a tight, bitter smile. "Of course not," he said courteously. Then he knocked on the roof of the coach and it rolled to a stop. "When we arrive, you'll say your hellos, then plead exhaustion and retire to your tent. And if you do anything reckless, I will torture the tracker until he begs me to take his life."

And he was gone.

I rode the rest of the way into Kribirsk alone, trying to stop trembling. *Mal is alive*, I told myself. *That's all that matters*. But another thought crept in. *Maybe the Darkling is letting you believe he's still alive just to keep you in line*. I wrapped my arms around myself, praying that it wasn't true.

I pulled back the curtains as we rode through Kribirsk and felt a pang of sadness as I remembered walking this same road so many months ago. I'd nearly been crushed by the very coach I was riding in. Mal had saved me, and Zoya had looked at him from the window of the Summoners' coach. I'd wished to be like her, a beautiful girl in a blue *kefta*.

When we finally pulled up to the immense black silk tent, a crowd of Grisha swarmed around the coach. Marie and Ivo and Sergei rushed forward to greet me. I was surprised at how good it felt to see them again.

As they caught sight of me, their excitement vanished, replaced by worry and concern. They'd expected a triumphant Sun Summoner, wearing the greatest amplifier ever known, radiant with power and the favour of the Darkling. Instead, they saw a pale, tired girl, broken by misery.

"Are you all right?" Marie whispered when she hugged me.

"Yes," I promised. "Just worn out from the journey."

I did my best to smile convincingly and reassure them. I tried to feign enthusiasm as they marvelled at Morozova's collar and reached out to touch it.

The Darkling was never far from view, a warning in his eyes, and I kept moving through the crowd, grinning until my cheeks hurt.

As we passed through the Grisha pavilion, I caught sight of Zoya sulking on a pile of cushions. She stared greedily at the collar as I passed. *You're welcome to it*, I thought bitterly, and hurried my steps.

Ivan led me to a private tent close to the Darkling's quarters. Fresh clothes were waiting on my camp cot along with a bath of hot water and my blue *kefta*. It had only been a few weeks, but it felt strange to wear Summoners' colours again.

The Darkling's guards were stationed all around the perimeter of my tent. Only I knew they were there to monitor as well as protect me. The tent was luxuriously appointed with piles of furs, a painted table and chairs, and a Fabrikator mirror, clear as water and inlaid with gold. I would have traded it all in an instant to shiver beside Mal on a threadbare blanket.

I had no visitors, and I spent my days pacing back and forth with nothing to do but worry and imagine the worst. I didn't know why the Darkling was waiting to enter the Shadow Fold or what he might be planning, and my guards certainly weren't interested in discussing it.

On the fourth night, when the flap of my tent opened, I nearly fell off my cot. There was Genya, holding my dinner tray and looking impossibly gorgeous. I sat up, not knowing what to say.

She entered and set down the tray, hovering near the table. "I shouldn't be here," she said.

"Probably not," I admitted. "I'm not sure that I'm supposed to have visitors."

"No, I mean I shouldn't be *here*. It's incredibly dirty."

I laughed, suddenly very glad to see her. She smiled slightly and settled herself gracefully on the edge of the painted chair.

"They're saying you've been in seclusion, preparing for your ordeal," she said.

I examined Genya's face, trying to glean how much she knew. "I didn't have a chance to say goodbye before I . . . went away," I said carefully.

"If you had, I would have stopped you."

So she knew I'd run. "How's Baghra?"

"No one's seen her since you left. She seems to have gone into seclusion too."

I shuddered. I hoped that Baghra had escaped, but I knew it was unlikely. What price had the Darkling exacted for her betrayal?

I bit my lip, hesitating, and then decided to take what might be my only chance. "Genya, if I could get word to the King. I'm sure he doesn't know what the Darkling is planning. He—"

"Alina," Genya interrupted, "the King has taken ill. The Apparat is ruling in his stead."

My heart sank. I remembered what the Darkling had said the day that I'd met the Apparat: *He has his uses.*

And yet, the priest hadn't just spoken of toppling Kings, but Darklings as well. Had he been trying to warn me? If only I'd been less fearful. If only I'd been more willing to listen. More regrets to add to my long list. I didn't know if the Apparat was truly loyal to the Darkling or if he might be playing a deeper game. And now there was no way to find out.

The hope that the King might have the desire or will to oppose the Darkling had been a slim one, but it had given me something to hold on to over the last few days. Now that hope was undone too. "What about the Queen?" I asked with faint optimism.

A fierce little smile passed over Genya's lips. "The Queen is confined to her quarters. For her own safety, of course. Contagion, you know."

That was when I realised what Genya was wearing. I'd been so surprised to see her, so caught up in my own thoughts, that I hadn't really taken it in. Genya was wearing red. Corporalki red. Her cuffs were embroidered with blue, a combination I had never seen before.

A chill slid up my spine. What role had Genya played in the King's sudden illness? What had she traded to wear full Grisha colours?

"I see," I said quietly.

"I did try to warn you," she said with some sadness.

"And you know what the Darkling plans to do?"

"There are rumours," she said uncomfortably.

"They're all true."

"Then it has to be done."

I stared at her. After a moment, she looked down at her lap. Her fingers pleated and unpleated the folds of her *kefta*. "David feels terrible," she whispered. "He thinks he's destroyed all of Ravka."

"It's not his fault," I said with an empty laugh. "We all did our part to bring about the end of the world."

Genya looked up sharply. "You don't really believe that." Distress was written on her face. Was there a warning there as well?

I thought of Mal and the Darkling's threats. "No," I said hollowly. "Of course not."

I knew she didn't believe me, but her brow cleared, and she smiled her soft, beautiful smile at me. She looked like a painted icon of a Saint, her hair a burnished copper halo. She rose, and as I walked with her to the flap of the tent, the stag's dark eyes loomed up in my mind, the eyes I saw every night in my dreams.

"For what it's worth," I said, "tell David I forgive him." *And I forgive you too*, I added silently. I meant it. I knew what it was to want to belong.

"I will," she said quietly. She turned and disappeared into the night, but not before I saw that her lovely eyes were full of tears.

Chapter 21

I picked at my dinner and then lay down on my cot again, turning over the things that Genya had said. Genya had spent nearly her entire life cloistered away in Os Alta, existing uneasily between the world of the Grisha and the intrigues of the court. The Darkling had put her in that position for his own gain, and now he had raised her out of it. She would never again have to bend to the whim of the King and Queen or wear a servant's colours. But David had regrets. And if he did, maybe others did too. Maybe there would be more when the Darkling unleashed the Shadow Fold's power. Though by then, it might be too late.

My thoughts were interrupted by Ivan's arrival at the entrance to my tent.

"Up," he commanded. "He wants to see you."

My stomach twisted nervously, but I got up and followed him. As soon as we stepped out of the tent, we were flanked by guards who escorted us the short distance to the Darkling's quarters.

When they saw Ivan, the *oprichniki* at the entryway stepped aside. Ivan nodded towards the tent.

"Go on," he said with a smirk. I desperately wanted to smack that knowing look right off his face. Instead, I lifted my chin and strode past him.

The heavy silks slid closed behind me, and I took a few steps forward, then paused to get my bearings. The tent was large and lit by dimly glowing lamps. The floor was covered in rugs and furs, and at its centre burned a fire that crackled in a large silver dish. High above it, a flap in the roof of the tent allowed the smoke to escape and showed a patch of the night sky.

The Darkling sat in a large chair, his long legs sprawled out before him, staring into the fire, a glass in his hand and a bottle of *kvas* on the table beside him.

Without looking at me, he gestured to the chair across from him. I walked over to the fire, but I did not sit. He glanced at me with faint exasperation and then looked back into the flames.

"Sit down, Alina."

I perched on the edge of the chair, watching him warily.

"Speak," he said. I was starting to feel like a dog.

"I have nothing to say."

"I imagine you have a great deal to say."

"If I tell you to stop, you won't stop. If I tell you you're mad, you won't believe me. Why should I bother?"

"Maybe because you want the boy to live."

All of the breath went out of me and I had to stifle a sob. Mal was alive. The Darkling might be lying, but I didn't think so. He loved power, and Mal's life gave him power over me.

"Tell me what to say to save him," I whispered, leaning forward. "Tell me, and I'll say it."

"He's a traitor and a deserter."

"He's the best tracker you have or ever will have."

"Possibly," said the Darkling with an indifferent

shrug. But I knew him better now, and I saw the flicker of greed in his eyes as he tilted his head back to empty his glass of *kvas*. I knew what it cost him to think of destroying something he might acquire and use. I pressed this small advantage.

"You could exile him, send him north to the permafrost until you need him."

"You'd have him spend the rest of his life in a work camp or a prison?"

I swallowed the lump in my throat. "Yes."

"You think you'll find a way to him, don't you?" he asked, his voice bemused. "You think that somehow, if he's alive, you'll find a way." He shook his head and gave a short laugh. "I've given you power beyond all dreaming, and you can't wait to run off and keep house for your tracker."

I knew I should stay silent, play the diplomat, but I couldn't help myself. "You haven't given me anything. You've made me a slave."

"That's never what I intended, Alina." He ran a hand over his jaw, his expression fatigued, frustrated, human. But how much of it was real and how much was pretence? "I couldn't take chances," he said. "Not with the power of the stag, not with Ravka's future hanging in the balance."

"Don't pretend this is about Ravka's welfare. You lied to me. You've been lying to me since the moment I met you."

His long fingers tightened around the glass. "Did you deserve my trust?" he asked, and for once, his voice was less than steady and cold. "Baghra whispers a few accusations in your ear, and off you go. Did you ever stop to think of what it would mean for me, for all of Ravka, if you just disappeared?"

"You didn't give me much choice."

"Of course you had a choice. And you chose to turn your back on your country, on everything that you are."

"That isn't fair."

"Fairness!" he laughed. "Still she talks of fairness. What does fairness have to do with any of this? The people curse my name and pray for you, but you're the one who was ready to abandon them. I'm the one who will give them power over their enemies. I'm the one who will free them from the tyranny of the King."

"And give them your tyranny in return."

"Someone has to lead, Alina. Someone has to end this. Believe me, I wish there were another way."

He sounded so sincere, so reasonable, less a creature of relentless ambition than a man who believed he was doing the right thing for his people. Despite all he'd done and all he intended, I did almost believe him. Almost.

I gave a single shake of my head.

He slumped back in his chair. "Fine," he said with a weary shrug. "Make me your villain." He set his empty glass down and stood. "Come here."

Fear shot through me, but I made myself rise and close the distance between us. He studied me in the firelight. He reached out and touched Morozova's collar, letting his long fingers spread over the rough bone, then slide up my neck to cradle my face with one hand. I felt a jolt of revulsion, but I also felt the sure, intoxicating force of him. I hated that it still had an effect on me.

"You betrayed me," he said softly.

I wanted to laugh. *I* had betrayed *him*? He had used me, seduced me, and now enslaved me, and I was the betrayer? But I thought of Mal and swallowed my anger and my pride. "Yes," I said. "I'm sorry for that."

He laughed. "You're not sorry for any of it. The only thought you have is for the boy and his miserable life."

I said nothing.

"Tell me," he said, his grip tightening painfully, his fingertips pressing into my flesh. In the firelight, his gaze looked unfathomably bleak. "Tell me how much you love him. Beg for his life."

"Please," I whispered, fighting the tears that welled in my eyes. "Please spare him."

"Why?"

"Because the collar can't give you what you want," I said recklessly. I had only one thing with which to bargain and it was so little, but I pressed on. "I have no choice but to serve you, but if Mal comes to harm, I will never forgive you. I will fight you any way that I can. I will spend every waking minute looking for a way to end my life, and eventually, I'll succeed. But show him mercy, let him live, and I will serve you gladly. I will spend the rest of my days proving my gratitude." I nearly choked out the last word.

He cocked his head to one side, a small, skeptical smile playing about his lips. Then the smile disappeared, replaced by something I didn't recognise, something that looked almost like longing.

"Mercy." He said the word as if he were tasting something unfamiliar. "I could be merciful." He raised his other hand to cup my face and kissed me softly, gently, and though everything in me rebelled, I let him. I hated him. I feared him. But still I felt the strange tug of his power, and I couldn't stop the hungry response of my own treacherous heart.

He pulled away and looked at me. Then, his eyes locked on mine, he called for Ivan.

"Take her to the cells," the Darkling said when Ivan appeared in the doorway of the tent. "Let her see her tracker."

A sliver of hope entered my heart.

"Yes, Alina," he said, stroking my cheek. "I can be merciful." He leaned forward, pulling me close, his lips brushing my ear. "Tomorrow, we enter the Shadow Fold," he whispered, his voice like a caress. "And when we do, I will feed your friend to the volcra, and you will watch him die."

"No!" I cried, recoiling in horror. I tried to pull away from him, but his grip was like steel, his fingers digging into my skull. "You said—"

"You may say your goodbyes tonight. That is all the mercy traitors deserve."

Something broke loose inside me. I lunged at him, clawing at him, screaming my hate. Ivan was on me in moments, holding me tight as I thrashed and strained in his arms.

"Murderer!" I shouted. "Monster!"

"All of those things."

"I hate you," I spat.

He shrugged. "You'll tire of hate soon enough. You'll tire of everything." He smiled then, and behind his eyes I saw the same bleak and yawning chasm I had seen in Baghra's ancient gaze. "You will wear that collar for the rest of your very, very long life, Alina. Fight me as long as you're able. You will find I have far more practice with eternity."

He waved his hand dismissively, and Ivan pulled me

from the tent and down the path, still struggling. A sob tore from my throat. The tears I had fought to hold back during my conversation with the Darkling gave way and streamed unchecked down my cheeks.

"Stop that," Ivan whispered furiously. "Someone will see you."

"I don't care."

The Darkling was going to kill Mal anyway. What difference did it make who saw my misery now? The reality of Mal's death and the Darkling's cruelty were staring me in the face, and I saw the stark and horrible shape of things to come.

Ivan yanked me into my tent and gave me a rough shake. "Do you want to see the tracker or not? I'm not going to march a weeping girl through camp."

I pressed my hands against my eyes and stifled my sobs.

"Better," he said. "Put this on." He tossed me a long brown cloak. I slipped it over my *kefta*, and he yanked the large hood up. "Keep your head down and stay quiet, or I swear I'll drag you right back here and you can say your goodbyes on the Fold. Understand?"

I nodded.

We followed an unlit path that skirted the perimeter of the camp. My guards kept their distance, walking far ahead and far behind us, and I quickly realised that Ivan did not want anyone to recognise me or to know that I was visiting the gaol.

As we walked between the barracks and tents, I could sense a strange tension crackling through the camp. The soldiers we passed seemed jumpy, and a few glared at Ivan with blatant hostility. I wondered how the First

Army felt about the Apparat's sudden rise to power.

The gaol was located on the far side of camp. It was an older building, clearly from a time predating the barracks that surrounded it. Bored guards flanked the entrance.

"New prisoner?" one of them asked Ivan.

"A visitor."

"Since when do you escort visitors to the cells?"

"Since tonight," Ivan said, a dangerous edge to his voice.

The guards exchanged a nervous glance and stepped aside. "No need to get antsy, bloodletter."

Ivan led me down a hallway lined with mostly empty cells. I saw a few ragged men, a drunk snoring soundly on the floor of his cell. At the end of the hall, Ivan unlocked a gate, and we descended a set of rickety stairs to a dark, windowless room lit by a single guttering lamp. In the gloom, I could make out the heavy iron bars of the room's only cell and, sitting slumped by its far wall, its only prisoner.

"Mal?" I whispered.

In seconds, he was on his feet and we were clinging to each other through the iron bars, our hands clasped tightly together. I couldn't stop the sobs that shook me.

"Shhhh. It's okay. Alina, it's okay."

"You have the night," said Ivan, and disappeared back up the stairs. When we heard the outer gate clang shut, Mal turned to me.

His eyes roved over my face. "I can't believe he let you come."

Fresh tears spilled over my cheeks. "Mal, he let me come because . . ."

"When?" he asked hoarsely.

"Tomorrow. On the Shadow Fold."

He swallowed, and I could see him struggle with the knowledge, but all he said was, "All right."

I let out a sound that was half laugh, half sob. "Only you could contemplate imminent death and just say 'all right'."

He smiled at me and pushed the hair back from my tear-stained face. "How about 'oh no'?"

"Mal, if I'd been stronger . . ."

"If I'd been stronger, I would have driven a knife through your heart."

"I wish you had," I muttered.

"Well, I don't."

I looked down at our clasped hands. "Mal, what the Darkling said in the glade about . . . about him and me. I didn't . . . I never . . ."

"It doesn't matter."

I looked up at him. "It doesn't?"

"No," he said, a little too fiercely.

"I don't think I believe you."

"So maybe I don't believe it yet either, not completely, but it's the truth." He clutched my hands more tightly, holding them close to his heart. "I don't care if you danced naked on the roof of the Little Palace with him. I love you, Alina, even the part of you that loved him."

I wanted to deny it, to erase it, but I couldn't. Another sob shook me. "I hate that I ever thought . . . that I ever—"

"Do you blame me for every mistake I made? For every girl I tumbled? For every dumb thing I've said? Because if we start running tallies on stupid, you know who's going to come out ahead."

"No, I don't blame you." I managed a small smile. "Much."

He grinned and my heart flip-flopped the way it always had. "We found our way back to each other, Alina. That's all that matters."

He kissed me through the bars, the cold iron pressing against my cheek as his lips met mine.

We stayed together that last night. We talked about the orphanage, the angry rasp of Ana Kuya's voice, the taste of stolen cherry cordial, the smell of the new-mown grass in our meadow, how we'd suffered in the heat of summer and sought out the cool comfort of the music room's marble floors, the journey we'd made together on the way to do our military service, the Suli violins we'd heard on our first night away from the only home either of us could remember.

I told him the story of the day I'd been mending pottery with one of the maids in the kitchen at Keramzin, waiting for him to return from one of the hunting trips that had taken him from home more and more frequently. I'd been fifteen, standing at the worktop, vainly trying to glue together the jagged pieces of a blue cup. When I saw him crossing the fields, I ran to the doorway and waved. He caught sight of me and broke into a jog.

I had crossed the yard to him slowly, watching him draw closer, baffled by the way my heart was skittering around in my chest. Then he'd picked me up and spun me in a circle, and I'd clung to him, breathing in his sweet, familiar smell, shocked by how much I'd missed him. Dimly, I'd been aware that I still had a shard of the blue cup in my hand, that it was digging into my palm, but I didn't want to let go.

When he'd finally set me down and ambled off to the kitchen to find his lunch, I had stood there, my palm dripping blood, my head still spinning, knowing that everything had changed.

Ana Kuya had scolded me for getting blood on the clean kitchen floor. She'd bandaged my hand and told me it would heal. But I knew it would just go on hurting.

In the creaking silence of the cell, Mal kissed the scar on my palm, the wound made so long ago by the edge of that broken cup, a fragile thing I'd thought beyond repair.

We fell asleep on the floor, cheeks pressed together through the bars, hands clasped tight. I didn't want to sleep. I wanted to savour every last moment with him. But I must have dozed off because I dreamed again of the stag. This time, Mal was beside me in the glade, and it was his blood in the snow.

The next thing I knew, I was waking to the sound of the gate being opened above us and Ivan's footsteps on the stairs.

Mal had made me promise not to cry. He'd said it would only make it harder on him. So I swallowed my tears. I kissed him one last time and let Ivan lead me away.

Chapter 22

Dawn was creeping over Kribirsk as Ivan brought me back to my tent. I sat down on my cot and stared unseeingly at the room. My limbs felt strangely heavy, my mind a blank. I was still sitting there when Genya arrived.

She helped me wash my face and change into the black *kefta* I'd worn to the winter fete. I looked down at the silk and thought of tearing it to shreds, but somehow I couldn't manage to move. My hands stayed limp at my sides.

Genya steered me into the painted chair. I sat still as she arranged my hair, piling it onto my head in loops and coils that she secured with golden pins, the better to show off Morozova's collar.

When she had finished, she pressed her cheek against mine and led me to Ivan, placing my hand on his arm like a bride. Not a word had passed between us.

Ivan led me to the Grisha tent, where I took my place at the Darkling's side. I knew that my friends were watching me, whispering, wondering what was the matter. They probably thought I was nervous about entering the Fold. They were wrong. I wasn't nervous or frightened. I wasn't anything.

The Grisha followed us in an ordered processional all

the way to the dry docks. There, only a select few were permitted to board the sand skiff. It was larger than any I'd seen and equipped with three enormous sails emblazoned with the Darkling's symbol. I scanned the crowd of soldiers and Grisha on the skiff. I knew Mal must be on board somewhere, but I couldn't see him.

The Darkling and I were escorted to the front of the skiff, where I was introduced to a group of elaborately dressed men with blond beards and piercing blue eyes. With a start, I realised they were Fjerdan ambassadors. Beside them, in crimson silks, stood a delegation from the Shu Han, and next to them, a group of Kerch tradesmen in shortcoats with curiously belled sleeves. An envoy of the King stood with them in full military dress, his pale blue sash bearing a golden double eagle, a stern expression on his weathered countenance.

I studied them curiously. This must be why the Darkling had delayed our trip into the Fold. He'd needed time to assemble the proper audience, witnesses who would attest to his newfound power. But just how far did he intend to go? A feeling of foreboding stirred inside me, disturbing the lovely numbness that had held me in its grip all morning.

The skiff shuddered and began to slide over the grass and into the eerie black mist of the Fold. Three Summoners raised their arms and the great sails snapped forward, swelling with wind.

The first time I'd entered the Fold, I'd feared the darkness and my own death. Now, darkness was nothing to me, and I knew that soon death would seem like a gift. I'd always known I would have to return to the Unsea, but as I looked back, I realised that some part of me had anticipated it. I had welcomed the chance to prove myself and – I cringed when I thought of it – to please the Darkling. I had dreamed of this moment, standing by his side. I had wanted to believe in the destiny he'd laid out for me, that the orphan no one wanted would change the world and be adored for it.

The Darkling stared ahead, radiating confidence and ease. The sun flickered and began to disappear from view. A moment later, we were in darkness.

For a long while, we drifted in the black, the Grisha Squallers driving the skiffs forward over the sand.

Then, the Darkling's voice rang out. "Burn."

Huge clouds of flame burst from the Inferni on either side of the skiff, briefly illuminating the sky. The ambassadors and even the guards around me stirred nervously. The Darkling was announcing our location, calling the volcra directly to us.

It didn't take long for them to answer, and a tremor ran up my spine as I heard the distant beat of leathery wings. I felt fear spread through the passengers on the skiff and heard the Fjerdans begin to pray in their lilting tongue. In the flare of Grisha fire, I saw the dim shapes of dark bodies flying towards us. The volcras' shrieks split the air.

The guards reached for their rifles. Someone began to weep. But still the Darkling waited as the volcra drew closer.

Baghra had claimed that the volcra had once been men and women, victims of the unnatural power unleashed by the Darkling's greed. It might have been my mind playing tricks, but I thought I heard something not just horrible, but human in their cries.

When they were almost upon us, the Darkling gripped my arm and simply said, "Now."

That invisible hand took hold of the power inside me, and I felt it stretch, reaching through the darkness of the Fold, seeking the light. It came to me with a speed and fury that nearly knocked me from my feet, breaking over me in a shower of brilliance and warmth.

The Fold was alight, as bright as noon, as if its impenetrable darkness had never been. I saw a long reach of blanched sand, hulks of what looked like shipwrecks dotting the dead landscape, and above it all, a teeming flock of volcra. They screamed in terror, their writhing grey bodies gruesome in the bright sunlight. *This is the truth of him*, I thought as I squinted in the dazzling light. *Like calls to like.* This was his soul made flesh, the truth of him laid bare in the blazing sun, shorn of mystery and shadow. This was the truth behind the handsome face and the miraculous powers, the truth that was the dead and empty space between the stars, a wasteland peopled by frightened monsters.

Make a path. I wasn't sure if he had spoken or thought the command that reverberated through me. Helpless, I let the Fold close in around us as I focused the light, making a channel through which the skiff could pass, bordered on both sides by walls of rippling darkness. The volcra fled into the dark, and I could hear them crying in rage and confusion as if from behind an impenetrable curtain.

We sped over the colourless sands, the sunlight spreading in glimmering waves before us. Far ahead, I saw a flash of green, and I realised I was seeing the other side of the Shadow Fold. We were looking into West

Ravka, and as we drew closer, I saw their meadow, their dry docks, the village of Novokribirsk nestled behind it. The towers of Os Kervo gleamed in the distance. Was it my imagination, or could I smell the salt tang of the True Sea on the air?

People were streaming from the village and crowding onto the dry docks, pointing at the light that had split the Fold open before them. I saw children playing in the grass. I could hear the dockworkers calling to each other.

At a signal from the Darkling, the skiff slowed, and he lifted his arms. I felt a spike of horror as I understood what was about to happen.

"They're your own people!" I cried desperately.

He ignored me and brought his hands together with a sound like a clap of thunder.

It all seemed to happen slowly. Darkness rippled out from his hands. When it met the darkness of the Fold, a rumbling sound rose up out of the dead sands. The black walls of the path I'd created pulsed and swelled. *It's like it's breathing*, I thought in terror.

The rumble grew to a roar. The Fold shook and trembled around us and then burst forward in a terrible cascading tide.

A frightened wail went up from the crowd on the docks as darkness rushed towards them. They ran, and I saw their fear, heard their screams as the black fabric of the Fold crashed over the dry docks and the village like a breaking wave. Darkness enveloped them, and the volcra set upon their new prey. A woman carrying a little boy stumbled, trying to outrun the grasping dark, but it swallowed her too.

I reached inside myself desperately, trying to expand

the light, to drive the volcra off, to offer some kind of protection. But I could do nothing. My power slid away, pulled from me by that invisible, taunting hand. I wished for a knife to drive into the Darkling's heart, into my own heart, anything that would make this stop.

The Darkling turned to look at the ambassadors and the King's envoy. Their faces were identical masks of horror and shock. Whatever he saw there must have satisfied him, because he separated his hands and the darkness stopped pushing forward. The rumbling faded.

I could hear the anguished cries of those lost in the dark, the shrieks of the volcra, the sounds of rifle fire. The dry docks were gone. The village of Novokribirsk was gone. We were staring into the new reaches of the Fold.

The message was clear: today it had been West Ravka. Tomorrow, the Darkling could just as easily push the Fold north to Fjerda or south to the Shu Han. It would devour whole countries and drive the Darkling's enemies into the sea. How many deaths had I just helped to bring about? How many more would I be responsible for?

Close the path, commanded the Darkling. I had no choice but to obey. I pulled the light back until it rested around the skiff like a glowing dome.

"What have you done?" whispered the envoy, his voice shaking.

The Darkling turned on him. "Do you need to see more?"

"You were meant to undo this abomination, not enlarge it! You've slaughtered Ravkans! The King will never stand—"

"The King will do as he's told, or I'll march the Shadow Fold to the walls of Os Alta itself."

The envoy sputtered, his mouth opening and closing soundlessly. The Darkling turned to the ambassadors. "I think you understand me now. There are no Ravkans, no Fjerdans, no Kerch, no Shu Han. There are no more borders, and there will be no more wars. From now on, there is only the land inside the Fold and outside of it, and there will be peace."

"Peace on your terms," said one of the Shu Han angrily.

"It will not stand," blustered a Fjerdan.

The Darkling looked them over and said very calmly, "Peace on my terms. Or your precious mountains and your saintsforsaken tundra will simply cease to exist."

With crushing certainty, I understood that he meant every word. The ambassadors might hope it was an empty threat, believe that there were limits to his hunger, but they would learn soon enough. The Darkling would not hesitate. He would not grieve. His darkness would consume the world, and he would never waver.

The Darkling turned his back on their stunned and angry expressions and addressed the Grisha and soldiers on the skiff. "Tell the story of what you've seen today. Tell everyone that the days of fear and uncertainty are over. The days of endless fighting are over. Tell them that you saw a new age begin."

A cheer went up from the crowd. I saw a few soldiers muttering to each other. Even some of the Grisha looked unnerved. But most of their faces were eager, triumphant, shining.

They're hungry for this, I realised. Even after they've seen what he can do, even after watching their own people die. The Darkling wasn't just offering them an end to war, but an end to weakness. After all these long years of terror and suffering, he would give them something that had seemed permanently beyond their grasp: victory. And despite their fear, they loved him for it.

The Darkling signalled to Ivan, who stood behind him, waiting for orders. "Bring me the prisoner."

I looked up sharply, a fresh bolt of fear shooting through me as Mal was led through the crowd to the railing, his hands bound.

"We return to Ravka," said the Darkling. "But the traitor stays."

Before I even knew what was happening, Ivan shoved Mal over the edge of the skiff. The volcra screeched and beat their wings. I ran to the railing. Mal was on his side in the sand, still within the protective circle of my light. He spat sand from his mouth and pushed himself up with his bound hands.

"Mal!" I cried.

Without thinking, I turned on Ivan and punched him hard in the jaw. He stumbled back against the railing, stunned, and then lunged at me. *Good*, I thought as he grabbed me. *Throw me over too.*

"Hold," said the Darkling, his voice like ice. Ivan scowled, his face red with embarrassment and anger. He relaxed his grip but didn't let go.

I could see the confusion of the people on the skiff. They didn't know what this show was about, why the Darkling was troubling with a deserter or why his most valued Grisha had just punched his second in command.

Pull it back. The command rang through me and I looked at the Darkling in horror.

"No!" I said. But I couldn't stop it; the dome of light began to contract. Mal looked at me as the circle shrank closer to the skiff, and if Ivan hadn't been holding me, the look of regret and love in his blue eyes would have sent me to my knees. I fought with everything I had, every bit of strength, everything Baghra had taught me, and it was nothing in the face of the Darkling's power over me. The light inched closer to the skiff.

I gripped the railing and cried out in rage, in misery, the tears streaming down my cheeks. Mal was standing at the edge of the gleaming circle now. I could see the shapes of the volcra in the swirling dark, feel the beat of their wings. He could have run, could have wept, could have clung to the sides of the skiff until the darkness took him, but he did none of those things. He stood unflinching before the gathering dark.

Only I had the power to save him – and I was powerless to save him. In the next breath, the darkness swallowed him. I heard him scream. The memory of the stag reared up before me, so vivid that for a moment the snowy glade swam in my vision, the image of it transposed over the barren landscape of the Fold. I smelled the pines, felt the chill air on my cheeks. I remembered the stag's dark, liquid eyes, the plume of his breath in the cold night, the moment when I knew that I would not take his life. And finally, I understood why the stag had come to me every night in my dreams.

I'd thought the stag was haunting me, a reminder of my failure and the price my weakness would exact. But I was wrong.

The stag had been showing me my strength – not just the price of mercy but the power it bestowed. And mercy was something the Darkling would never understand.

I had spared the stag's life. The power of that life belonged to me as surely as it belonged to the man who had taken it.

I gasped as understanding flooded through me, and I felt that invisible grip falter. My power slid back into my hands. Once more, I stood in Baghra's hut, calling the light for the first time, feeling it rush towards me, taking possession of what was rightfully mine. This was what I had been born for. I would never let anyone separate me from it again.

Light exploded from me, pure and unwavering, flooding over the dark place where Mal had stood only moments before. The volcra that had hold of him shrieked and released its grip. Mal fell to his knees, blood streaming from his wounds as my light enveloped him and drove the volcra back into the darkness.

The Darkling looked momentarily confused. He narrowed his eyes, and I felt his will descend on me again, felt that invisible hand grasping. I shrugged it off. It was nothing. He was nothing.

"What is this?" he hissed. He raised his hands and skeins of darkness spooled towards me, but with a flick of my hand, they burned away like mist.

The Darkling advanced, his handsome features contorted with fury. My mind was working frantically. I knew he would have liked to kill me where I stood, but he couldn't, not with the volcra circling outside the light that only I could provide.

"Seize her!" he shouted to the guards surrounding us. Ivan reached out.

I felt the weight of the collar around my neck, the

steady rhythm of the stag's ancient heart beating in time with mine. My power rose up in me, solid and without hesitation, a sword in my hand.

I lifted my arm and slashed. With an ear-splitting crack, one of the skiff's masts split in two. People bleated in panic and scattered as the broken mast fell to the deck, the thick wood gleaming with burning light. Shock registered on the Darkling's face.

"The Cut!" Ivan gasped, taking a step backwards.

"Don't come any closer," I warned.

"You aren't a murderer, Alina," said the Darkling.

"I think the Ravkans I just helped you slaughter would disagree."

Panic was spreading through the skiff. The *oprichniki* looked wary, but they were closing in on me just the same.

"You saw what he did to those people!" I cried to the guards and Grisha around me. "Is that the future you want? A world of darkness? A world remade in his image?" I saw their confusion, their anger and fear. "It's not too late to stop him! Help me," I begged. "Please, help me."

But no one moved. Soldier and Grisha alike stood frozen on the deck. They were all too afraid, afraid of him and afraid of a world without his protection.

The *oprichniki* inched closer. I had to make a choice. Mal and I wouldn't have another chance.

So be it, I thought.

I glanced over my shoulder, hoping Mal understood, and then I dived for the side of the skiff.

"Don't let her reach the railing!" the Darkling shouted.

The guards surged towards me. And I let the light go out.

We were plunged into darkness. People wailed and, above us, I heard the volcra screeching. My outstretched hands struck the railing. I ducked under it and hurled myself onto the sand, rolling to my feet and running blindly towards Mal as I threw the light ahead of me in an arc.

Behind me, I heard the sounds of slaughter on the skiff as the volcra attacked and clouds of Grisha flame exploded in the darkness. But I couldn't stop to think of the people I'd left behind.

My arc of light flashed over Mal, crouched in the sand. The volcra looming above him screeched and whirled away into the dark. I sprinted to him and pulled him to his feet.

A bullet pinged against the sand beside us and I plunged us into darkness again.

"Hold your fire!" I heard the Darkling shouting over the chaos on the skiff. "We need her alive!"

I threw out another arc of light, scattering the volcra that were hovering around us.

"You can't run from me, Alina!" the Darkling shouted.

I couldn't let him come after us. I couldn't take the chance that he might survive. But I hated what I had to do. The others on the skiff had failed to come to my aid, but did they deserve to be abandoned to the volcra?

"You can't leave us all here to die, Alina!" the Darkling shouted. "If you take this step, you know where it will lead."

I felt a hysterical laugh burble up inside me. I knew. I knew it would make me more like him.

"You begged me for clemency once," he called over the dead reaches of the Fold, over the hungry shrieks of the horrors he had made. "Is this your idea of mercy?"

Another bullet hit the sand, only inches from us. *Yes*, I thought as the power rose up inside me, *the mercy you taught me.*

I raised my hand and brought it down in a blazing arc, slashing through the air. An earth-shaking *crack* echoed through the Fold as the sand skiff split in half. Raw screams filled the air and the volcra shrieked in their frenzy.

I grabbed Mal's arm and threw a dome of light around us. We ran, stumbling into the darkness, and soon the sounds of battle faded as we left the monsters behind.

We emerged from the Fold somewhere south of Novokribirsk and took our first steps in West Ravka. The afternoon sun was bright, the meadow grass green and sweet, but we didn't stop to savour any of it. We were tired, hungry and wounded, but our enemies wouldn't rest, and neither could we.

We walked until we found cover in an orchard and hid there until dark, afraid of being spotted and remembered. The air was thick with the smell of apple blossoms, but the fruit was far too small and green to eat.

There was a bucket full of fetid rainwater sitting beneath our tree, and we used it to wash the worst stains from Mal's bloodied shirt. He tried not to wince as he pulled the torn fabric over his head, but there was no disguising the deep wounds the volcra's claws had left across the smooth skin of his shoulder and back.

When night came, we began our trek to the coast. Briefly, I'd worried that we might be lost. But even in a strange country, Mal found the way.

Shortly before dawn, we crested a hill and saw the broad sweep of Alkhem Bay and the glittering lights of Os Kervo below us. We knew we should get off the road. It would soon be bustling with tradesmen and travellers who were sure to notice a cut-up tracker and a girl in a black *kefta*. But we couldn't resist our first glimpse of the True Sea.

The sun rose at our backs, pink light gleaming off the city's slender towers then splintering gold on the waters of the bay. I saw the sprawl of the port, the great ships bobbing in the harbour, and beyond that blue, and blue, and blue again. The sea seemed to go on forever, stretching into an impossibly distant horizon. I had seen plenty of maps. I knew there was land out there somewhere, beyond long weeks of travel and miles of ocean. But I still had the dizzying sense that we were standing at the edge of the world. A breeze came in off the water, carrying the smell of salt and damp, the faint cries of gulls.

"There's just so much of it," I said at last.

Mal nodded. Then he turned to me and smiled. "A good place to hide."

He reached out and slid his hand into my hair. He pulled one of the gold pins from the tangled waves. I felt a curl slide free and slither down my neck.

"For clothes," he said as he dropped the pin into his pocket.

A day ago, Genya had placed those golden pins in my

hair. I would never see her again, never see any of them. My heart twisted. I didn't know if Genya had ever really been my friend, but I would miss her just the same.

Mal left me waiting a little way off the road, hidden in a stand of trees. We'd agreed it would be safer for him to enter Os Kervo by himself, but it was hard to watch him go. He'd told me to rest, but once he was gone, I couldn't seem to find sleep. I could still feel power thrumming through my body, the echo of what I'd done on the Fold. My hand strayed to the collar at my neck. I'd never felt anything like it, and some part of me wanted to feel it again.

And what about the people you left there? said a voice in my head that I desperately wanted to ignore. Ambassadors, soldiers, Grisha. I had as good as doomed them all, and I couldn't even be sure that the Darkling was dead. Had he been torn apart by volcra? Had the lost men and women of the Tula Valley finally had their revenge on the Black Heretic? Or was he, at this very moment, hurtling towards me over the dead reaches of the Unsea, ready to bring down his own kind of reckoning?

I shuddered and paced, flinching at every sound.

By late afternoon, I was convinced that Mal had been identified and captured. When I heard footsteps and saw his familiar form emerge through the trees, I nearly sobbed with relief.

"Any trouble?" I asked shakily, trying to hide my nerves.

"None," he said. "I've never seen a city so crowded with people. No one even gave me a second glance."

He wore a new shirt and an ill-fitting coat, and his

arms were laden with clothes for me: a sack-like dress in a red so faded it looked almost orange and a nubbly mustard-coloured coat. He handed them to me and then tactfully turned his back so that I could change.

I fumbled with the tiny black buttons of the *kefta*. There seemed to be a thousand of them. When the silk finally slid over my shoulders and pooled at my feet, I felt a great burden lift from me. The cool spring air pricked my bare skin and, for the first time, I dared to hope that we might really be free. I quashed that thought. Until I knew the Darkling was dead, I would never draw an easy breath.

I pulled on the rough wool dress and the yellow coat. "Did you deliberately buy the ugliest clothes you could find?"

Mal turned to look at me and couldn't restrain a smile. "I bought the *first* clothes I could find," he said. Then his grin faded. He touched my cheek lightly, and when he spoke again, his voice was low and raw. "I never want to see you in black again."

I held his gaze. "Never," I whispered.

He reached into his coat pocket and pulled out a long red scarf. Gently, he wrapped it around my neck, hiding Morozova's collar. "There," he said, smiling again. "Perfect."

"What am I going to do when summer comes?" I laughed.

"By then we'll have found a way to get rid of it."

"No!" I said sharply, surprised by how much the idea upset me. Mal recoiled, taken aback. "We can't get rid of it," I explained. "It's Ravka's only chance to be free of the Shadow Fold."

It was the truth – just not all of it. We did need the collar. It was insurance against the Darkling's strength and a promise that someday we'd return to Ravka and find a way to set things right. But what I couldn't tell Mal was that the collar *belonged* to me, that the stag's power felt like a part of me now, and I wasn't sure I wanted to let it go.

Mal studied me, his brow furrowed. I thought of the Darkling's warnings, of the bleak look I'd seen in his face and in Baghra's.

"Alina . . ."

I tried for a reassuring smile. "We'll get rid of it," I promised. "As soon as we can."

Seconds passed. "All right," he said at last, but his expression was still wary. Then, he pushed the crumpled *kefta* with the toe of his boot. "What should we do with this?"

I looked down at the heap of tattered silk and felt anger and shame roll over me.

"Burn it," I said. And we did.

As the flames consumed the silk, Mal slowly pulled the rest of the golden pins from my curls, one by one, until my hair tumbled around my shoulders. Gently, he pushed my hair aside and kissed my neck, right above the collar. When the tears came, he pulled me close and held me, until there was nothing left but ashes.

After

The boy and the girl stand at the railing of the ship, a true ship that rolls and rocks on the heaving back of the True Sea.

"*Goed morgen, fentomen!*" a deckhand shouts to them as he passes by, his arms full of rope.

All the ship's crew call them *fentomen*. It is the Kerch word for ghosts.

When the girl asks the quartermaster why, he laughs and says it's because they are so pale and because of the way they stand silent at the ship's railing, staring at the sea for hours, as if they'd never seen water before. She smiles and does not tell him the truth: that they must keep their eyes on the horizon. They are watching for a ship with black sails.

Baghra's *Verloren* was long gone, so they had hidden in the slums of Os Kervo until the boy could use the gold pins from her hair to book passage on another ship. The city buzzed with the horror of what had happened in Novokribirsk. Some blamed the Darkling. Others blamed the Shu Han or Fjerdans. A few even claimed it was the righteous work of angry Saints.

Rumours began to reach them of strange happenings in Ravka. They heard that the Apparat had disappeared, that foreign troops were massing on the borders, that the

First and Second Armies were threatening to go to war with each other, that the Sun Summoner was dead. They waited to hear word of the Darkling's death on the Fold, but it never came.

At night, the boy and the girl lie curled around each other in the belly of the ship. He holds her tight when she wakes from another nightmare, her teeth chattering, her ears ringing with the terrified screams of the men and women she left behind on the broken skiff, her limbs trembling with remembered power.

"It's all right," he whispers in the darkness. "It's all right."

She wants to believe him, but she's afraid to close her eyes.

The wind creaks in the sails. The ship sighs around them. They are alone again, as they were when they were young, hiding from the older children, from Ana Kuya's temper, from the things that seemed to move and slither in the dark.

They are orphans again, with no true home but each other and whatever life they can make together on the other side of the sea.

Acknowledgments

Thanks to my agent and champion, Joanna Stampfel-Volpe. I feel lucky every day to have her on my side, as well as the wonderful team at Nancy Coffey Literary: Nancy, Sara Kendall, Kathleen Ortiz, Jaqueline Murphy and Pouya Shahbazian.

My sharp-eyed and intuitive editor, Noa Wheeler, believed in this story and knew exactly how to make it better. Many thanks to the remarkable people at Holt Children's and Macmillan: Laura Godwin, Jean Feiwel, Rich Deas and April Ward in design, and Karen Frangipane, Kathryn Bhunida and Lizzy Mason in marketing and publicity. I'd also like to thank Dan Farley and Joy Dallanegra-Sanger. *Shadow & Bone / The Gathering Dark* could not have found a better home.

I'm grateful to everyone at Orion and Indigo who helped bring the Grisha Trilogy to the UK including Fiona Kennedy, Jenny Glencross and Nina Douglas.

My generous readers, Michelle Chihara and Josh Kamensky, lent me their supergenius brains and cheered me on with relentless enthusiasm and patience. Thanks also to my brother Shem for his art and long-distance hugs, Miriam "Sis" Pastan, Heather Joy Kamensky, Peter Bibring, Tracey Taylor, the Apocalypsies (especially Lynne Kelly, Gretchen McNeil and Sarah J. Maas, who gave me my first review), my fellow WOART Leslie Blanco, Johannah Playford, and Dan Moulder, who was lost to the river.

I blame Gamynne Guillote for fostering my megalomania and encouraging my love of villains, Josh Minuto for introducing me to epic fantasy and making me believe in heroes, and Rachel Tejada for way too many late-night movies. Hedwig Aerts, my fellow pirate queen, put up with long hours of late-night typing. Erdene Ukhaasai diligently translated Russian and Mongolian for me over Facebook. Morgan Fahey kept me in cocktails, conversation and delicious fiction. Dan Braun and Michael Pessah kept the beat.

Many books helped to inspire Ravka and bring it to life, including *Natasha's Dance: A Cultural History of Russia*, by Orlando Figes; *Land of the Firebird: The Beauty of Old Russia*, by Suzanne Massie; and *Russian Folk Belief*, by Linda J. Ivanits.

And finally, many thanks to my family: my mother, Judy, whose faith never wavered, and who was first in line to order her *kefta*; my father, Harve, who was my rock, and whom I miss every day; and my grandfather Mel Seder, who taught me to love poetry, seek adventure and throw a punch.

Leigh Bardugo, March 2012

Coming soon in
The Grisha Trilogy

The
Shadow
Fold